———————— ★ ————————

"SO HOW ABOUT A NICE CUP OF TEA, DAVIE? AND ALSO A PIECE OF SCHNECKEN?"

"I can take it or leave it, Mom."

"You better take it. You'll need your strength and your brainpower. We've got a lot to talk about tonight."

I recognized the glitter in her eyes, and I felt my heart beating a little faster. "You know who the murderer is? You've got the answer?"

"I've got the question. Sometimes that's more important."

"What question? You're deliberately being mysterious, you know how that drives me up the wall."

"Excuse me. I don't want you driving up walls, you could have a bad accident."

———————— ★ ————————

"Mom's a hoot!"
        —Sue Feder's Magical Mystery Tour

"When a Jewish mother is on the case, there are two certainties: detection will take place at the table, and there will be absolutely no loose ends."
        —New York Daily News

Mom
DOTH MURDER SLEEP

James Yaffe

WORLDWIDE.

TORONTO • NEW YORK • LONDON
AMSTERDAM • PARIS • SYDNEY • HAMBURG
STOCKHOLM • ATHENS • TOKYO • MILAN
MADRID • WARSAW • BUDAPEST • AUCKLAND

MOM DOTH MURDER SLEEP

A Worldwide Mystery/June 1992

First published by St. Martin's Press Incorporated.

ISBN 0-373-26098-9

Mom
DOTH
MURDER
SLEEP

PROLOGUE

Dear Roger,

GETTING THIS LETTER from me will be a big surprise for you. Especially since I could call you up on the phone and ask you over for a cup of coffee and talk to you straight into your face. But I didn't want to do this because I thought maybe it would be embarrassing for you, talking about such things to another person, especially an old lady. I know how it is at your age, practically everything is embarrassing. Believe it or not, I was twenty-two years old myself once.

So I'm putting all the facts into this letter and personally driving to your house to slide it under your door. And the reason I'm doing this, I have a good idea what's going on inside of you right now. My son Davie told me you spoke to the girl today, and what she said to you. It wouldn't take any Albert Einstein to figure out how this made you feel. My heart goes out to you like I was your own mother. In fact, if your mother was here now, instead of a thousand miles away, I'm positive she'd do for you what I'm going to do.

For the last few months already I knew these facts. I kept them locked up inside of me because I was afraid the truth could hurt you. But since you're hurting anyway, what harm can it do if you hear it? Maybe it could even do you some good.

So here it is, the truth about those murders, the whole truth, and nothing but...

ONE

Dave's Narrative

MY FIRST CONTACT with those cockamamy murders came on the night of September 29, a Sunday, when I was having dinner at Mom's house.

I didn't know at the time, of course, that the conversation during that dinner would turn out to be the preview—like the coming attractions in a movie theater—for a murder case. I wasn't thinking along such lines, if you want the truth. I was thinking—let's face it, worrying—about Roger Meyer, my young assistant, who was having dinner with Mom and me. I was asking myself, as I'd been doing for weeks now, what was going on in the kid's head.

Before I get to the relevant parts of the conversation, though, I should give a little background information about the three people who were sitting at that dinner table.

First, me. I'm an ex-New York cop who got as high as lieutenant on the Homicide Squad in my forties, which is no small accomplishment. Ten years later I gave it all up, when my wife died and New York wasn't a place I could live in anymore. So I came out here to the city of Mesa Grande, a hundred and eighty thousand people, "nestled in the foothills of the Rockies," as our Chamber of Commerce likes to put it. I became the chief and for a while the only investigator for the public defender's office.

Second, presiding over the table, was my mother. She was widowed at a much younger age than I was widowered. She brought me up in an apartment in the Bronx, held on in New York for a year or so after I left, and finally gave in to my nagging and coaxing and came out here to join me. Not to live with me, though. She bought a little house of her own and settled into it nicely, telling me she'd already used up her youth and middle age waiting "hands and feet" on helpless males (meaning my father and me), and she intended to have an enjoyable old age by living alone and spoiling herself.

And, third and last, was Roger Meyer. He graduated from Yale a year or so ago, with a degree in sociology and a specialty in criminology. A week later, our City Council having voted to increase the public defender's budget accordingly, Roger came out here to be my assistant. How I met this kid in the first place and why I gave him the job is a complicated story that has nothing to do with this particular murder (though it had a lot to do with a totally different murder that I've described elsewhere).

At any rate, Mom had been putting food into him since he got to town the previous June. Whenever she sees a human being under the age of thirty, her first impulse is to feed him or her. (Her second impulse is to find out if he or she is married and to take it from there.)

So the three of us were having dinner together during one of those incredible Septembers that we're lucky enough to get every few years. The air was as mild and balmy as the springtime of your dreams, the mountains glittered at you from the end of every street. If you were standing in one of the older sections of town, that is. If you were standing out east, where the malls have been spawning like salmon in recent years, for all you'd get to see of the mountains you might as well be in Kansas.

To tell the truth, I'm still a little suspicious of those mountains. Part of me still believes that they're made of cardboard and canvas. The Chamber of Commerce puts them up before sunrise every morning to please the tourists, and takes them down again after dark and stores them away backstage.

Back to dinner. We were eating one of Mom's chicken pot pies, with dumplings that spring back from your fork like rubber but go down your throat like honey. Everybody becomes talkative under the influence of Mom's chicken pot pie. So Roger started telling us about the big explosion that had just occurred at the rehearsal of the play he was in, produced by our local amateur repertory company.

"They're nice people, I like them a lot," he said, "but sometimes they don't seem to have much self-control or maturity. They seem to be living in some kind of dream-world."

"That's what actors get paid for, no?" said Mom. "So they can take us away from the real world and make us enjoy ourselves someplace better."

"I don't actually agree with that," Roger said, and he launched into a long speech about how art, through the use of illusion and selection, interprets and enhances reality, et cetera, et cetera. Well, he *had* just graduated from college, so you had to make allowances.

And finally he got back to his original point. "Anyway, I do like them. Okay, I know the Mesa Grande Art Players aren't exactly the Royal Shakespeare Company, but some of them are really talented. Only what happened at rehearsal this afternoon was upsetting. I mean, all of a sudden this bunch of nice creative people started acting like babies.''

Then, for the next half hour or so, he gave us the details.

TWO

ACTUALLY there were two mysteries, and one of them I managed to solve. The one I didn't solve was the murders, for which I'm still kicking myself; I should have seen a lot more than I did. And the other one was my boss's mother.

My boss—he wants me to call him Dave, not mister—is the chief investigator for the public defender's office here in Mesa Grande. I'm his chief assistant—his only assistant, as a matter of fact—ever since the City Council voted the funds for the public defender to expand her investigative staff.

I wouldn't blame anybody for wondering why Dave hired me, a kid right out of college, with a few criminology courses under my belt, and absolutely no experience. One reason was that the funds the Council voted weren't enough to attract anybody who looked halfway professional. Another was that when I was out here a year and a half ago at Christmastime, visiting my parents, Dave and I were thrown together a lot and I made an obnoxious pest of myself letting him know how much I wanted to work under him. And another reason, which I didn't find out about until much later, was that his mother—this nice old lady, she must be seventy or eighty years old—went to bat for me.

Anyway, here I've been since last June. My parents were still living here then. They moved out to Mesa Grande after Dad retired from business, because he had been stationed here when he was in the Army in World War II and he liked the mountains, the fresh air, and the peace and quiet. Well, the peace and quiet turned out to be strictly an illusion. I won't go into the grisly details, but the upshot was that he and my mother decided to go back to Detroit, where they had lived and worked since they first got married and where all their friends were.

But they had this little house here in Mesa Grande, in a nice quiet section of town with a good view of the mountains, and instead of selling it, they offered it to me. They said they were planning to leave it to me someday anyway; without selling it, they had enough money to buy a little apartment in Detroit. Even so, I told them I wouldn't take it unless they were willing to let me pay rent.

So I've been living here in Mesa Grande ever since. I admit it isn't the most exciting town in America. The population is two hundred thousand; in the next five years it'll shoot up to two hundred and fifty, but what have we got to show for it? Do we have a concert hall, gourmet restaurants, a choice of bookstores, a decent theatre company? No, we don't. What we *do* have is an escalating crime rate, a lot of drugs, a lot of homeless people sleeping under bridges, a pollution problem, and a shortage of parking places downtown.

But the worst of it is that there isn't a single movie house in town that shows anything with subtitles or anything that isn't the latest Hollywood schlock. Movies, let's face it, are my food and drink. I'll go to see any movie at all, of course, but without some good ones, I feel like I'm living on a diet of McDonald's hamburgers and Dr. Pepper.

The job makes up for a lot. Not that I've always exactly distinguished myself. I wasn't on it two weeks before I made that huge boner with the little Korean girl from the massage parlor. Poor little loser, I told myself from the heights of my superior intelligence, she's so stupid and ignorant, she can't even understand simple English, I have to explain everything to her twice as many times as I would to anybody else. Result: I let her know exactly what *we* knew, without finding out one damn thing *she* knew, and that was the end of her as a witness for our client. (Luckily we got him off anyway, though it wouldn't have been any tragedy if we hadn't, since the son of a bitch was guilty as hell.)

Dave wasn't shy about pointing out to me how badly I'd fouled up, and that night I had my suitcase up from the basement, I was all ready to pack and go back to Detroit. But instead, thank God, Dave's mother invited me for breakfast the next morning. She didn't talk to me about that massage-parlor case at all; in fact, mostly what she talked about were things that had happened to people she knew in the old days, when Dave was on the New York Homicide Squad and she was living in the Bronx. But somehow the stories she told seemed to apply to my own situation, and I went away from that breakfast thinking that maybe I could give the criminal investigation business another few months.

And it was only a few weeks later I had my big triumph. A certain VP in one of our local Savings and Loans had an alibi for the night the safe got robbed, which meant that our client, his secretary, could have gone to the cooler for ten years. His alibi, which his wife corroborated, was that he spent the night of the break-in watching an old Bogart movie on his VCR. In repeating the plot of this movie, he said the villain was Sidney Greenstreet, big and fat and smiling. Well, I knew that flick inside and out, I could reel off whole scenes from it by heart, so I knew Sidney Greenstreet wasn't in it, the villain was actually

Peter Lorre, small and thin and shifty-eyed. Ann Swenson, the public defender, caught this Savings and Loan guy in that lie right up on the witness stand, and he broke down and confessed everything, and even screamed at his wife for not being able to tell the difference between Greenstreet and Lorre.

All right, enough about me. I'll move on to Sunday afternoon, September 29, and the rehearsal of that play I was in.

I anticipate the question: How did it happen that a young hotshot investigator for the public defender's office found himself acting in a play by Shakespeare?

The answer is that it probably couldn't happen in a city like New York or even my hometown Detroit. It had to happen in a city like Mesa Grande, where there's no professional theatre, where the only public entertainments that most people go to see are rodeos, football games, and Indiana Jones movies, where people mostly like to sit home and watch the top ten TV shows. So whatever theatre there is falls into the hands of amateurs.

I found out about the Mesa Grande Art Players from a small item in *The Republican-American,* our local rag, saying that casting was being done for their forthcoming production of *Macbeth,* and urging all interested people, whether or not they had any previous stage experience, to try out. My previous stage experience consisted of a high school production of *Our Town.* I played Editor Webb, and loved the part because it gave me a chance to suck at a pipe for two hours. But something in me has always got a kick out of acting, no matter how badly I do it, so I asked myself why the hell not.

I went down to this rickety little theatre that was attached to the back of the local convention hall. The director sat a table up on the bare stage, and a couple of dozen

of us read lines from the paperback copy of *Macbeth* that
he gave to us, and that seemed to be that. A few days later
the stage manager called me at the office and told me I had
a part if I wanted it. Three or four parts, in fact, all of
them about three or four lines long.

I had to get Dave's permission first, even though all the
rehearsals would be at night, except for Sunday afternoon, since practically everybody in the cast was holding
down some kind of daytime job. I asked Dave if he could
possibly see his way clear to giving me every night off for
the month of rehearsals, and Thursday, Friday, and Saturday nights for the month of performances. (Productions by the Mesa Grande Art Players run only on
weekends, because this area doesn't exactly have an un-
limited supply of theatregoers in it. And usually the run
lasts for only three weekends; in scheduling *Macbeth* for a
fourth weekend, the Players were indulging in wild optimism.)

Dave was very nice about it. Any emergencies that came
along, he could handle them by himself, he said. For what
I was being paid, why should I have to work nights?

And when his mother heard about it, she positively
bubbled over. "It's a wonderful thing to do," she told me,
when she had Dave and me over for dinner that night.
"I'm crazy from actors! In New York I went all the time
to the theatre. *Macbeth* by Shakespeare—I saw it years ago
on Broadway with Morris Evans and that Anderson girl.
The way she washed her hands when she was walking in
her sleep, goose bumps it gave me! You say there's a lot of
people going to be in this production? Some of them are
young people, I hope? Any nice young girls?"

The Mesa Grande Art Players was founded about ten
years ago by Lloyd Cunningham, who owns an electron-
ics store. He never talks about it himself, but several peo-

ple have told me that he graduated from the American Academy of Dramatic Arts when he was in his twenties, that he had tramped the pavement around Broadway for a couple of years, and even had a few small parts in a few small plays. Then he got married, to a girl from Mesa Grande, and she quickly became pregnant. His father-in-law had a very successful business selling TVs and phonographs, and so nature took its course. The Players, I suppose, has been Cunningham's way for the last ten years of smuggling a little theatre into his life.

As rehearsals got underway, I began to realize that the same thing was true about many of the other actors in *Macbeth*. Like Cunningham, the hard-core members of the Players—the ones who paid dues—had dreamed once upon a time of getting into the profession. Casting calls for all productions are open, and a lot of stagestruck citizens like me always show up for them, but the hard-core members play most of the leads.

This particular production, as I soon found out, wasn't typical. Up till then, the Players had been specializing in Neil Simon and other popular American playwrights. They thought they had reached the pinnacle of dramatic art a couple of years ago when they did *A Streetcar Named Desire*. So why, all of a sudden, were they jumping headfirst into Shakespearean tragedy?

The explanation was the director, Martin Osborn. A tall, weedy man in his fifties, with bushy black hair and a bulldog jaw, he looked familiar to me the moment I set eyes on him at that first audition. Pretty soon I found out why. He had once been a character actor in Hollywood; not the most famous character actor in the business, but I watch a lot of movies. I've been known to look at TV till three in the morning just to catch some 1950s grade-B mystery. I recognized Osborn from several of these.

He had retired from the movies a dozen years ago to marry a meat-packing heiress and manage her investments. His wife had died recently, and Osborn, now a wealthy man, had settled in Mesa Grande last April. Right away he'd taken an interest in the Players, and the inevitable happened. The Players are always in desperate financial straits, always on the verge of folding for lack of funds. How could they resist being seduced by an experienced pro who was willing to dig down in his own pocket to guarantee the season? In return, of course, he expected to get his way.

Lloyd Cunningham and a few of the other old-guard members had wanted to open the season with *The Odd Couple,* but Osborn had laid down the law: not only would they open with *Macbeth* but nothing by Neil Simon would be done at all. And having chosen *Macbeth,* he chose himself as its director, a position that usually went to Lloyd Cunningham.

Still worse, Cunningham didn't even get the leading part, though he was certainly the best actor in town. Instead, Osborn brought in a friend of his, Randolph Le Sage, a professional actor from New York who worked off-Broadway and on TV soap operas. Ordinarily Actors' Equity, the national actors' union, won't allow its members to appear in any production in which all the other actors aren't Equity members too. But occasionally (though Equity doesn't like to publicize this) they'll make an exception to the rule. Only under certain conditions though; one of them is that the company must operate strictly on a nonprofit basis. Well, you couldn't get any more nonprofit than the Mesa Grande Art Players, so Osborn inveigled a special Equity dispensation for his old friend.

The unspoken message in all this—but it came across loud and clear—was that nobody in this hick town could possibly be good enough to handle such a demanding role. Cunningham was cast as Macbeth's fellow soldier Banquo, who gets killed off halfway through the play.

So there was a lot of tension during rehearsals. Everybody, even the stage crew, kept saying what a success the show was going to be. Osborn kept telling us what a superb job we were doing: "It's about time this town got exposed to some *real* theatre!" But the fact was, you could cut the tension with a knife.

And then came that Sunday afternoon, the twenty-ninth, four days before opening night.

THE CAUSE of all the trouble was that Allan Franz sat in on the rehearsal.

Everybody was pretty excited about that, naturally, Franz being one of the biggest directors in Hollywood today. He comes out with a new picture every three or four years, and I've seen and loved them all, even the last one, that big epic about the building of the Panama Canal, and how the United States corrupted the natives.

He was in town that week because his daughter Laurie, who was starting her sophomore year at Mesa Grande College, was playing Lady Macduff. Osborn told us he never knew Allan Franz back in his Hollywood period, but that didn't stop him from asking the great man to make a few comments afterward to the cast.

I recognized Franz right away, because I'd seen pictures of him in film magazines. He was a middle-sized man, in his fifties, not too fat or too thin, with a bald head and thick horn-rimmed glasses; he looked more like your garden-variety shoe salesman than a Hollywood big shot. He spoke with just a touch of a Brooklyn accent. He was born and brought up in Brooklyn, and he had never been ashamed to tell that to the interviewers.

He began his comments after the run-through by clearing his throat a few times, running his hand around his collar, looking up at the ceiling and down at the floor.

"It's good," he said. "It's a very creditable effort. I've seen plenty of professional productions of the Scottish play that weren't nearly as creditable."

I'd better explain that remark. Actors are notoriously superstitious—who wouldn't be, in such a risky profession?—and one of their oldest superstitions is that *Macbeth* is jinxed, that productions of it are disaster-prone. This doesn't mean that it's never performed; as a matter of fact, it's performed more often than any of Shakespeare's tragedies except *Hamlet.* But precautions are always taken to keep the bad luck away, and one of the most important is that the name of the play must never be spoken out loud inside the theatre—unless the actors *have* to speak it in the course of rehearsals and performances. "The Scottish play" is the most popular euphemism by means of which the roof of the theatre is prevented from crashing down on everybody's head.

All of this, incidentally, I learned from Martin Osborn, in the speech he made at the beginning of our very first rehearsal. When somebody asked him if he really believed in that superstitious crap, Osborn drew himself up and said, "Of course I don't. What do you think I am, some gibbering old gypsy crone? I haven't got a superstitious bone in my body. However, I don't see the point of taking unnecessary chances."

Anyway, as Allan Franz started talking, most of us were sitting around on the stage, gazing down, hanging on his words, and he was leaning back and looking up at us from the aisle seat. Osborn was sitting in the seat next to him.

"One thing I like," Franz said. "You're doing it fast, with plenty of cuts. All Shakespeare plays should be done with plenty of cuts. He was a big overwriter, that was the style in those days. He'd never get away with it these days. That's why I'll never make a movie out of one of his things. If you trim the fat the way you ought to, the college professors and the critics jump on you. If you leave him alone, you bore millions of people to death, and you die at the box office.

"Now, here's some other things you're doing that I like. Macduff and our hero, that's a good sword fight at the end. You're really working up a sweat. Lots of grunting and thrashing around, practically Kurosawa. Shakespeare always threw in a good fight at the end, he knew he had to make up for all those long dull speeches. Only suggestion I'd make to you fellows—go even further, throw yourselves into it even harder, draw *blood.*

"Also, I very much like the scene with Banquo's ghost. The way he comes rising up from the trapdoor, looking like Boris Karloff in *Frankenstein,* and the kid who's serving dinner drops the tray—that's good strong horror stuff. And you deserve praise that you don't use that trapdoor any other time in the play. Most amateur theatres, if they've got a trapdoor they can't keep their hands off it, they're sending people up and down it so often it's like a public elevator.

"Now about your directional concept, Marty. Setting the Scottish play in the old West and dressing everybody up in cowboy suits. It's interesting all right. It's original. Makes the audience look at the play in a fresh light."

"That was the idea, Allan—"

"Only problem I've got with it is the language. That's pretty fancy English you've got those cowboys talking. Thee's and thou's, and blank verse, and all those complicated metaphors. But maybe, after a while, people won't notice. They just take it for granted this is the way cowboys talked in Elizabethan times.

"Now I've got some suggestions for some of you actors specifically. Most of you are doing a terrific job, understand that? If I give you a suggestion, it's not because I think your performances aren't great. It's because I think you could make them even greater. Okay, let's start with the leading role..."

And Franz ran down the cast list, one person at a time, always finding something to praise before he got to something he didn't like. He even touched on me, for a second or two. "Fleance, Banquo's son, that's a good scream for help you're letting out in the murder scene. Could you make it even louder and more bloodcurdling on the night of the show? Doesn't matter how sophisticated people are, a good old-fashioned bloodcurdling scream is still surefire."

Then Franz turned his attention to Laurie. She was his daughter, a tall redhead with incredibly delicate features and a body there was only one word for, *willowy*. Franz addressed her just as impersonally as he had everybody else. "Lady Macduff, I like your general idea about the character. I agree that she's a tough Scotswoman who's been through the wars. I *am* getting tired of teary, trembling Lady Macduffs who faint away at the sight of blood. But if I can give you one word of advice—watch out you don't carry it to the other extreme. She isn't some kind of floozie selling her body along Hollywood Boulevard. She's a *lady*. She's got class, elegance, education, self-control. When she pleads with the murderers to spare her son, she isn't coming on to them for an evening's trade. Not that you're creating that effect all the way through, just here and there, so I'm only asking you to be careful.

"Now who else? Oh yeah, the little fellow that's play-ing the Third Murderer? I like what you're doing, Mr. er—uh—It's only five or six lines, but you're making the most of them. I like that funny little lisp you're giving him. That's a terrific idea, this murderer has a lisp, he's a kind of pansy, right? Makes him even more sinister and fright-ening. Positively Hitchcock!"

The Third Murderer was Harold Hapgood, who ran an insurance agency in the daytime. He was very short, shorter than anybody else in the case, and he had a round face that looked as if it wasn't quite out of baby fat, though he was probably in his early thirties. The lisp that Franz had praised so much was Harold's normal way of talking, but this didn't stop him from blushing and mur-muring, "Thank you, Mr. Franz. It's so gratifying. You try your best. No such thing as a small part, only a small actor—"

Franz had already turned away from him and was blinking around behind his thick glasses. "Have I covered everybody? No, there's one performance I left out."

He turned in Lloyd Cunningham's direction. "I've been saving you for last, Banquo, because you're the one per-formance that I think is seriously wrong. I mean, all wrong."

Cunningham, who was tall and broad-shouldered, with a lot of beef on him, met Franz's gaze without flinching, a faint smile on his face. I had to admire his cool.

"You'd be doing a terrific job, Banquo, giving a great performance," Franz said, "if you happened to be acting in some other play. You're supposed to be Banquo in the Scottish play, or am I mistaken? So why are you playing Hamlet? All that sweetness and gentleness and nobility! Didn't it ever occur to you that Banquo is *sore* at M—at his friend? They both got predictions from the weird sisters, but the only one who's benefiting from them is the other guy. And that's because he's taken matters into his own hands, right? Banquo would like a little slice of the pie himself. Why should he be left out in the cold, especially since he knows for sure what his friend's been up to? In other words, you're turning him into a lily-livered pansy. Hamlet, did I say? What *you're* playing is *Torch Song Trilogy*."

All through rehearsals Cunningham had been careful to keep himself under control, to be cooperative, to take direction patiently, even though Osborn had done him out of being the director *and* the star. Cunningham was the closest thing to a professional that the Players had. But what Franz had just said to him, it seemed to me, was enough to make any actor hit the ceiling.

And it got even worse, because Osborn, like a damn fool, had to speak up too. Couldn't resist the temptation to brownnose the great Franz.

"I'm glad you agree with me about that, Allan," Osborn said. "I've been telling Lloyd exactly that since the first rehearsal. Give it some anger, some threat, some *balls*. All that sweetness and nobility is getting too sticky and boring. But Lloyd just hasn't been able to see the point. Actors get stuck in a bad interpretation, and it takes dynamite to blast them out of it. Well, maybe he'll listen to *you*."

Cunningham started looking dangerous. He had let it drop once that he worked out every morning at a gym. But he didn't get violent, he kept his explosion to words. "Okay, Martin, you don't like how I'm playing Banquo, you want more anger and hostility? I'm glad to oblige. I'm feeling nothing but anger and hostility for how you're screwing up this play! And since I never *have* enjoyed funerals, I'm quitting as of now!" Then Cunningham threw his script across the stage, and it hit Osborn right in the nose. After a lucky shot like that, how could Cunningham find an exit line to top it?

Well, he did. He strode across the stage, turned to face the group, and said, "Good luck to all of you. I hope you have a big success—with *Macbeth!*" He spit out the last word and disappeared into the wings.

The rest of us had our jaws hanging open. I suppose everybody was thinking what I was thinking: This was Sunday, and Thursday was the opening. How were we going to make it? Was the old *Macbeth* jinx starting to operate already?

But the Banquo problem disappeared a few seconds later. As soon as Cunningham was out of there, Osborn announced he would take over the part of Banquo himself. Years ago, when he was an actor in New York, he had played it to great critical acclaim—as he had already told us about a thousand times during rehearsals—and he knew all the lines. In my opinion, he didn't look particularly unhappy that the whole thing had happened.

But Cunningham's blow-up seemed to set off a delayed reaction in everybody else. All the tension that had been building up for the last three weeks came bursting out in one big tidal wave: people screaming at Osborn, people defending him and cursing Cunningham, people turning on each other and saying all the things they had been too polite to say up to then. A lot of hostility was directed at Randolph Le Sage, the New York actor who was playing Macbeth. Some people were saying he was the cause of all the trouble; Osborn never should've brought in this outsider, and he wasn't giving that good a performance either.

The person saying this the loudest was Sally Michaels, who was playing Lady Macbeth. Sally taught third grade in one of the public schools, but she had been acting with the Players for years; she did most of the leading women over forty.

She was rather tall and busty, went in for long strings of beads and gaudy knitted sweaters, and had the world's heartiest laugh. She used a brand of perfume that she referred to as "Magnolia Blossoms, inspired by *Gone With the Wind*." I kind of liked her, to tell the truth, and I could see why a lot of men found her attractive. I don't think she meant badly, it was just that she couldn't keep her mouth shut.

Naturally, Le Sage wasn't going to sit quietly while she attacked him, so he hit right back with some remarks about the unprofessionalism of his fellow cast members, especially female cast members who jumped into bed promiscuously with every male in sight. The louder and more vulgar the male, the better they seemed to like him. If there was anything Le Sage deplored, in or out of the theatre, it was vulgarity and bad taste.

Sally turned a few shades of red and purple at this. I don't think she minded being called promiscuous nearly as much as being told she had bad taste.

Then Bernie Michaels joined in on the free-for-all. Bernie was a chiropractor in real life, and also Sally's exhusband. They had split up years ago but were still on friendly terms, so naturally he couldn't let Le Sage insult her. Bernie had struck me from the start as one of the gentlest, most easygoing guys in the world, perfect casting for King Duncan, whom he was playing in *Macbeth*. It really amazed me to see him turning into a towering inferno when the old chivalric knight in him got aroused.

While all this ensemble screaming went on, Allan Franz had his chin down and was huddled in his aisle seat. He looked sort of pained and brooding, as if he was blaming himself for stirring up this storm and praying for it to die down.

A personal note: During the storm the only thing I could think about was poor Laurie. I could see her in her corner of the stage, looking bewildered and stricken and all those other things that make your heart go out to a pretty girl in trouble. So I started across the stage to her, but there were too many people in the way, yelling at each other and in no mood to step aside for me, and before I could reach her I saw her jump off the stage and run down the aisle to the back of the theatre.

Her father saw her too. The sight seemed to jolt him out of his brooding silence. He got to his feet and followed Laurie down the aisle. So I decided to hell with it.

Martin Osborn had joined the shouting match now. For some reason he had decided to pursue one of his favorite beefs against Sally. "Good God, are you wearing that horror again? I hope you're not planning to expose our audience to that piece of junk on opening night!"

He was referring to Sally's ring, a heavy silver band with a huge red stone that more or less looked like a grinning face, whether animal or human was hard to tell. Sally had been wearing this eyesore to rehearsals, and Osborn had been nasty about it two or three times already.

As usual, Sally put on her dignity act. "As I've explained to you till I'm blue in the face, I chose this ring especially for my role in this play. It's been in my jewelry box for years, ever since it was given to me, in happier, more innocent days, by one who truly loved me. Hopelessly, I'm sorry to say. Feelings *can't* be forced. But I always revered and respected his love, though unable to return it, because he was a person of impeccable good taste, as this beautiful heirloom of his family clearly proves!"

"It looks like something he picked up on the board-walk in Atlantic City," said Osborn. "You're supposed to be Lady Macbeth, Queen of Scotland, a woman of the highest classiness. You wear that monstrosity in a per-formance, the audience'll think you're a dance-hall host-ess. They'll laugh you off the stage."

"I don't perform," Sally said, "for the type of louts and rowdies that apparently form *your* circle of acquaintance. This ring happens to be *perfect* for Lady—for the Scot-tish lady. This ring is every inch the queen. You might as well know I have no intention of taking it off. I expect to wear it on opening night and for every performance after that."

Osborn looked as if he'd be happy to go on with the ar-gument, but by that time it was six o'clock and he had to let us go. So I got in my car and drove uptown to Dave's mother's house for dinner.

DURING THAT DINNER I told Dave and his mother about the rehearsal, doing my best to make the story coherent in between mouthfuls of food. I finished along with the des-sert, and was wolfing down one of the strawberry tarts and using my coffee to soften it up for the trip, when the old lady leaned forward. Her voice was very casual. "This girl you were feeling bad for, this movie director's daughter? You got to know her well since the rehearsals started?"

I pretty much knew what this question was all about—I do have a mother of my own—but I made my voice casual too. "We've been out for coffee a couple of times."

"You like her maybe?"

"She's a wonderful person. She's had everything she ever wanted all her life, being brought up in Hollywood and all, but you wouldn't know it from the way she be-haves. She's just as simple and unspoiled—"

"Maybe, after the play starts, you could bring her here for dinner. She eats food, don't she, like ordinary people?"

Dave broke in at this point; I think he felt sorry for me and was trying to rescue me by changing the subject. "Do you suppose Lloyd Cunningham could've been planning this all along, Mom? He was mad because he didn't get to direct *Macbeth* or play the lead. So maybe he accepted the part of Banquo intending to quit at the last moment and ruin the production."

"His *is* sort of cynical and sarcastic," I said. "But I don't think he'd do anything really malicious—"

"The trouble with your theory," the old lady said to Dave, "is it isn't logical."

"Since when is revenge ever logical?"

"That an actor who didn't get a part should try to ruin the play," the old lady said, "this I couldn't argue with. But such a stupid way to do it! If he wants to ruin the play, why does he quit four days before opening? Knowing the director is an actor too, and what's more, played the same part once and has the lines memorized? Why don't we wait till the opening night, the curtain is ready to go up, and *then* he should quit?"

"All right then," Dave said, "you *don't* think there was anything fishy about Cunningham's blow-up."

"On the other hand—" The old lady stopped and frowned. "There's something. This much you're right about, Davie. About this blowing-up is something that isn't kosher. So what is it, what is it?" She gave her lower lip a tug for a long time, but her frown didn't go away.

Finally she looked up at us, smiling again. "Who says you're going now? You didn't have a second piece yet of the strawberry tart. Believe me, there's plenty more in the kitchen."

She bustled off through the swinging door, and I noticed Dave watching me.

I turned my eyes away from him, suddenly feeling a little guilty, though Dave couldn't possibly have known what was going on in my mind. I was thinking about the old lady's questions and comments. Pretty sharp questions and comments, I thought. They reminded me of certain things I'd been wondering about lately....

THREE

Dave's Narrative

PERSONALLY I've never been a big fan of the theatre. A good movie costs one-fifth as much, and the actors never forget their lines.

Mom is the theatre nut in our family. Ever since she was a young girl and her parents brought her to New York from the old country, she went to as many plays as she could. In the early days, when she didn't have the money, she waited in line for hours for standing room or cut-rate seats, and she didn't care how high up she was sitting. The actors could look like little dolls and sound as if they were whispering to her from the next block, she'd still say, "By me it has to be flesh-and-blood people. I can't get interested in talking photographs."

So even if Roger hadn't been in it, Mom would have gone to *Macbeth*. She was one of the small band of regular subscribers to the Mesa Grande Art Players, and nothing could keep her away from any of their productions, not even the amateurish acting, the rickety scenery, or the undependable lights.

So Mom and I got two tickets for the opening night, Thursday, October 3. And then, that morning, she called me at the office. "I can't go out tonight," she said. "I'm coughing and sneezing, I've got the bug. Didn't you tell me, when I left New York, that out here, with the fresh air and the mountains, there aren't any bugs?"

I never told her anything of the sort, but I let it pass.

"I'll skip the play myself," I said, "and come over and keep you company."

"Positively not. One of us has to be there, we shouldn't disappoint Roger. Mrs. Minetta from next door is coming in to put my dinner on the stove and play a little gin rummy with me afterward."

I should have realized that Mom would have a contingent of neighborly souls all ready to rally round in an emergency. She attracts friends the way a dog attracts fleas. Maybe for the same reason: she feeds them. She not only gives them chicken soup for their stomachs, she also listens with a sympathetic ear to their troubles.

I tried to find somebody to go to the opening night with me, but I didn't have any luck. The woman I was most interested in at the time, who works as a paralegal for one of the local judges, was committed to baby-sit for her married daughter's little girl.

I asked Ann Swenson, my boss, if she'd care to use the extra ticket. Her husband, a surgeon, was often busy at night. But she said she had too much work to do, getting her final arguments ready for the jury in the rape case that was just finishing up. She'd have to see Roger's performance later in the run. I also offered the ticket to Mabel Gibson, our secretary in the office; she's a white-haired motherly type, and she treated all of us like her chicks; she certainly intended to do some clucking over Roger the actor. But she told me that Thursday was her husband's bowling night, and her obligation to keep him company and boost his morale was sacred.

So I went down to the theatre by myself.

To tell the truth, I was feeling more than a little self-sacrificial about this. My attitude toward Roger, at this particular time, wasn't totally positive. I still couldn't forget the look on his face last Sunday, after Mom came out with her deductions about Lloyd Cunningham. Was he beginning to guess certain things? About the relationship between Mom and me, particularly regarding some of my cases?

By the time I got to the theatre for the opening night of *Macbeth*, one thing was absolutely clear to me. In the future I had to make sure that Roger didn't see nearly as much of Mom as he'd been doing lately.

THE PERFORMANCE WAS scheduled to begin at seven, earlier than usual, because our local drama critic, who also reviewed concerts, lectures, movies, and ice shoes, had to make a midnight deadline if his review was going to be in tomorrow morning's paper. It was beyond me why the Players went to all that trouble for such a reason. That drama critic, moonlighting from his job as a physics professor at Mesa Grande College, always panned their shows anyway.

The theatre had been built in 1927, tacked on to the back end of the old city auditorium, where wrestling matches, antique fairs, and revivalist preachers still held forth. It was a nice little theatre, actually, with a thick velvet curtain and decent acoustics, and seating for about two hundred people. The architect had given it a name too: the Ramon Novarro Theatre, in honor of the famous silent-movie heartthrob who spent a week in Mesa Grande, visiting his nephew, back in 1925. Traveling repertory companies doing Shakespeare and other classics were supposed to be enticed by this theatre to stop at Mesa Grande on their triumphant national tours. Not too many of them ever did. The stock market crashed and, even more fatally, talking pictures were invented. The Ramon Novarro Theatre sank into limbo for more than half a century. The two hundred seats got old and broken; the stage became a storing place for all the overflow debris of whatever was going on in the auditorium.

Until four or five years ago, when Lloyd Cunningham discovered the old wreck and persuaded the City Council to put a little money into refurbishing it; not exactly to make it a splendid little jewel but at least to clean it up enough so an audience could be put into it. Since then, the Mesa Grande Art Players paid the city a reasonable rent and used the theatre as their permanent home during their regular season, from October to May.

The entrance to the theatre didn't have any long marquee with neon lights. It was one small door, with a sign over it that said "Ramon Novarro Theatre"; under the sign was the great heartthrob's face, painted on wood in black and white. When you went through this entrance door, you didn't find yourself in a spacious lobby with gilt-painted box offices. What you got was a narrow corridor with a table at the end of it where some harried volunteer, usually the wife of one of the actors, would be selling tickets right up to curtain time.

A few people were ahead of me at the ticket table, but it didn't take me long to get my turn. I told the lady at the table that I had an extra ticket to turn in, and she quickly said, "No refunds." I told her I didn't expect any, and she breathed a sigh of relief.

On the way to my seat, I recognized a lot of people in the audience. That's the thing about Mesa Grande that always puzzles outsiders. With a population of two hundred thousand people, we go on being a small town in one respect: we still don't have the blessing of privacy, of anonymity, that a big city can offer. Maybe this is because most of our new population are blue-collar workers or second-rank office help who have pushed into the outlying districts to the north and the east that have clustered around jerry-built malls, and half of whom will probably move somewhere else in the next five years. Maybe it's because of all the military bases that surround us.

Whatever the reason, the power structure and social makeup of the town are pretty much as narrow and limited as they were twenty years ago. The same names, rich old families who have been here for generations, show up regularly on letterheads and boards of directors; you see the same people at every so-called cultural event; you run into them at Rotary luncheons, school-board meetings, sessions of the City Council, lectures at our local liberal arts college. From this fairly small group come the people who run for office or otherwise get their names in our one and only newspaper. The same clergymen—ministers of the leading Episcopal, Presbyterian, Baptist, and Roman Catholic churches, and occasionally even our only local rabbi—are constantly being quoted on public issues. Just like in any small town, you keep seeing the same faces over and over again, and if you don't recognize *them*, they're sure to recognize *you*, and often they know more about your personal business than you know yourself.

So it wasn't surprising that the audience at the opening of *Macbeth* should be full of familiar faces. Some of them were the affluent-looking middle-aged types who patronized the symphony, the summer opera, the concerts and lectures at Mesa Grande College. They were local doctors and lawyers, officers of banks, retired military, widows and dowagers of the older families in town. And there weren't all that many of them; their money and patronage had to be spread awfully thin.

Mixed in with these were the types that showed up only for theatrical events, a younger, seedier group who worked as clerks in local stores or taught at the local schools. They decorated their small rooms with old movie posters, clinging fiercely to the edges of what passed for artistic life in Mesa Grande. Among this group a higher than normal proportion were gay, or at least the men cultivated the exaggerated gestures and high-pitched voices that they thought belonged to the gay world in bigger, more sophisticated cities.

The two groups, wealthy patrons and scruffy mavericks, kept pretty much apart, sat in their own sections of the theater, and talked only to others in the same group. They seemed to tolerate each other pretty well, though, maybe because they knew instinctively that they had one thing in common. They were all dedicated to something that practically everybody else in Mesa Grande looked down on with contempt if not downright hostility.

My seat was in the third row. On the aisle, so that I had to maneuver my way past him, was a neatly dressed man, with a bald head, horn-rimmed glasses, and a mellow suntan. I recognized him from Roger's description as the famous movie director Allan Franz.

I turned to him and introduced myself, and told him how pleased my young assistant had been to meet him the other day. I asked him how he was enjoying his stay in Mesa Grande.

He shrugged and said, "It seems like a nice little town. The only trouble with it is, if I put it in a movie who'd believe it? I keep seeing people on the streets with cowboy hats, they look as if they came from Central Casting. And all the stores that sell nothing but guns for hunting! No offense, but it's Middle America set up on the main lot."

I laughed and said I occasionally had the same feeling.

"And all this fresh air you've got here," Franz went on. "I'm sure it's doing no end of damage to my lungs. I always sleep like a top, thank God, even in strange hotel rooms, but I'll feel safer when I get back to that healthy Los Angeles smog."

Then Franz gave me a grin, slightly sardonic but not unfriendly. "So your boy was present at the big bang the other day?" he said. "Now which one was he? Oh yeah, Fleance. Not too bad. Reasonably tolerable, in fact."

"He says you didn't say much to him about his performance."

"Why should I have? He seems like a nice kid. Definitely an amateur, but that's okay. The best Hamlet I ever saw was an amateur. Your boy—what's his name, Roger?—was saying his lines the way he thought a human being might say them. No fancy business, no highfalutin airs and poses, no Method, for Christ's sake! What I mean is, he was one of the few people on that stage who wasn't, God help us, ecting. So what would've been the point of telling him so? Then he might've got self-conscious and stopped doing it. Or *started* doing it, if you follow my meaning."

"And the rest of them *were* 'ecting'?"

"At the top of their voices. Or with no voices at all, mumbling into their underwear. Depending on who they think they are, Gielgud or Brando."

"But Roger says you paid every one of them a compliment."

"Sure I did. And then I told every one of them what they were doing that was terrible. The compliment helps the insult go down smoother. Like chocolate milk with a pill. Remember how the doctor used to do that to you when you were a kid? Actors are all little kids."

He gave a big sigh. "You want to know the truth? Last Sunday was one of the saddest afternoons I ever spent in my life. Actors are depressing enough under ordinary circumstances. The lives they lead, the shit they take from everybody! And where does it get them? Ninety per cent of them are out of work ninety per cent of the time, and even the ones that manage to make a living at it for a while mostly end up dead broke, living off charity in old actors' homes.

"The point I'm making is, real actors are sad enough, but *would-be* actors, for Christ's sake! Like the ones we're about to see in this play. They put on all the mannerisms, all the stupid poses you get from professionals. They call each other 'darling,' they show you what somebody once told them was their 'good' profile, they even snort-coke from time to time, though they sure as hell can't afford it. But it all comes out wrong, you know what I mean? Like a rotten performance. If 'players' are walking shadows, which is what old Shakespeare calls them at the end of the ordeal we're facing tonight, the players in this town must be the shadows of shadows.

"And you know what's the craziest part of it? These people all have decent jobs. They're hardware salesmen, insurance agents, teachers. And they're eating their hearts out because they can't run off to the West Coast or the East Coast, and descend into hell!"

"But if this is what makes their lives bearable to them—"

"Excuse the expression, Dave, that's a lot of horse manure. Nobody would say something like that about any other profession or business in this world. You're a policeman, right? If you had somebody working for you who was rotten at the job, who couldn't do anything right, you'd fire him, wouldn't you? You wouldn't choke up and tell him it's okay for him to be a dumb incompetent cop if this is what makes life bearable to him."

Franz broke off with a shake of his head. Then he grinned and started in again. "You know what most of the actors I know would say, if they heard me talking to you like this? Typical director's crap! He couldn't make it as an actor himself, so now he goes around bad-mouthing the profession. All directors are frustrated actors, that's received wisdom where I come from.''

"Does it apply to you?''

His grin broadened. He didn't seem to be the least bit offended. "Sure it does. I wanted to be an actor when I was a kid. That was in Brooklyn. My father owned a hardware store. Did I ever help him take care of it? No, I pounded the pavements around Times Square for three years, waiting on tables to keep alive, giving up jobs so I could go to casting calls where imbeciles looked me over like I was raw meat, blew cigar smoke in my face, and told me I didn't amount to shit. Until I got smart, and decided *I'd* be one of the imbeciles and blow cigar smoke in *other* people's faces. Of course, if I'd known what I know now—''

"Being a director has its problems too?''

"You can say that again. A director—especially a movie director—has to develop the ability to live with fear and uncertainty. You're in charge of a gigantic business enterprise, you've got hundreds of employees, millions of dollars riding on you—and all the time, in your heart, you don't know how the hell anything is going to turn out.''

"Surely you work from a script?''

"Scripts don't mean a thing. Believe me. The script gives you a general outline, but the details along the way keep changing. Every day it's a new emergency, an unexpected obstacle. So you have to improvise, roll with the punches, take crazy chances. Come to think of it, if you're going to survive in this business, you have to *enjoy* fear and uncertainty, you have to get your *kicks* out of them.''

"Roger tells me that your daughter wants to be an actress?"

"Your boy tells you that, does he? I had my eye on him during that rehearsal last Sunday. The way he was looking at Laurie—I guess I know good old-fashioned lust when I see it. Young people haven't changed much in *that* respect since our day."

"I guess they haven't. You don't hold it against him?"

"Far from it. Laurie brings out the lust in plenty of young men; she'd worry me if she didn't." He laughed, then grew more serious. "You ought to warn your young assistant, though, he might be heading for a bad pain in the heart. Laurie's not interested in any long-term relationships just now. She's very serious about this acting business. When she gets out of college in a couple of years, she plans to go to one of those big acting schools back east. Yale or Carnegie Mellon, one of those places."

"She must have a lot of talent," I said.

"She's pretty damn good, if I say so myself. And her looks are on her side too. She's a tall redhead, that's always surefire. Takes after her mother, thank God."

"You're not worried about her becoming an actress? Everything you were saying just now, about what a competitive profession it is—"

"Sure I'm worried. I'd be out of my mind if I wasn't. But if that's what the kid wants . . . and she *does* have the temperament for it. Sensitive. Big swings from high to low and back again. This summer, when she was home with me in Beverly Hills, I never knew *what* she was going to be from one day to the next. One night last August, for instance, she goes to bed happy as a clam, like Juliet when Romeo climbs up her balcony, and she comes to breakfast the next morning snapping everyone's head off. Like Juliet when she see Romeo's dead body."

"Actors are like that usually?"

"Never knew one who wasn't. Life isn't exactly real to them, you know what I mean? They've always got to be playing a part—"

Before he could go any further, the house lights started to dim. Franz immediately swiveled around to look at the stage. His daughter wouldn't be on it for a few hours, but he was already giving it his full attention.

I took another quick glance around the audience. Sitting in one of the back rows, way off to the side, was Lloyd Cunningham. I recognized him from other plays I'd seen the Players do, and once I'd bought some stereo equipment from his store.

He was too far away for me to see the expression on his face.

So now came *Macbeth*.

It began in the dark. Actually I don't think it was supposed to be that dark, I think the lights weren't working quite right. Anyway, these three dim figures were sitting around a big pot in the center of the stage. And once you adjusted your eyes with a lot of hard squinting, you could just about make out that they were women. They were waving their hands over the pot and muttering to themselves, like three hobos trying to keep warm over their rabbit stew.

It was a little hard to make out what they were saying, since they tended to put a lot of squeaks and screeches between the words. Aside from that, the voices were awfully ladylike and genteel. "Fair is foul, and foul is fair," I made out one of them saying, as she dropped something in the pot, and it was clear from her tone that she was pouring at some tea party for the local gentry and one of the guests had just asked for two lumps.

My program told me the names of the actresses who were playing these three characters. I recognized them as a local kindergarten teacher, a departmental secretary at Mesa Grande College, and the wife of a retired Air Force colonel.

Finally they took their pot and left the stage. The lights went up, and several men in cowboy suits came striding in. Their purposeful masculine movements, as well as the guns and holsters around their waists, left you in no doubt that they were military types. Leading them, and standing half a head taller than any of them, was Bernie Michaels, the chiropractor. The one thing you could say for Bernie's acting was that it was loud; he had a voice that filled the hall. On account of this, plus his long white beard—and in spite of the Stetson on his head, a little too big for him, with a tendency to slip down over his eyebrows—you could easily believe he was a big shot of some sort.

These cowboys were suffering from a peculiar delusion: they thought they were Scotsmen and that Bernie was their king, Duncan of Scotland. But pretty soon I got used to this. To tell the truth, I was beginning to get caught up in the play. I even began to enjoy it.

Don't get me wrong, I'm not giving *Macbeth* any rave reviews. The great Randolph Le Sage, from New York, was one of those actors who read their speeches with a lot of round reverberating "O" sounds. He produced his own echo as he talked, and he did so much spitting that you wanted to throw a towel to his fellow actors. And once, in the scene where Lady Macbeth is egging him on to kill the king, he kept trying to interrupt one of her long speeches, only she wouldn't let him.

And Sally Michaels's Lady Macbeth was pretty much like everything else I had ever seen her do. Before she addressed any remarks to other people on the stage, she took a couple of steps in their direction and pointed at them, in case the audience couldn't figure out who she was talking to. When she finally spoke, she enunciated each word with great care, pretty much the way she must have spoken to her third-grade classes.

Even so, the performance moved fast, most of the cast snapped out their lines, and you could understand what everybody was saying. It didn't take long for me to forget about that crazy cowboy idea, to ignore the Wild West outfits and enjoy the show.

And one thing in this production was really first-rate. You knew from the moment he first opened his mouth that Martin Osborn, in the role of Banquo, was the best actor on the stage. He spoke his lines so naturally that they didn't sound like lines at all; they sounded like exactly what this particular man might take it into his head to say at this particular moment.

After a while I got curious about something, so I turned my neck to try and look at Lloyd Cunningham. I wanted to see how he was reacting to Osborn's performance. I couldn't satisfy my curiosity, though; Cunningham wasn't in his seat anymore.

All this time, of course, I had been paying special attention to Roger, who wasn't bad at all. Which started me thinking about how there has to be a little bit of ham, or at least con man, in every good detective. Roger had several small parts, where he got to say some lines of the "Yes, sire" and "No, sire" variety, but his best part was Fleance, Banquo's teenage son, and he had one nice little scene with his father. Before and after that scene he showed up as several different hangers-on in King Duncan's court.

All the minor actors doubled or tripled as somebody else in this production: the three witches, with their black dresses traded in for blue ones, showed up as ladies in King Duncan's court; the dying Sergeant early in the play got himself resurrected in time to be the drunken Porter who opened Macbeth's gate; as I saw from the program that little Harold Hapgood, as the Old Man who made a gloomy weather report right after Duncan's death, was scheduled to show up later on as the Third Murderer.

So finally we got to the scene of Banquo's murder. Shakespeare hasn't actually given Banquo's son Fleance any lines in this scene, but Osborn had. Roger was supposed to stick in shouts of "Help!" and "Murder!" and "What ho!" while the Third Murderer grabbed him; then he fought his way free and went rushing off. I knew all this because he'd been practicing it around the office for the past four weeks.

The scene began with a dark stage again. Not quite as dark as it had been for the witches but enough so that it wasn't easy to make out people's faces. And it didn't help that the three murderers wore black masks on their faces, like outlaws in a Western movie.

Then Banquo and Fleance came on, strolling along, enjoying the night air, and suddenly the murderers were on them. Two of them had Banquo by the arms, and the third one, identified in the program as Harold Hapgood, had his left arm around Fleance's waist and his right hand flat against his chest just below his chin. Very poor mugging technique, I thought, remembering my years as one of New York's Finest. The left arm should have been around the neck.

Then Fleance pulled away from the Third Murderer. To tell you the truth, he didn't seem to need much strength to do it; the Third Murderer was awfully cooperative about letting him go. Then Banquo yelled at him, "O treachery!

Fly, good Fleance, fly, fly, fly!'' And Fleance, letting out horrendous shouts with obvious gusto, flew into the wings.

The murderers then turned their attention to Banquo. The first two had him pinned by the arms. The Third Murderer pulled out a big ugly-looking knife from under his black cloak and, aiming it directly at Banquo's middle, he charged at him with a fierce yell. The knife went straight into Banquo's chest; the Third Murderer pulled it out again, and drove it in again. Banquo's arms and legs thrashed; the other two murderers seemed to be having a hard time holding on to him. The Third Murderer pulled the knife out again, and a cry came out of Banquo, thick and hideous but cut off short. The two murderers let him go, and he sank to the ground.

Shakespeare, as I didn't find out till later, has the three murderers hang around and whisper some lines to each other at this point. But Osborn had cut these lines. The Third Murderer dropped his bloody knife and dashed offstage in the same direction Fleance had just gone; the first two murderers escaped in the opposite direction. Banquo, sprawled on the ground with his arms stretched out and one leg kicked under the other, remained alone onstage.

He lay there awhile. The lights didn't go out, the curtain didn't go down. Was he supposed to be dead, was there just enough life in him to gasp out a dying speech?

That's what I was waiting for, and the rest of the audience must have been waiting for it too, because there wasn't a cough or whisper or even heavy breathing in the whole house.

And then the silence was broken by a shout. "My God!"

I didn't realize at first that it had come from Allan Franz, sitting on my left. Only he wasn't sitting anymore, he was on his feet and running up the aisle. With amazing speed and agility for a man who looked as if he got most of his exercise in a swivel chair, he scrambled onto the stage, ran over to where Banquo was lying, and got down on his knees. I could see him lifting Banquo's hand, holding it a second, then letting it drop. Then he was on his feet again—the whole process hadn't taken more than thirty seconds—and he was facing the audience and shouting out, "For God's sake, is there a doctor out there? I think this man is dead!" There were gasps in the audience, and a woman gave a half scream.

There were half a dozen doctors out there, and one of them was on the stage in a few moments. Franz moved away, looking a little sick, as the doctor bent down to Osborn, put an ear to his chest, then looked up and muttered something. I couldn't hear what he was saying, but the look on his face told it all.

"See?" I heard a voice from the maverick section say loudly. "I told you about the curse, didn't I? The play is cursed!"

And finally I reacted. It had taken me a long time to remember that I was a policeman, a sworn officer of the law, even though I worked for the public defender. If a crime had been committed, it was up to me to take charge of things until the regular cops could be called.

So I got to my feet and followed Franz's and the doctor's routes up the aisle and onto the stage. The doctor was on his feet now, but I didn't have to get down on my knees in his place to see that Osborn was a dead man. The legs were pulled up, the right fist was clenched. There are positions that arms and legs can get into in death that they just don't get into when that person is alive. If I'd been up on the stage when he got stabbed, instead of out in the audience, I might have realized right away what had happened.

Also I saw a lot of blood, and lying a few feet away from the body, I saw the knife. Long glittering blade, black handle, big as the knife Mom uses to carve her pot roast.

I stepped forward and shouted at the audience, who were just beginning to break out of their trance and make hysterical noises. "Everybody stay seated till the police come! Shut the doors in back! One of you ushers, shut those doors and lock them!" I turned my shouting toward the wings. "Nobody leaves backstage either! Roger, are you there? See to it that nobody leaves! Lock the back doors!"

I saw him galvanized into life, so I turned back to the audience. "All right, be calm, everybody, get back to your seats. Is there a telephone in this theatre?"

A voice yelled at me from behind the stage, "There's a pay phone down in the basement!"

It was the stage manager, a heavyset man with bulging biceps and a two days' growth of beard. But right now as I joined him backstage, he was looking a little green around the gills.

He led me down a short flight of steps into the basement, then along the damp, musty corridor, with four or five doors off it. On the floor next to one of the doors lay a couple of stick brooms, a beat-up old whisk broom, and a wrung-out mop. We stepped over all this, turned a corner, and there was the pay phone attached to the wall. I put in my quarter, dialed police, and snapped out my message. I was told they'd be along in ten minutes.

I decided I'd better get back on the stage and do what I could to keep the mob from getting out of hand. So I retraced my steps along the basement corridor. And stopped suddenly.

From behind a door to my right, I heard banging noises and the sound of a muffled voice. It was the door with the brooms and the mop scattered on the floor in front of it.

"It's the janitor's closet," said the stage manager.

I tried the door. It was locked.

The stage manager pulled out a collection of keys on a chain, fumbled through them, and finally got the door open. Harold Hapgood, with his hair flying in every direction and his face very red, came stumbling out and landed in my arms.

"Who did this to me? Who's the son of a bitch—"

I asked him what he was talking about, and his voice with its lisp much more pronounced than usual, rose to a squeal. "They hit me over the head! My head hurts! The son of a bitch—"

Then he clapped his hand to his forehead. "My God, I've got to get up there! It must be my cue pretty soon! I never missed a cue in my life!"

"What cue?" I ran after him, grabbing him by the arm.

"For the murder scene! Let go of me, for heaven's sake! They can't do the murder scene without *me*! I'm the Third Murderer!"

FOUR

Roger's Narrative

I GOT FOUR HOURS of sleep on the night of the murder. Not enough for a growing boy, as my mother would say.

The cops and the district attorney's men kept hammering at me till one in the morning, first at the theatre, then down at headquarters. I was an important witness. I was the person who had got closest to the Third Murderer while he was on the stage. He had grabbed me and held on to me for a while before he moved on to killing Banquo. So why wasn't I able to say who it was? It made them mad as hell that I couldn't.

It was two o'clock before I got to sleep, and at seven my phone rang.

"I just read it in the morning papers," Dave's mother said. "How are you feeling, terrible? I'll come right over, I'll make you some coffee and some breakfast. After what you went through you shouldn't have to do it for yourself."

"I didn't go through so much," I managed to mumble into the phone. "It's really nice of you, but I don't have any breakfast stuff in the house."

"Not even an egg? Not even a piece toast? This is how you take care of yourself? Your mother would have a fit she should find out! She wouldn't forgive me in a million years!"

So eventually I told her I'd get up right away, take my shower, and drive over to her house so that she could have breakfast waiting for me. The only thing that worried me, I told her, was being late for work, but she answered that she'd square it with my boss. ''I've got influence with him. I knew him when he was in his diapers.''

The morning *Republican-American* was on my front porch as I left the house. Every once in a while, the paper boy manages to make the porch, instead of some narrow unreachable hole under the hedge. I stopped to look at the headlines; sure enough, the biggest were devoted to Osborn's murder, crowding Congressional ethics and terrorists down to the lower half of the front page.

PROMINENT ACTOR MURDERED ONSTAGE; SHAKESPEARE PLAY BECOMES BLOODBATH

The article began:

Hollywood actor-director Martin Osborn was stabbed to death last night in full view of an audience of two hundred people who had gathered at the Ramon Novarro Theatre for what they thought would be an evening of high culture. . . .

And in a small box next to the article was this announcement: ''Turn to page 5 for our critic's review of the performance.''

On page 5, under the familiar photograph of the paper's plump, beaming reviewer, I read the following:

The Mesa Grande Art Players' production of Shakespeare's *Macbeth* was interrupted last night by tragedy (described on page one). It must be reported, unfortunately, that this was the only note of genuine tragedy that occurred in the course of the evening.

Your reviewer, of course, along with the rest of the audience, had a chance to see only the first half of the production. The second half might have risen above the generally plodding and uninspired level of what we did see, though your reviewer has strong doubts, given the ineptitude of most of the major performances....

Still, I glanced through the rest of it to see if my name was mentioned. Yes, there it was. "The ill-fated Banquo's son Fleance, played by Roger Meyer, produced no startling revelations of characterization...."

I shrugged this off—what did *he* know?—and turned to the movie page, where I learned that the new Paul Newman flick, in which he invents the atomic bomb, would be opening on Friday. I made a mental note to see it as soon as possible. The invention of the atomic bomb, even by Paul Newman, wasn't likely to run very long in Mesa Grande. Now if it had been Sylvester Stallone dropping some of them on Latin American drug traffickers...!

I drove across town to the old lady's house. She lives in a much nicer neighborhood than I do. My neighborhood is new and still not very densely populated, but cracker-barrel houses, which in a few years will look like shanties, are springing up around me all the time. Her neighborhood is older, the lawns are wider, the houses are father apart, and everybody's doesn't look exactly like everybody else's. Her house is two stories high, white, red-shuttered and lace-curtained, kind of homey and inviting.

I pulled up right behind a dusty old Ford that I recognized immediately. Dave was getting out of it. He waited for me on the front walk, wearing that wry, slightly wary expression.

"Your mother was nice enough to ask me for breakfast," I said, as I went up to him. "She thought I'd be too tired to fix my own, on account of what happened last night. She didn't tell me you were going to be here too."

"Didn't she?" he said. "I guess that was before she developed her headache and discovered she was out of aspirin."

We walked up to the front door together, and a few seconds later the old lady was smiling at us and motioning for us to come in.

"Here's your aspirin, Mom," Dave said. "But are you sure you ought to be on your feet? Especially since you had the bug last night?"

"I started feeling better a couple minutes ago," she said. "I tried to call you but you left already. So you don't have a kiss for your mother?"

He gave her a kiss, though the wry look didn't leave his face. "And look who happened to drive up at the same time," he said. "You forgot to mention you were having Roger for breakfast this morning?"

"My headache pushed it right out of my mind." The old lady moved past him and planted a kiss on my cheek. "So come into the kitchen, the omelets are ready."

"Omelets! And enough for three people," Dave said as she took us both by the arm and steered us into her kitchen. "And do I smell blueberry muffins? And look at that fresh-squeezed orange juice! And all this you did while you were suffering from that headache!"

The old lady smiled gently, pointing us to our seats. "At my age the only cure for aches and pains is to think about something else."

In a few minutes those muffins and that omelet had eased the exhaustion out of my eyes and my bones. As I finished my coffee the old lady said, "So you both had an interesting night last night. I'll get you another cup coffee while you tell me about it.''

DAVE MADE A remark, apparently addressed to the ceiling, about singing for your supper and that there's no such thing as a free breakfast. Then he started in.

He repeated everything he'd seen and heard from his position in the audience. He repeated all conversations verbatim. I'd marveled before at his memory. The trick was to keep your eyes and ears open, to *notice* what was happening around you, not just to let it wash over you like your morning shower. I'd been practicing this trick for months, but I wondered if I would ever learn to do it as neatly as Dave did.

All the time his mother listened intently, her head cocked forward a little. Once or twice she interrupted him to ask him to repeat something. Like she was his superior officer, and he was her subordinate delivering an official report.

This thought made me squirm. That crazy suspicion was coming into my head again.

"It took the cops about ten minutes to get there," Dave was saying. "Sammy Sierra. He's the lieutenant that gets the important homicides. We've got a pretty good working relationship. Which naturally didn't stop him and his crew from grilling Roger and me twice as long as anybody else in the place."

"They talked to everybody that was in the theatre?" the old lady asked.

"They got names and statements from the whole audience, and from everybody that was on the stage and behind the stage. And some of them, including Roger, they hauled down to headquarters so the assistant DA could give them a going-over."

"Do you happen to know, did they find out if anybody got out of the theatre before you yelled that the doors should be locked?"

"I wouldn't know about that, Mom, Sammy wasn't telling me. I was pretty quick about getting them to shut the auditorium doors, and Roger was just as quick about the doors in back, but there were still a couple of minutes after Franz said Osborn was dead when there was a lot of confusion, people shouting, some of them starting up the aisle."

"And the murderer himself," I put in, "could've left the theatre through one of the back doors as soon as he got offstage."

The old lady shook her head. "No, this isn't possible. If the murderer left the theatre right after doing the murder, everybody would've noticed he was missing."

"You're assuming the murderer was somebody everybody knew," Dave said, "somebody in the cast or the backstage crew. You can't automatically make such an assumption."

"Assumptions I don't make automatically. I make them logically. This murderer is somebody who knew how the character he acted was dressed up, with a long black coat and a mask over his face. Who knew when he was supposed to walk on the stage, where he was supposed to stand, how he had to grab hold of Roger, how the other two actors would hold on to the victim so he could stab him nice and easy, how he'd run off the stage right afterward. Who also knew what lines he had to say, that he could say them in a whisper so nobody could recognize his voice, that he had to put on a little lisp like the regular actor did. In other words, this was somebody that belonged with the play, an actor or one of the stage crew. If such a person suddenly disappeared after the murder, everybody would miss him.''

''Maybe he's not actually in the play,'' I said. ''Maybe he's the husband or wife or a close friend of one of the actors, something like that. And the person who's in the play *told* the murderer all those details—''

''Not so stupid.'' The old lady turned a soft, approving smile on me, and I found myself blushing a little, the way I used to do as a kid if the teacher praised me in front of the class. ''Definitely a possibility. But not a likelihood. Hearing what happens secondhand, from somebody else's description, is different from seeing it yourself, with your own eyes. If you only heard it secondhand, you'd be crazy you should go up on the stage and try to do it right the first time, when you're committing the murder. This would be like acting in a play in front of an audience before you ever had any rehearsals.'' She turned back to Dave. ''So where did the police find the costume?''

''What do you mean, Mom?''

''This murderer had to get rid of the black cloak and the mask after he finished doing the murder. Did he drop them somewhere on the floor in the back of the stage? Where did the police find them?''

''As far as I know, they haven't been found yet. Sammy Sierra didn't mention them to me last night.''

''Did he say who is it the police are suspecting right now?''

''He didn't even drop a hint. Maybe Roger can answer that. He was down at headquarters for an hour after I went to bed.''

The old lady turned her gaze on me.

''I was questioned by one of the assistant DAs,'' I said. ''The new one, he's kind of young-looking. He didn't say it in so many words, but I got the feeling they're not sold on Harold Hapgood's story. He kept asking me if I was sure it wasn't Harold who grabbed me, how come I didn't react in some way if it was a different person. As if they think maybe Harold did the murder himself and invented that conk on the head to give himself an alibi.''

"So what story did you tell to the police?"

"It doesn't really amount to much," I said. "I was in position for the murder scene, just as I'd been dozens of times at rehearsal. Upstage, to the left, facing my father. Banquo, that is. Martin Osborn, that is. The Third Murderer came up behind me, the way he always did in rehearsal—"

"You could hear his footsteps?"

"Well, Fleance isn't supposed to, of course, but I always can. What I have to do is pretend I'm being taken by surprise. Well, a second later he had his left arm around my waist, pinning my arms to my side, and his right arm around my neck—no, around my chest, with his right hand flat against it, a couple of inches below my chin. Well, what I did then, I struggled a little. Not so hard that I'd break away from him too soon. I waited for my cue, when Banquo yells, 'Fly, good Fleance!' Then I broke loose from the Third Murderer and started yelling 'Help, murder!' and so on, and I ran offstage to the left."

"And there wasn't anything you noticed when this Third Murderer was holding on to you? Anything that maybe could be a clue who it was?"

"I sure can't think of anything. I didn't even see what he was dressed like or what his face looked like."

"You keep calling him 'he,'" Dave put in. "So you could tell it was a man, right?"

"No, I'm not even sure about *that*. I *expected* it to be a man, because it was usually Harold who did it to me. But now that I think of it, there wasn't anything particularly man-like about him. Or woman-like. The other people onstage could say a lot more about who it was, *they* were facing him—her. And later on, when he ran offstage—"

"You saw him when he ran offstage?" the old lady said.

"Just for a split second. Because I didn't go straight down to my dressing room in the basement, the way I usually do after that scene. I stood in the wings for a few minutes."

"How come you did that?"

"Well, to tell the truth, it's the first time we ever did the play in front of an audience. And the murder of Banquo was the end of the first half. So I was curious, after the curtain went down—"

"You were curious would there be any applause from the audience?" The old lady laughed, which somehow made me blush again. "So after you ran off the stage, you stood in the wings—this is what they call them? Like birds? And you saw maybe the murder happening?"

"No, I couldn't actually see Banquo being stabbed. That was on the right-hand side of the stage, there was no way of seeing it from where I was standing. But after it happened, the Third Murderer came running offstage on my side and went past me, to the stairs a few feet away from me, and down into the basement."

"You saw his face then?"

"No, he was moving much too fast. All I really saw was a streak of black. And the face was black too, he was still wearing that mask."

"Did it seem to you he was running like a man or like a woman?"

"I just can't answer that. With that cloak flapping around him, I couldn't see his legs or his arms, I had no sense of *how* he was running. Except that he was in one hell of a hurry."

"This didn't strike you as peculiar?"

"I suppose it did. But I wasn't letting myself think about it. I still wanted to hear that applause from the audience. I turned back to look at the stage, and a minute or two after that—well, all hell broke loose. Then Dave was up onstage yelling at me to lock the back doors, and that's about all I had any time to think about."

"Did anybody get out the back doors before you locked them?"

"I didn't see anybody. But if they made it before I got there, I *wouldn't* have seen them, would I?"

"And you didn't see this murderer anywhere either? Or the black coat and the mask he was wearing?"

"I'm afraid not. Lieutenant Sierra and the assistant DA weren't too happy with my story either. They made it pretty clear they think I know more than I'm telling."

"So don't you?"

The old lady settled back in her chair and took a nibble out of a piece of coffee cake.

"What are you getting at, Mom?" Dave said. "Roger wouldn't lie about this."

"Who's talking from lying? Sometimes what's in your memory gets lost in the back of your head. Isn't this what the psychoanalyzers are for? You lie down on a couch, you talk about when you were a baby and you got toilet trained, and suddenly you remember what you forgot." She turned back to me. "You didn't *see* anything about this murderer when he grabbed hold of you. So did you *hear* anything? Anything he said, even the way he sounded when he breathed?"

"Nothing at all."

"And the way he smelled?"

"I didn't notice anything. I suppose he smelled no different from the way *Harold* usually smelled."

"When he grabbed hold of you, was there something peculiar about how it felt?"

"No, I don't think so. I remember noticing afterwards that my neck wasn't sore— Wait a second!"

The old lady was beaming again. "You figured it out finally, am I right?"

"The way he held me when he grabbed hold of me! In rehearsals he always threw his right arm around my neck. He got carried away sometimes, he held on too tight, my neck was usually a little sore afterward. But last night he didn't touch my neck. He put his right arm over my *chest*, his right hand flat against it. But what's this supposed to prove? That last night's Third Murderer wasn't Harold Hapgood, because he grabbed me differently than Harold did?"

The old lady frowned and shook her head. "This I have to think about a little more. Right now I couldn't tell you what this proves."

As soon as she said this, I found myself feeling a twitch of disappointment. Like I really expected her to come up with the answers, to dig deeper into the truth than other people could.

But why didn't I expect this from *Dave?* Plenty of times, since I started working for him, I'd seen him unravel cases that baffled everybody else, I'd heard him come out with amazing logical deductions. So why was I turning to his mother now, instead of him?

"Damn it, it's after nine, we're late for work already!" Dave's voice cut sharply into my thoughts. "This conversation is a waste of time anyway, Mom. The police haven't arrested anybody, the public defender hasn't got a client, so Roger and I don't have any reason to think about this case."

He had his hand on my arm, and I barely had time to thank his mother for the breakfast before he hustled me out the front door.

FIVE

Dave's Narrative

DRIVING DOWN to my office, I thought about my relationship with Mom. Plenty of love and affection, but with a strong lacing of exasperation. I mean, there always came a time when we'd use the umbilical cord to play tug-of-war. No sooner do I decide, for instance, that the Meyer kid has to start seeing less of her than she not only invites him for dinner, she invites him for *breakfast* too.

What's more, if she'd planned it deliberately, could she have done a better job of letting him in on exactly what I didn't want him to be let in on? No wonder that puzzled look came onto his face halfway through the omelet and was still there when I finally got him out of the house!

All right, there was only one thing to do. I'd make a date to meet Mom for lunch today, and I'd explain to her how important it was that a certain distance be maintained between a man in a position of authority and the people working under him.

I'd explain it, but how would she take it? This question almost made me run a red light. I could hear the tone of Mom's voice, so soft and gentle and full of scorn. Her talent for making me feel like a naughty little kid was as impressive as ever, even after all these years. For the sake of my irrational childish vanity, was she going to deprive herself of the pleasure of shoveling food into this sweet earnest kid, fixing him up with nice Jewish girls, administering chicken soup when he had a cold? For her it was just like having a son in his early twenties again, instead of a grouchy old widower in his fifties who insisted on leading his own life and resisted all her matrimonial schemes.

My office is located in the new courthouse in downtown Mesa Grande. A magnificent-looking structure if your taste goes to mongrels: half ancient Greece, with columns and a portico, and half Spanish-pueblo, with pink adobe and a bell tower. The magnificence extends to the courtrooms, judges' chambers and jury rooms on the first and second floors, and to the suite of rooms occupied by the district attorney and his minions on the third floor; but the architects and decorators ran out of magnificence by the time they got to the public defender's quarters on the fourth floor.

We're shoved into the back with a spectacular view of the dark alley next to the side wall of the county jail. Moving through a frosted-glass door, our clients find themselves in a tiny waiting room with a couple of hard benches. This connects to a slightly larger room for Ann Swenson and to a cubbyhole that my self-respect requires me to call "my office." Just about enough space in it for my desk, my chair on one side of it, and a second chair on the other side of it. This second chair is where Roger spends much of his time when he isn't off doing legwork for me and Ann. Having increased the public defender's budget so I could hire an assistant, the City Council hasn't seen fit to provide anywhere for him to work.

We both reached the waiting room that morning within a few seconds of each other, but there was no chance for me to give Roger his orders for the day. Half a dozen cases were in various stages of investigation, there was plenty for him to do, but Mabel Gibson, who manned the waiting-room reception desk, forestalled all that. "Oh my goodness," she cried, "You're twenty minutes late, and she's been asking for you since nine!"

Mabel's children are all grown and her husband is a large, unemotional man, like a solid brick wall. With nobody to fuss over at home anymore, she does her fussing over the three of us.

We went into Ann's office and found a visitor with her, sitting in the chair across from her desk. It was Bernie Michaels, the chiropractor, who had played King Duncan in last night's *Macbeth*. He was a tall, broad-shouldered man whose grizzly beard and solemn blue eyes gave him a look of great dignity. With the Mesa Grande Art Players he specialized in kings, business executives, kindly old doctors, and, in one production, Abraham Lincoln.

He scrambled to his feet and shook my hand and Roger's warmly. He was sweating a little around his whiskers.

"You both know Mr. Michaels, I see," Ann said, cool and businesslike as always, without a word about our being late. "So we can get straight to the matter at hand. The murder at the theatre last night. The police have arrested Mr. Michaels's ex-wife."

"It isn't true," Bernie said. "Sally wouldn't ever do such a thing. I know she gets excited, maybe she says things she doesn't really mean. But that's only because she's got this—this dramatic side to her. She always wanted to be a stage actress, and she kind of likes to play parts."

Ann cut in, "Mrs. Michaels has asked us to handle her defense. She sent Mr. Michaels to us for that purpose."

"I guess that sounds kind of funny," Bernie said. "On account of Sally and me being divorced. But you have to know, there was never any bitterness, we've gone on being friends."

I didn't comment. I hadn't been in town yet at the time of the divorce, but I'd heard the rumors. As the gossipmongers told it, very few men of Sally's acquaintance, if they were over sixteen and more or less presentable, hadn't found their way to her bed.

"What makes them think she did it?" I said.

"They didn't tell her much when they arrested her this morning," Bernie said. "Something about witnesses."

"That couldn't be you, could it?" Ann turned to Roger. "Did you tell them anything that might lead them to think the person who grabbed you was Mrs. Michaels?"

I could see the kid gulping a little. Stronger types than him have been forced to back down under Ann's cross-examination. "I certainly don't *think* I did—"

Ann turned back to the rest of us. "All right, if the DA has witnesses, they must be the other two actors who were onstage when the murder took place. Who are they?"

"Jeff Greenwald and Danny Imperio," Roger said. "They play the first two murderers. Jeff's a senior at General Wagner High. Danny's a waiter at the Richelieu Hotel."

General William Henry Harrison Wagner, a hero of the Indian Wars, founded Mesa Grande about a hundred and twenty years ago; lots of things in town are named after him. And the Richelieu Hotel is the big posh resort on the outskirts of town, an object of awe and reverence to local merchants because of the tourist trade it brings in.

"Talk to them this morning," Ann said to me. "Also anybody else who was backstage at the time. Maybe the DA's got hold of somebody who got a good look at the murderer when he—or she—was running off the stage. And while you're at it, how about checking what they were all doing while Osborn was getting killed. Some of them ought to be able to give each other alibis."

"I'll get started on that," Roger said. "I know Jeff and Danny pretty well. I'll get in touch with them."

He left the room, while I turned back to Bernie, keeping my voice friendly. "What were *you* doing while Osborn was onstage being killed?"

"I'm King Duncan. Macbeth and his wife murder me early in the play. I wasn't even in the theatre when it happened."

"Where did you go?"

"I went to the movies. The Mesa Grande Triplex, just a couple of blocks from the theatre. I had two hours to kill, and I get restless if I just sit around backstage."

"Didn't you want to see how the play was going over?" Ann asked.

"Not particularly. All this theatre stuff, this acting and all, doesn't mean much to me. My father was a plumber. Back east, in Newark, New Jersey, that's where I was raised. While I was growing up, I hardly even knew there *were* such people as actors."

"How did you happen to get into acting then?"

He grinned a little. For a second there was something in his expression, under the gray beard and the royal dignity, that almost reminded me of a little boy. "When I married Sally, how else? *She* was crazy about it, you know, and I thought a husband ought to share his wife's interests. So they'd have things in common that they could talk about together. So I went down with her that first year when Lloyd Cunningham started the Players, and I tried out with her. She got to be the girl's mother in *Our Town*, and I got to be this college professor that gives all the statistics at the beginning. It's a pretty small part, so you probably don't remember it."

"But you and Mrs. Michaels broke up six or seven years ago," Dave said. "How come you're still acting?"

He spread his hands. "You know how it is. You get into the habit of something. They keep asking me to be in things. Whenever there's an old-man part, and it's so dull nobody else wants it—"

"Go on with what you did last night," I broke in, "at the time of the murder."

"Like I told you, I went to the movies. I expected to get back to the theatre in time for the curtain calls. I've been timing it at rehearsals, so I knew exactly how long I had."

"You weren't afraid the play might finish up earlier than usual?"

"Oh, no. Once we get set, we perform it at pretty much the same speed every time. I was planning to give it ten minutes leeway or so, in case somebody forgot their lines and skipped a page or two. I was sure I wouldn't need more than that. But of course—" a troubled look came over his face—"it didn't work out that way last night. I mean, I got out of the movies at ten o'clock, which should've been plenty of time, but when I got to the theatre the place was surrounded by police cars."

"So what did you do then?"

"My first thought was that somebody had an accident, somebody got hurt. Sally, maybe. I tried to get into the theatre; the police told me I couldn't. I'm afraid I got pretty excited. It took me a while to convince them I belonged there. Well, finally they let me through, and I looked all over for Sally. She was being questioned by one of the district attorney's people, and after he finished he told her she'd have to wait around until the assistant DA gave orders they were through with her. So I waited with her. And actually they let her go about half an hour later."

"You went home after that?"

"Well, I took Sally home first. She was exhausted, poor girl, so I didn't go into the house with her. *Then* I went home. I slept for a few hours, and then, just an hour ago, Sally called me from the jail. You *will* handle her case, won't you? She can't afford a lawyer, she hasn't got a dime. You know what grade-school teachers get paid, and Sally never saves any of her money." He lifted his chin. "If *I* had the money, I'd gladly—I mean, what else have I got to spend it on? But if you want to know, I'm pretty close to dead broke myself. You know what the economy is in this town these days. My practice is just about breaking even."

"You don't have any savings?" I asked. "The economy was pretty good a few years ago."

"Oh yes, I did pretty well for a while, I built up a pretty good bank account. But—well, that's all gone now. In the last few years there've been expenses."

He didn't say any more, but he didn't have to. I was sure his ex-wife had never hesitated to put the bite on him whenever she ran out of funds.

"Bernie," I went on, "what was the movie you saw last night?"

"It was one of those—oh my God, it was one of those mad slasher things! Blood spurting all over the place—" He broke off, his face slightly yellow. "I came in at the middle and didn't leave till it got around to the part where I'd come in."

"Didn't it bother you that you'd see the second half first and first half second?"

"What's the difference? I'm not much of a moviegoer, television is so much easier and cheaper. I went to the movies a lot when I was a kid, but I lost interest after I grew up. I'll bet this is the first one I've been to in ten years. All I really cared about was passing the time and getting back to the theatre before the curtain call."

We had no more questions for Bernie, so Ann told him he could leave it to us from now on. We'd try to arrange bail for Sally, and we'd be in touch with him on our progress. Meanwhile he should do as little worrying as possible.

ROGER CAME BACK after Bernie was gone, saying he had appointments with the two murderers. Till then, I told him, he was to go down to the Ramon Novarro Theatre, find the stage manager, and get a list of everybody in the cast and crew who was backstage at the time of the murder. Then he was to find out what as many of them as possible had been doing, whom they had been with, and if any of them could alibi others.

Meanwhile, Ann and I started our working day by going down to the second floor, where we had an appointment with the assistant DA who was handling the murder.

His name was Leland Grantley III, and he had replaced George Wolkowicz, who had been offered a higher-paying assistantship in San Diego, with a classier, more affluent criminal element. Already, though Wolkowicz had left less than a month ago, the feel of the office was completely different. Wolkowicz's desk had always been a disaster area, but now it was incredibly neat: empty new blotter, a row of sharpened pencils, a blank notepad, an empty In tray and a full Out tray.

And the pictures on the walls were different. Wolkowicz had gone in mostly for photographs, showing himself sitting at banquet tables, shaking hands with local celebrities, or grinning servilely at our esteemed district attorney, Marvin McBride. In each case McBride was wearing his friendliest, dumbest grin, which showed the pictures had been taken in the late afternoon, after he had lubricated himself with his usual quota of daylight martinis; pictures taken of him in the morning always showed him looking angry, not at the rise of the crime rate but at the effect of this morning's hangover on his digestion.

But Wolkowicz had evidently taken his photographs with him to San Diego, and the new assistant DA had put up reproductions of famous paintings by Impressionists. The word was that he was an intellectual, right out of Harvard Law School, and had turned down two or three offers from Wall Street firms because he preferred a career of public service.

He stood up when Ann and I entered. Another radical break with tradition: Wolkowicz had never gone further than a nod and a grunt. Then he actually came around his desk so he could shake our hands. He was a thin, tan, old-young man, with stooping shoulders, thick black-rimmed glasses, and a two-piece gray pin-striped suit with a subdued blue-gray tie to match. The uniform of big-city Eastern yuppiedom, not usually seen in our parts. We have our own yuppies, of course—Mesa Grande is a growing community, not to be left out of present-day social progress—but their uniform involves open sports shirts with little alligators over the pocket.

"How are you, how are you, nice to see you again," he murmured at Ann and me; the Leland Grantley IIIs manage to express their emotions without ever raising their voices. "Please sit down. Is that chair comfortable enough for you, Mrs. Swenson? Well, I'm certainly glad you could see me this morning." He was behind his desk again, hands clasped in front of him. "When the public defender is handling a case I'm concerned in, I believe we should get together and talk out all the problems, bring our differences into the open. Cooperation, not competition, that's my policy."

"Have you discussed your policy with the DA?" Ann asked.

"Oh, yes. Mr. McBride is solidly behind me. 'A hundred and ten percent' is how he puts it. He's got a very colorful way of speaking, don't you agree? A salty character in every respect.''

He smiled, then his smile gave way to an earnest expression. ''Now I hear you'll be handling the defense for the Michaels woman. Sally Michaels, I believe, is the full name.'' From his desk drawer he pulled out a folder and contaminated the purity of his desk blotter as he ruffled through it.

''What we were hoping you'd explain to us,'' Ann said, ''is why you're charging Mrs. Michaels with this crime. A dozen or more people were backstage at the time of the murder. Not to mention a few hundred more in the audience, almost any one of whom could have slipped out of the auditorium and gone backstage when the lights were out.''

''Yes, that's true. It's seldom a murder is committed in such public circumstances. Makes this case terrifically fascinating.'' Grantley's face had taken on a gleam of boyish excitement. He forced himself to look earnest again. ''As to your question, though. You know, my predecessor in this office might have refused to answer it. Even though the law says we have to provide the defense with all the results of our investigations. Well, I don't operate the way he did. Frankly, I don't want to get convictions through trickery and unfairness. So I'll put my cards on the table right now. We've got two pieces of evidence against Mrs. Michaels. Either one might be the basis for a case, taken together they're conclusive. First of all, we've got eyewitnesses who are ready to swear it was Mrs. Michaels who dressed up as the Third Murderer and stabbed Mr. Osborn.''

''What eyewitnesses?'' Ann gave a gentle snort. ''Only three people, besides the victim, got close to the killer. One of them happens to work in my office, and I know *he* can't identify Mrs. Michaels.''

"Yes, young Meyer. I know what he *says,* of course. There may be some who might point out that he has a certain vested interest in Mrs. Michaels's being acquitted. But I won't make such a suggestion; I'm happy to assume he's telling the truth. The fact is, he never saw the killer from the front, did he? She was behind him all the time, until he left the stage.''

"In other words," I said, "your eyewitnesses are that high school student, Greenwald, and that waiter, Imperio. The actors who played the other two murderers. They weren't naming any names last night. How come they didn't accuse Mrs. Michaels right after they saw the murder?''

"They were in a state of shock last night," Grantley said. "They weren't sure what they'd seen, they hadn't thought it all through yet. But this morning, when they were calmer and steadier and had a chance to refresh their recollections—"

"With a battery of police officers doing the refreshing," Ann said.

"I assure you, Mrs. Swenson," Grantley said, with an injured look on his face, "nobody intimidated them in any way. *We* didn't bring up Mrs. Michaels to those two witnesses. It was what *they* told us—about the brief scene they played with the Third Murderer, before Roger Meyer and the victim came onstage—that suggested Mrs. Michaels to us. You remember no doubt that Harold Hapgood—is that his name? Yes, it's right here—who was supposed to be the Third Murderer, is unusually short, at least a head shorter than Greenwald and Imperio, who are fairly short themselves; they're both exactly five feet eight. Ordinarily, when they played their scene with Hapgood, they had to look down at him. But last night—so they tell us, and they're prepared to testify to this under oath—they played the scene with him at eye level. Do you see the significance of that? Last night the Third Murderer, *the* murderer, was exactly the same height as the other two.''

''I don't see how that justifies you in accusing Sally Michaels—''

''You agree, I'm sure, that the murderer has to be somebody with a close connection to the play, somebody who's seen the rehearsals, who knew the Third Murderer's lines and what actions he was supposed to perform. And somebody who's fairly close to five feet eight inches tall. Well, we've questioned everybody who's connected with the play, the cast and the backstage crew who were in the theatre last night. At the time of the murder, most of them were busy doing their jobs, and in full view of at least two other people. Only a handful have no alibis of that sort. All of them actors, by the way, none of them members of the stage crew. I'll be happy to supply you with a list of names, though no doubt you'll want to do your own questioning too. Well, of those five or six people whose whereabouts at the time of the murder can't be substantiated, all but one are too tall to have taken Hapgood's place onstage. Your client, Mrs. Michaels, happens to be the only one who's exactly five feet eight inches tall.''

''Ridiculous,'' Ann said. ''You've got no proof at all that the murder wasn't committed by somebody from the audience or by somebody who came in from outside. Doesn't Osborn have any family, any survivors? He had a lot of money. Who inherits it?''

''He never seems to have made a will,'' Grantley said. ''Actors' Equity has a few facts on file about his background, but it isn't much. He was born in Los Angeles, not far from the studios. Parents dead, no siblings; late wife had no relatives either. His Equity insurance goes to her, and he never bothered to change it after she died. So I'm afraid the mysterious sinister heir just isn't in the picture.''

''Even so, that business about the murderer's height sounds pretty thin to me. Why couldn't the murderer be a taller person who was stooping?''

Grantley gave a little laugh. ''Well, I suppose it's *possible,* Mrs. Swenson. But I rather believe no jury will find it *likely.* When you combine the matter of height, however, with our *second* piece of evidence—''

''Which is?''

''The Third Murderer's costume was supposed to be a black poncho, a bit too large for him, so it concealed most of his body. That costume plus the black mask was what made it hard to see who it was.''

''Wait a second,'' I broke in. ''He wasn't wearing any poncho. He was wearing a raincoat, a dark-colored raincoat, I'll swear to that.''

''Exactly the point.'' Grantley turned his pleased smile on me. ''Harold Hapgood had that poncho on when he was attacked in the basement, he still had it on when you found him in the broom closet. Evidently the killer didn't have time to pull it off him and put it on herself. Maybe she heard somebody coming down to the basement and had to stow Hapgood away fast. So she did the next best thing: she went onstage in her own raincoat, which she ordinarily wore to the theatre at night. It's a common type of cheap raincoat, nondescript dark gray in color, and with the lights dim nobody, not even the actors onstage with her, would be likely to identify it as hers. And nobody would have, except for the one bad break she got. When she came in close to stab Osborn, he must've shot his hand out and grabbed hold of one of the buttons on her raincoat. She pulled away from him, but the button came tearing off. We found it in the palm of the victim's hand.''

"I didn't see it when I looked at the body last night," I said.

"The victim's hand was closed over it. And you were being very careful not to touch the body, weren't you? So it's no wonder you didn't notice the button. But the doctor noticed it when he examined the body just before you. He left it where he found it and called it to the attention of the police when they got to the scene.''

I remembered now, Osborn's right fist *had* been clenched when I looked at the body. I saw no point in mentioning this, though.

"How can you be sure that button came from Mrs. Michaels's raincoat?" Ann said. "You just told us it's a common cheap brand.''

"We searched the theatre, and we found Mrs. Michaels's raincoat on the floor of her dressing room. As if she'd thrown it down there in a hurry. The middle button was torn from it, and the button Osborn was holding matches the others exactly. So there really isn't any doubt about it, I'm afraid.''

"I've got plenty of doubts," Ann said. "The murderer could've stolen Mrs. Michaels's coat from her dressing room, then thrown it back in there afterward. You've got nothing to connect her *directly* with the murder. The weapon, for instance." Ann narrowed her eyes. "I don't suppose you *can* connect her with the weapon?''

"No, as a matter of fact, we can't. The play murder was supposed to be committed with a prop knife, made of wood, that Hapgood carried in a pocket inside his poncho, but *that* knife was still there when he woke up in the broom closet. The *real* murder weapon is an ordinary kitchen knife, with a black rubber handle. It's mass-produced, most of the hardware stores in town carry it."

"And I gather you didn't find Mrs. Michaels's fingerprints on it. Or you certainly would've mentioned it a long time ago."

"There were *no* fingerprints on the knife. That type of handle wouldn't show any."

"Well, there you are then," Ann said. "And another thing—where's the motive? Why should Sally Michaels want to kill Martin Osborn?"

Grantley gave a little shrug. "We haven't uncovered her motive yet, I admit that. It's not necessary to prove motive in a murder case, I'm sure you know this better than I do. As long as you can prove everything else. Nevertheless, we're working on it, and I'm sure we'll come up with something. These theatrical people are such emotional types."

"What this all boils down to," Ann said, "is that you haven't got much of a case. Certainly not for such an early arrest."

Grantley smiled and got to his feet. "Well, it seems to be time for my next appointment. Mrs. Swenson, Dave, it's been a pleasure. And listen, now, I want you to know you can count on my full cooperation in your investigation. As District Attorney McBride said to me only the other day, this office isn't in the business of getting convictions. This office is in the business of making sure that justice is done."

YOU GET FROM the new court building to the new jail by an underground passageway, which already, though the buildings have been in existence only two years, smells as damp and musty as a men's shower room. Once at the jail, Ann and I were shown into the small basement room where prisoners get to confer with their attorneys. This room has a wooden table and a few metal chairs around it, and its only window is in the center of the heavy iron door. Outside this door sits a guard with a gun strapped conspicuously around his waist, to let the lawyers inside know that it would be useless for them to try to bust their clients out of jail.

Sally Michaels was led in a few minutes after Ann and I sat down at the table. The last time I had seen her she had been up onstage as the Queen of Scotland, cowboy-style, with an elegant evening dress circa 1890, and a diamond tiara (made of cardboard but convincingly painted) ringing her semi-blond hair. I remember thinking she might have been a handsome woman in her younger days.

Not much was elegant or queenlike about her now. After a morning in jail, the folds at her neck were flabby, her hair seemed mouse-gray, and the heavy dark smudges under her eyes made her look even older than her age, which was probably close to fifty.

When she saw us, she put on a big smile and sailed across the room to us, arms outstretched. "Oh, how good of you to come!" she cried. She was the fashionable hostess welcoming distinguished guests to her drawing room.

"Are you all right, Mrs. Michaels?" Ann said. "Are they treating you well?"

"Nothing to complain of at all—Mrs. Swenson, isn't it? I can assure you that people couldn't be more gracious and considerate to me. The staff, that is." Sally tried a charming toss of her head, but her eyes suddenly started filling with moisture. I looked down at my shoes.

"The judge has scheduled a hearing for bail at three o'clock this afternoon," Ann said. "We've got a good chance of getting you out then, the assistant district attorney seems to be willing to cooperate. But it can't be until three, I'm afraid."

"Oh, I've endured worse than this, believe me." A tinkling laugh from Sally. Lady Something-or-Other presiding over an Oscar Wilde tea party. "In my old theatre days, you should've seen some of the dressing rooms I got stuck with."

As far as I knew, Sally's theatre days had been confined to her appearances with the Mesa Grande Art Players. How much of her glamorous past, I wondered, had she talked herself into believing?

"So you think I've got a chance of being let out on bail?" she went on. "Who's the judge going to be?"

"Probably Judge Flannery," Ann said.

"Henry Flannery? His little grandson was in my third-grade class a few years ago. Henry's a charming man. A gentleman of the old school. The type who, if you don't mind my saying so in these days of women's lib, still holds to the old-fashioned notion that the female of the species should be treated with somewhat greater delicacy and respect than the male. Oh, I'm sure Henry will be—will fully appreciate—the difficulties of my situation and—and—"

Her voice trailed off. The eyes were filling up again.

"We'll certainly do our best," Ann said. "Meanwhile, not to waste any time, I'd like to go over last night's events with you."

"I've been over them a thousand times with the policemen and the district attorney. They woke me up at five-thirty this morning. Five-thirty, good God; I haven't been up that early since I was a kindergartner! They didn't even give me a chance to put on a decent-looking dress or take trouble with my makeup or put a drop of Magnolia Blossoms behind my ear. And I seem to have been doing nothing but telling that same damn story ever since."

"I'm sorry," Ann said, "but I'm afraid it's still necessary for me, as your attorney—"

"No, no, it's all right, I apologize for making such a fuss. You're my lawyer, you know what has to be done. Well, let me see." Sally put one pudgy finger to her chin and frowned prettily, her "thinking" pose. "It would be six o'clock or so when I got to the theatre last night. The curtain wasn't due to go up till seven, but we had to get there early for makeup and costumes and so forth. I've got my own dressing room for this show, because there are so few women in the cast. Only little Laurie Franz, our Lady Macduff, and those three frightful old biddies who play the witches. If you can call it a dressing room, more like a hole in the wall, but at least I have it all to myself. And freezing! Would somebody please explain to me why the dressing rooms in this theatre are always so cold, even when it isn't cold outside!"

"Did you happen to see Mr. Osborn before the show began?"

"Oh, yes. He had us all gather on the stage around a quarter of seven—with the curtain down, of course—and he gave us the usual pep talk that directors give you on opening night. He told us how wonderful we all were, and what a brilliant performance we were going to give. We always know it's bullshit, you understand, but we'd be terribly disappointed if the director ever left it out. Actors are such children."

"You went back to your dressing room after the pep talk?"

"Yes, I did. I chatted there for a while with Randy Le Sage. He's got the dressing room right next to mine, he's our big New York actor who was brought in at great expense to play Macbeth. To tell you the truth, till Martin mentioned his name I'd never heard of him. Small wonder! The way he kept stepping on my lines last night, trying to interrupt me. And *he's* supposed to be a professional? Well, anyway, after a few minutes Randy had to leave and be ready in the wings for his entrance with Banquo, where they see the weird sisters. And I do mean weird. I taught at the same school as Ella Feeney once, she's a kindergarten teacher, and everyone knows they turn into five-year-olds themselves after a few years, though most of them start off on that level—"

"How long was it before you went onstage yourself?"

"Another fifteen minutes. I begin with my letter scene, you know the one I mean, I'm sure. I read this letter from my husband, where he tells me what the weird sisters predicted, and all the time I've got this gleam of ruthless ambition in my eye."

She put a gleam of ruthless ambition in her eye, to show us what she meant.

"In your next few scenes," Ann said, "did you happen to see Harold Hapgood? He was supposed to play the Third Murderer, but I understand he had some other parts too."

"I certainly must've seen him, but I can't say I paid too much attention. Poor Harold is such a ... a *washed-out* actor, if you know what I mean. You hardly realize he's on the stage at all, even when he's saying his lines."

"Did you see him go onstage for that murder scene?"

"No, I wouldn't have. One of my biggest scenes comes right after intermission. The banquet scene, where Macbeth sees Banquo's ghost, and I keep telling the guests that nothing is wrong with him. It's an extremely taxing scene, it requires the most intense emotional concentration, so I was in my dressing room resting up for it. There's a little couch in there, a fairly dilapidated old piece of furniture, and I was stretched out on it all the time the...the murder was happening up on the stage."

"Did anyone see you in your dressing room at that time?" I said. "Or talk to you through the door?"

"Oh, dear me, no. When I'm resting before a big scene, working up my emotional concentration, I simply mustn't be disturbed. Everybody in the company knows that. Randy Le Sage likes to rest up before the banquet scene too. Maybe *he* was in his dressing room, and he heard me tossing and turning. Those walls are as thin as paper, no privacy at all."

"Was it your black raincoat that you wore to the theatre last night?"

"I always do, everybody knows that about me. It's a mangy old thing, but I'd never bring one of my really *nice* coats into that grubby old barn."

"The police say they found it on your dressing room floor, with one of the buttons torn off."

"Yes, they told me that, I just can't understand it. That button wasn't torn off when I got to the theatre at six. I'm positive I would've noticed."

"You don't lock your dressing room whenever you leave it?"

"Good heavens, nobody does that. And certainly not *me*. As a matter of fact, most of the time when I leave my dressing room I don't even bother to shut the door behind me. I'm such a trusting person, it's my one big fault. You'll never convince me that people aren't innately good."

She raised her chin on these words, and I remembered that the Mesa Grande Art Players had done *The Diary of Ann Frank* a few years ago.

"Everybody in the company," I said, "knows how you feel about locks and doors, I suppose?"

"I imagine so. Everybody knows *everything* about me. I'm just not the type to conceal my feelings."

"Last night, when the police took your raincoat away with them," Ann said, "didn't that worry you a bit?"

"Why should it?" She met Ann's eyes steadily. "I didn't have anything to feel guilty about."

Ann gave a little grunt. "One last point, Mrs. Michaels. Did you have any reason to kill Martin Osborn?"

"Certainly not!"

"If there *is* such a reason, *anything* in your relationship with him, I advise you to tell me all about it right now. I can promise you, the police will dig it up sooner or later."

Ann fixed her eyes on Sally in that riveting way Ann is so good at. Sally stared back for a while, and then her eyes lowered. "Martin and I were—we'd been having a rather close relationship. We made no secret about it. We didn't exactly send announcements to the newspapers, either, you understand, but I suppose there must be people who know about it."

"How long had it been going on?"

"Three or four months. Since last June, when he came up with the idea of doing *Macbeth,* and he consulted me about it and asked for my support at the Players meeting, and told me what a perfect Lady Macbeth I'd be."

"All right, now go on being frank with me, will you. What was the status of this relationship as of last night?"

"Well, the truth is, we broke up a week ago. He told me . . . well, you know how people's minds work. If a man and a woman break up their relationship, people assume that *he* dumped *her,* and naturally she's furious with him. Hell hath no fury—"

"*Did* he dump you?"

"No! Things haven't been going too well lately. We've *both* been feeling it. We knew we had to move on, it was necessary for our personal growth. The fact that *he* was the first one to find somebody else is entirely irrelevant to—"

"He started an affair with somebody else? Who was it?"

"I haven't the slightest idea. All he told me was that there *was* somebody. Of course I can make a pretty good guess."

"And what *is* your guess?"

"Well, when a play is in rehearsal, who does the director get thrown in with night and day, he doesn't even have *time* for other people? The members of the cast, that's who. And who are the other women in this cast? I certainly can't see Martin coming on to one of those fat frumpy witches!"

"You're saying," I put in, "Osborn is having an affair with Laurie Franz?"

"I'm not *saying* anything. You asked me what I was *guessing*." She gave a little flounce and sat back in her chair. "At any rate, it's ridiculous to think that my breaking up with Martin gave me a motive to *kill* him. I've had plenty of relationships. It's almost seven years since Bernie and I got divorced, you don't imagine I've lived like a nun all that time? I'm a deeply emotional person, I have a need for love. If I went around murdering every man I've broken up with, I'd be one of those serial killers."

She held her head high for a few moments after this, but then her lips trembled a little. "I don't want you to think— I'm not promiscuous. I never go with more than one man at a time. It's always somebody I truly care about. It's just that...a woman who's all alone nowadays...and nobody to talk to at work except a lot of eight-year-olds..."

A little later I signaled for the guard to open the door. Sally marched out of the room, chin up, eyes flashing.

"Katharine Hepburn in *Mary of Scotland*," Ann said. "It was one of the late movies on TV last week."

By now it was almost noon. Ann had to go back to her desk and munch a sandwich while she got ready for the bail hearing that afternoon. I had to meet Mom at the courthouse cafeteria for lunch. The purpose of which was to explain to her why she had to stop paying so much attention to my assistant.

I didn't have much appetite.

SIX

Roger's Narrative

I SPENT Friday morning at the theatre, talking to the stage crew and the stage manager. They were there, even though the play had been shut down, because there hadn't been any time to clean up the stage last night. Also, since the theatre would be closed for a while, props and furniture had to be locked up in a storeroom.

I talked to every one of these people and found out they'd all had something important to do during the Banquo scene, and each of them did it with at least two of the others. So they alibied each other perfectly.

Also none of them could remember noticing anything particular about the masked and raincoated actor who had played the Third Murderer. A few of them got a glimpse of him standing in the wings before he went onstage, a few of them saw him moving fast as he left the stage, but nobody had any helpful details to offer.

It was lunchtime before I finished at the theatre, so I went back to the office to give Dave my report. No Dave, though. Mrs. Gibson told me he was having lunch at the courthouse cafeteria; he had left a message for me to join him.

I went downstairs to the basement where the cafeteria was located. It was crowded, of course, with the usual mix of lawyers and cops and jurors and felons. You can tell the felons from the others by the anxious looks on their faces. I spotted Dave at a table in the corner, and was surprised to see he had his mother with him. I waved at them till I caught their attention, then motioned I was going through the line to get my food.

I got chicken à la king, because at the courthouse cafeteria seeing what you're eating can only depress you. Then I joined them at their table.

"Didn't expect you in here today," Dave said, giving me a glare that didn't look particularly welcoming.

"Mrs. Gibson said you left a message for me to meet you here."

"I'm the one left the message," said Dave's mother. "I asked you should have lunch with us. Excuse me, Davie, did your secretary get it mixed up?"

Dave gave her a hard look. "She's been working for me three years, and I've never yet known her to get a message mixed up."

"It only goes to prove, nobody's perfect."

The old lady turned her smile on me and said, "So sit down, be comfortable. That's all you're having for lunch, that puddle? No green vegetables? All right, it's *your* health. So you both had busy mornings, didn't you? Davie was telling me just now about his. How about yours?"

This made me very uncomfortable. It occurred to me that Dave wouldn't want me to come out with a confidential report in front of somebody who had no official position.

"Why so shy?" the old lady said. "You're the old-fashioned type that wouldn't talk about business to a woman? You think a woman wouldn't understand such complicated things that you do at your office?"

The corners of Dave's mouth were turned down, his bad-smell expression that I had come to know and pretty much dread. He gave a weary wave of his hand. "Okay, you may as well make your report. It'll save time later."

So I reported, the old lady nodded and said, "So now it's pretty obvious, isn't it? The murderer wasn't wearing your client's raincoat by accident. He didn't pick it up just because it happened to be handy. He went out of his way he should be wearing it. He took it from her and put it on so she should get arrested."

"What makes you think that, Mom?"

"Because when this Hapgood got knocked out and locked up in the broom closet, he had his costume on already, the black poncho that he ordinarily used for the murder scene. So why didn't the murderer take this poncho off and wear it himself? Wouldn't that be easier to do than go to all the trouble stealing Sally Michaels's raincoat from her dressing room? The only logical explanation: he wanted she should be blamed."

"Unless our client wore her own raincoat, Mom," Dave said. "Unless she's guilty to begin with."

"This," said the old lady, "isn't a possibility."

"How can you be so sure of that?"

"From everything you told me about her so far. What is it in life that means more to her than anything else? Playing big parts in front of audiences, am I right? If she killed this Martin Osborn, what was she doing except closing down the play and giving up her chance to act Lady Macbeth? And halfway through yet, before she gets to do the scene where she's sleepwalking! This is the scene that plenty actresses would die happy they should only be asked to act it in public. Believe me, Davie, if your client wanted to kill Martin Osborn, she'd wait till the last night of the play."

She turned back to me now. "You did good questioning the witnesses. It's too bad you couldn't do just as good questioning yourself."

"I don't know what you—"

"Certainly you know. Now it's time you should *know* that you know. Do me a favor, all right? Ask yourself one question—only don't just answer it right away, off your head, but give it a little bit thought."

"Sure I will. What is it?"

"This morning you remembered how the murderer grabbed you from behind and put his hand on your chest. So can you push a little harder? Did you see something else, only it's gone to sleep in the back of your mind?"

I shut my eyes and tried to think back to that moment. It was hard. It had all happened so fast, and I had been standing onstage in front of two hundred people, worrying about screwing up my lines.

"I wish there *was* something," I said. "But I just can't—"

"Take it piece by piece, maybe it'll wake up," she said. "When I'm giving a dinner party, and I'm trying to remember at the last minute if there's something I forgot, what I do is I take it piece by piece. First I see myself meeting people at the door. It's a cold night maybe, they'll have hats and coats; have I got enough places to hang them all up? Then I see them coming into the living room; I'm offering them drinks and appetizings. Did I pick up the crackers for the chopped liver? Have I got enough chairs for them to sit in? You see what I mean?"

"Yes I do. I'll try it."

I shut my eyes again and went through it piece by piece. Third Murderer tiptoeing up behind me. The sound of soft breathing. The hands grabbing me. First the left hand around my waist, my arms being crushed to my sides. Then the right against my chest. High up, applying pressure. My eyes blinking down, a quick flash of that hand on my chest. A couple of fingers. Curling.

But that was it. Nothing more would come to me. I shook my head, furious with myself. "I'm sorry. *Something's* kicking around in there—"

"All right, all right," the old lady pushed in. "You did good. Now forget about it."

Dave broke in at this. "Wait a second, Mom, if he's getting close—"

"Don't be so impatient, Davie. Just like when you were a little boy." She reached across the table and patted my hand. "There's a time to concentrate, and there's a time to put the problem out of your mind and think about other things. Let it simmer on the back of the stove for a while."

I could see Dave doing some simmering of his own, but he didn't raise any objections.

SEVEN

Dave's Narrative

I NEVER HAD such a frustrating lunch. I was alone with Mom for about fifteen minutes, during which time I told her about my morning with the assistant DA and with Sally Michaels. Then, just as I was getting up the nerve to read her the riot act about the way she was treating Roger, along comes the kid himself. And it turns out Mom invited him! As if she'd known all along what I wanted to say to her, and she was making sure I couldn't say it.

Right after lunch, before I could send Roger off to question those two actors and maybe have a few minutes alone with Mom, she announced that she had shopping to do, slid into her little Japanese car, and went tootling off. Pulling away from the curb a little too fast, as usual, with a screeching of gears and tires. And the insurance companies raise their rates for teenagers!

So Roger headed to a phone booth, to find out if Greenwald and Imperio, the two actors who played First and Second Murderer, were home and able to see him. And I headed east to drop in on Harold Hapgood at his insurance agency. I didn't call up first. I decided I'd have better luck if I took him by surprise.

My destination was one of the malls that have been springing up to the east over the last ten years, since Mesa Grande started its big spurt of growth. (Nothing can spring up to the west, because the Rocky Mountains are standing in the way; our local real estate interests would love to figure out how to raze them, but so far they haven't been able to swing it.) Each mall is surrounded by a collection of identical cracker-barrel houses, and each collection has its own fancy name, Buckingham Acres or Hidalgo Towers or Chateau des Alpes. It's amazing how out here in the West, where people pride themselves on being plain down-to-earth Americans and look down their noses on those decadent foreigners, nothing sells a piece of dry rocky real estate better than giving it an old aristocratic European name.

Harold Hapgood's insurance agency was in a small building next to the mall des Alpes. He lived in an apartment on the second floor, above his office. A frosted-glass door had the words "Hapgood and Hillary, Insurance" painted neatly on it. In the outer room, which didn't seem to be a waiting room but an office in its own right, a short, skinny, pasty-faced man, probably in his forties, with a long nose and bloodshot eyes, sat behind a desk; next to the desk was a wheelchair. I had done a little research on Hapgood and his partner, Theodore Hillary, Jr.—I have a valuable friend who works in the morgue at *The Republican-American*—and I remembered that there had been some kind of an auto accident a few years back and Hillary had lost the use of his legs.

I introduced myself. This usually produces a look of surprise and sometimes even anxiety on people's faces; not too many people can take the unannounced visit of a detective in their stride. But Hillary didn't even bat an eyelash. He gave a dry grating cough and said, "Harold's busy with a client. If you don't have time to wait, he'll call your office and set up an appointment."

"I've got all the time in the world," I said, settling myself into a chair.

"Well, *I* don't." The words seemed to come spitting out of him. "This happens to be where I work. If you don't want to buy any insurance, I'd appreciate it if you left your number and went on your way."

This reception was pretty much what I had expected. Hillary—according to my friend at the newspaper morgue—came from an old Mesa Grande family (third generation is old in his neck of the woods) and had been brought up with money. Most of it had been taken away from him by his older, more respectable relatives once they became aware of his "life-style": that's the word people use here to label things they don't want to sully their lips with by describing more specifically. Since then Hillary had gone into the insurance business, buying this office space and living quarters above it. Ten years ago he had taken in twenty-two-year-old Harold Hapgood as his partner, on the second floor as well as the first. But breeding shows, in spite of everything: Hillary still talked to the hoi polloi in the same abrupt plantation-owner manner he had been brought up to.

Before he and I could fight it out any further, a door at the other side of the room opened, and Hapgood appeared. He was blinking, looking bewildered and a little flustered: in other words, his normal look. "What's going on?"

"I *told* this 'gentleman'"—it was easy to hear the quotation marks that Hillary put around the word—"we're tied up. You go back to work, Harold, I'm quite capable of dealing with this."

"Cut it out, Teddy, the man's a police officer." Hapgood turned his blink in my direction. "I'll be happy to talk to you. Of course I will."

I followed Hapgood into his office, which was just as small as Hillary's. The desk and chairs looked as if they had been picked up at one of the secondhand furniture close-out sales that were held in town regularly. The walls were unadorned, except for a framed insurance license and a photograph of a much younger Hapgood and Hillary, slightly out of focus, standing side by side. Hapgood smiling a little vaguely, Hillary scowling angrily.

"I appreciate your giving me the time, Mr. Hapgood," I said, pursuing my usual strategy: very respectful at the beginning, so they won't be ready for it when the gloves come off later on. "I'll be as quick as I possibly can. In case you haven't heard, the police arrested Sally Michaels for the murder of Martin Osborn."

"Yes, I *had* heard." Hapgood gave a quick little nod, and licked his lips nervously.

"Mrs. Michaels has asked the public defender to handle her case, and as the chief investigator for the public defender's office, it's my job to talk to everybody who might have any information about the crime."

"And who says *he* has to talk to *you*?" These words came snapping out from the other room.

The door was still open. Hapgood sighed, got to his feet, and crossed the room to shut the door.

"You'd better let me sit in on this, Harold! You'll be grateful for a witness—"

"You do understand, Mr. Hillary," I said, "the public defender has the same legal status as the district attorney. Citizens have the same obligation to answer our questions—"

"I know all about that. But there's no law says a citizen has to let you browbeat him and claim afterward that he said things he didn't really say."

"Really, Teddy," Hapgood put in, "I'm sure it's all right—"

"You're not sure of anything. That's why I'm around. Or God knows what would've happened to you all these years!"

Hapgood shut the door gently and returned to his desk. He gave me an apologetic half-grin. "If you'll tell me how I can help you."

"I know you've been all over this with the assistant DA," I said, "but I want you to describe exactly what happened to you last night. When you were attacked and locked in the broom closet."

"It was terrible, awful," he said, "I was walking along the corridor in the basement, on the way to the stairs—"

"What were you doing in the basement?"

"I'd been in my dressing room. Changing into my costume for the murder scene. I was playing the role of Third Murderer. He's a very mysterious figure. He isn't in the earlier scene, when Macbeth hires the first two murderers to kill Banquo, and nobody knows why Shakespeare put him into the later scene. One theory has it that the Third Murderer is actually Macbeth himself, in disguise. Mr. Osborn wasn't taking that view in the present production, of course—"

"For God's sake, Harold," came the voice from the other side of the door, "stick to the point! You'll keep this man here forever!"

"It's all right, Mr. Hapgood," I said. "I've always been interested in Shakespeare. And you seem to know a good deal about him."

A small smile flickered on Hapgood's face. "Well, I'm a great reader, that's what it is actually. Especially of dramatic literature. The theatre has always been one of my greatest . . . One gets so little opportunity in a community like this. . . ."

"Stagestruck, from childhood!" A contemptuous hoot came from the other side of the door. "Tell him about your idiotic daydreams, Harold! He still has them, believe it or not! Childish fantasies about running off to New York or Hollywood, and becoming an actor. An actor! With *his* height and looks? How much demand can there be in the movies for *midgets?* They already *made* the Wizard of Oz! You can talk till you're blue in the face, Harold, but you'll never get me to believe the big shots out there have lost their minds!"

Hapgood's face was red rather than blue. I spoke up fast. "Why were you changing into your costume such a short time before you had to go onstage?"

"Oh, Third Murderer isn't my only part in the play." Hapgood's lisp, hardly evident at all up to now, was suddenly more obvious. A sign of how agitated Hillary had made him, I guessed. "I was onstage only ten minutes earlier, as the Old Man who tells the audience about the sinister birds that have been flying all over the kingdom since King Duncan's death. I had to wear a headdress and an Indian blanket for that part. The Old Man is supposed to be an Indian medicine man, and was Marty Osborn's concept. And then I had very little time to get back to the dressing room and put on my mask and my poncho for the Third Murderer."

"Did anyone see you in the dressing room while you were making this change?"

"No, I don't think so. I do share the dressing room with several other people, those of us who have several small parts in the play. The first two murderers and the Meyer boy, who plays Banquo's son Fleance. But nobody came into the dressing room while I was changing into my Third Murderer costume. It took me only a few minutes, and then I started down the hallway to the stairs that lead up to the stage level. And then—well, I'm very confused as to just what happened then. That is, it was quite awful, like a sudden explosion inside my head—''

"You didn't hear anything or see anything before this explosion?"

"I just can't remember. There was no warning, I'm sure of that. No sounds behind me, no flash of movement or anything like that."

"Do you have any idea where the person who hit you came from?"

"I can't be sure. Maybe from one of the rooms along the hallway."

"Those are the other dressing rooms, aren't they?"

"Yes. And the broom closet itself."

"And you didn't notice, as you walked down the corridor before you were attacked, if any of those doors was open? Or even slightly ajar?"

"One of them might've been open, but it didn't register on my mind. To tell you the truth, I get so nervous before I go onstage, all I could think about was my opening line, which is absurd, because it happens to be only one word. The word is 'Macbeth.'"

"All right, so what happened after the explosion?"

"I have no idea. The blow knocked me out, I suppose. I was struck just below my left ear; it hasn't left much of a bruise, though it still aches quite a bit. Well, the next thing I'm sure of I was on the floor, propped up against a wall. Feeling quite horrible. And then, bit by bit, I became aware of this damp musty smell. Then I realized where I must be, though I didn't see any brooms, which struck me as peculiar. Later on, of course, I found out that my attacker had thrown the brooms into the corridor, to make room for me, I suppose. Well, after a few minutes, I got to my feet. It wasn't easy, I was terribly dizzy at first, quite close to throwing up, but I managed to try the door and found I was locked in. So I hammered on it with my fists for a while and called out for help, despairing that anybody would come. But pretty soon the stage manager opened the door, and—*you* were there too, weren't you?''

I told him I was, so he didn't have to go on with what he did next. "And what about your costume?" I said. "Were you still wearing it?"

"It took me a while to notice that. Whoever put me in the closet hadn't taken much from me. The black mask was gone, but I was still wearing my poncho. I still had the dagger too.''

"What dagger?"

"The one I'm supposed to stab Banquo with. It's long, with a heavy gold hilt, and the blade curves a little. Very ugly-looking. It's made of wood and papier-mâché, of course. Completely harmless.''

I looked at him hard for a moment, and suddenly his voice rose to a squeak. "I've told you the truth, I swear to God! The police know I'm not lying, they told me so when they talked to me this morning. Jeff and Danny say it wasn't me on the stage. They say the murderer was wearing Sally's raincoat, not my poncho.''

"You could've stolen the raincoat from her dressing room and put it back in there before you locked yourself in the broom closet.''

"I didn't! I didn't! And what about my motive? *Why* would I kill Martin Osborn?"

"He insulted everybody in the cast at one time or another. Maybe he insulted you once too often.''

"That's ridiculous!" A kind of bitter inward-turning titter came out of Hapgood. "Look at me, will you. What kind of person do you think I am? My parents were both doctors in this town, I went to high school in this town—

can you imagine what my childhood must've been like? Once people figured it out about me... Don't you think I've heard plenty of insults in my life? Don't you think I've had to swallow insults as long as I can remember? You've seen Teddy. Can you imagine what it is to live with—'' He broke off, raising his hands into the air. ''Oh, what's the use? In my whole life nobody's ever given me the benefit of the doubt, so why should I expect *you* to be any different? I'll say it once more, and then I'll keep quiet and you can believe whatever you want to believe. I didn't kill Marty Osborn. His getting killed is the *worst* thing that could've happened to me just now.''

''How do you figure that?''

''Because of the play. I'm doing really well in the play. I've done a lot of things with the Players before, but this is the first time—as the Old Man and the Third Murderer, and later on as Old Siward—I've really had a chance to make an impression. I mean, I'm doing those parts really *well*. Allan Franz himself told me, in person, what excellent work I was doing. And now, with Osborn getting killed, the play will be canceled, and nobody will ever see my work!''

His face was red and scrunched up. I was afraid he was going to cry.

But he didn't. Instead he looked up at me suddenly, with a sharp little gleam in his eyes. ''You don't care about the truth, do you? Anything to get your client off. After all, *I'm* not the one who had a fight with Martin Osborn and threatened to kill him!''

''You're saying that's what Sally Michaels did?''

''I heard her myself, didn't I? Just a few days ago. She and Martin were in her dressing room, and I was in mine just a little ways down, and they were talking so loud I could hear every word. Martin was telling Sally he didn't like the way she was doing the sleepwalking scene. '*Macbeth* is a play about royalty,' he said. 'Lady Macbeth is a queen, she's glorious, she's larger than life. In her sleep she's tormented by titanic bloodcurdling feelings of guilt over the crime she and Macbeth have committed. You're playing the scene as if she's a suburban housewife who's dissatisfied with the bathroom soap because it won't wash the grease stains off her hands.'

"Well, I don't blame Sally for losing her temper. Martin *could* be very cutting and unkind. 'How dare you say such a thing to me?' Sally said. 'I could kill you for that!' Then she walked out of her dressing room, and there was nothing else for me to hear."

"Was anyone with you when you overheard all this?"

"No, I was alone. That's why I was able to concentrate on it so intently. That's why it's positively engraved in my memory, word for word."

"Have you told the police about it?"

"Not yet. If you want to know, I was going to keep quiet about it so Sally wouldn't be in any worse trouble than she is already. I don't really believe she could kill anybody. I'm convinced she couldn't. But now, with you coming in here and making accusations against *me*—" He broke off and covered his face with his hands. The sobs, which had threatened to burst out of him before, made their entrance now.

And sure enough, the door flew open and Hillary, planted in his wheelchair, came plowing into the room. "What are you doing to him? We'll sue you! My cousin is a lawyer and he'll be glad to handle our case—"

I got to my feet and moved past Hillary to the door, careful to be completely calm and unperturbed. "Thank you, Mr. Hapgood," I said. "Sorry to disturb you."

"Never mind thank you!" Hillary swung the wheel-chair around to point it at me, as if he expected to run me over with it. "I'm reporting you to your superiors! We're taxpayers, we pay your salary—"

"By the way, Mr. Hillary," I said, "where were *you* sitting at the theatre last night?"

"Me? I wasn't there! I was at home, right upstairs, looking at television!"

"You didn't go to Mr. Hapgood's opening night?"

"You think I'm some kind of masochist? You think I deliberately watched him making a damn fool of himself, prancing around in front of strangers, pretending to be somebody he isn't? Isn't it bad enough he wastes *his* time on that idiocy? Now if you don't get out of here right this minute—"

I CALLED MY office from a phone booth in the mall, and Mabel Gibson told me that Leland Grantley had just sent over a list for me. It contained the names and addresses of everybody connected with *Macbeth* who didn't seem to have an alibi for the time of the murder.

I had her read the list to me over the phone, and I copied it down, which didn't take long because there were only five names on it:

Lloyd Cunningham
Randolph Le Sage
Sally Michaels
Bernie Michaels
Laura Franz

Sally and Bernie I had talked to already, so I decided to move on to Le Sage.

His address sounded familiar to me—1210 East Jalapeno Avenue. After a moment I realized it was the same address where Martin Osborn lived. I drove there and found one of the new condominiums, in Spanish style but with picture windows and sun porches, that were replacing the old residential houses in the downtown area.

I remember Roger telling me that Martin Osborn had bought this apartment shortly after coming to town last May. It hadn't been cheap.

The front of the building had a sweeping gravel driveway and a long blue awning, like a New York Park Avenue apartment house. But there was no Park Avenue doorman. You went into the small vestibule and looked up whom you wanted to see on the callboard and pushed the button. One of the cards on the board had "Osborn" printed on it, and scrawled underneath in pencil was "Le Sage."

I pressed the button, not knowing if I was going to get any response; once again I had thought it was a good idea to surprise him if I could. A few moments later Le Sage's voice was on the intercom, asking me who I was, and then the vestibule door clicked open.

I was in a small lobby with one elevator and a potted plant. I took the elevator up to the sixth floor and found Le Sage waiting for me in his doorway. Over his suit he was wearing a bathrobe, purple and heavy, and an ascot scarf was wrapped around his neck up to his chin. Onstage he had looked tall, with a clean, hawklike profile and long white hair sweeping in waves over the back of his neck. In person he looked smaller, the profile was a little more ragged, and the white hair had streaks of dirty gray in it. He looked older too, at least into his late fifties.

"I know you, don't I?" he said. He had thick whitish eyebrows and long lashes, and he blinked his eyes a lot. Some admiring theatre critic or girlfriend must have told him once that they were expressive.

I introduced myself again and reminded him that he may have seen me at the theatre last night. Then I started giving him my spiel about his obligation to answer my questions just like the district attorney's. He cut me off with a friendly laugh. "Delighted to tell you anything I can, my dear fellow. I've been over this all several times with various official-looking types, but I never resent telling a story more than once. Gives me a chance to polish my delivery, you know. An Actor is never off the stage."

I write "Actor" with a capital *A* because somehow that was the way he pronounced it.

"My only problem," he went on, "is that I'm expecting a rather important phone call at any moment, so I do hope we can make this as fast as possible."

He ushered me into the apartment, which had a large sunken living room, ornately decorated in a kind of up-to-date Art Deco style. Most of what was in it, from the slinky contour chairs to the hanging plants in the picture window, looked as if it had been delivered from the factory last week.

The exceptions to that were on the walls. Among the slick shiny reproductions of abstract expressionist paintings were several framed posters advertising various movies—grade-B horror movies from the fifties and sixties, as far as I could tell from a quick glance. Martin Osborn's name appeared on them all, though never above the title.

"Sit down, sit down." Le Sage waved me into one of the contour chairs—which, as always with that type of furniture, turned out to be a little too low and a little too hard for me. He himself dropped onto the sofa. The half-sofa, that is: it had one arm, and half a back, then it looked as if some machine had come along and chopped off the other half of it.

"It's a lovely flat, isn't it?" he said. "Poor Marty kindly offered to put me up here while I was doing the play. So much nicer than some cold impersonal hotel or motel."

I agreed that it was a nice place. I kept my words to a minimum. Le Sage was a talker, and the best thing you can do with a talker is sit back, keep your mouth shut, and let him enjoy his favorite music, the sound of his own voice.

"A real plus factor," Le Sage was going on, "is that Marty's digs are on the top floor. High enough so you can enjoy an unobstructed view of the mountains. Rather spectacular, aren't they? Though, of course, being a true New Yorker, I can take just so much of the great outdoors. Rodgers and Hammerstein did *Oklahoma!* so much better than God, don't you agree?"

I didn't bother to tell him I was a New Yorker myself.

"May I offer you a drink? A bit early for you, is it? Well, if you don't mind—" He poured himself a heavy order of Scotch from a liquor cabinet hidden in the bookshelf, splashed a little club soda into it, then resumed his position on the sofa. "You probably want to ask me what I was doing while poor Marty was being slaughtered in Shakespearean fashion up on the stage. And did I see anything suspicious, did I notice the masked figure before or after, et cetera. That's what the police, in and out of uniform, have been asking me. They swarmed over this place this morning, the ones who weren't questioning me were poking around in Martin's things, pulling clothes from his drawers and his closets. And they carted off several boxloads of papers from his desk. If there was anything among them useful to your client, it's all been destroyed by now, I suppose. That was my practice anyway when I was a district attorney."

I knew what he was saying, but I put a puzzled look on my face, because he obviously wanted me to.

He laughed when he saw it. "No, no, I don't mean I was ever in the law-enforcement game professionally. I *played* a DA once in a movie. Dreadful old stinker; anybody who says they made them better in the old days hasn't seen any of *my* masterpieces. I never hesitated to suppress evidence that would do the defense attorneys any good. Incidentally, I had the same low moral standard when I was a defense attorney."

He laughed again, polished off his drink, and refilled his glass. "If I'm giving you the impression I drink too much, that's quite right. Not on a regular basis, though. I don't touch a drop while I'm working, it's Martin's demise that's plunging me into the filthy habit today. If *Macbeth* ever gets started again, I'll be dry as a bone. Well, all of us alcoholics say that, don't we? We can stop anytime we like. That's what *I* always said when I was an alcoholic. On stage and screen, that is. In real life I'm *not* one. I gladly refer you to my wife and teenage children back in New York."

He took a quick look at his watch. "Twenty after already? That can't be right. Is that what *you* have, my dear fellow?"

I told him my watch said twenty after.

"Damn!" It came out of him in a low mutter. "What's keeping the bloody fellow? Said he'd call back in an hour!"

"You were talking about what you were doing at the time of the murder?" I said.

"Yes, certainly. In brief, my last scene, the one where I hire the two murderers to kill Banquo, is over about five minutes before Banquo's murder. Rather nice little scene, actually. These creatures fill me with disgust and horror, but I know I have to use them, so I put on a certain smarmy ingratiating manner, a subtle form of flattering them. Very underplayed. Well, you were at the performance, weren't you?''

He paused, his head cocked forward slightly. After a moment I got the idea. "Yes, that was a terrific scene," I said.

He leaned back again. "So nice of you to say so. At any rate, I went down to my dressing room right after the scene to stretch out a bit. Thank God I've got one of my own, though a dreadful cramped airless little cell it is. I was there no more than ten minutes or so when I heard the disturbance in the hallway. Loud voices, people running about, general hysteria. I moved down the corridor and found a cluster of people ahead of me, milling about. Shortly afterward I learned of the tragedy.''

"Did anybody see you when you went to your dressing room?"

"I don't believe so. I did knock briefly on the door of Sally's dressing room before I went into my own. Wanted to have a word with her about a scene we played together earlier, the scene in which Lady Macbeth taunts Macbeth into killing Duncan. Sally left out an entire speech in that scene—'Was the hope drunk wherein you dress'd yourself?' ending with 'the poor cat i' the adage?' Thus depriving me of one of my best lines, the one about doing 'all that may become a man.' She never left that speech out in any of the rehearsals, of course. Her idea was to make me look bad in front of an audience. *So* unprofessional. Well, at any rate, I never did get to talk to her about it, because she didn't answer my knock.''

"You're saying Mrs. Michaels wasn't in her dressing room?"

"Nothing of the sort. All I'm saying is that she didn't answer my knock.''

"Were you surprised when you heard about Osborn's murder?"

"I don't follow you exactly. I presume murder is always a surprise. And Marty was an old and valued colleague."

"Does it surprise you that he should have been a murder victim? Was he the type of man to make enemies?"

"Most of us make enemies, you know. Especially in the Profession. Actors are high-strung people, we're deeply ambitious and deeply insecure at the same time. An extremely explosive mixture."

"Can you think of anyone who might've hated Osborn enough to kill him?"

"My dear fellow, I'm certainly not going to name names. Since I've absolutely no proof, that would be slander, wouldn't it?"

"What about Mrs. Michaels? You know the police have arrested her?"

"Poor Sally. You'll never convince me there's a murderous bone in her body. All you have to do is look at the way she plays Lady Macbeth."

"Anybody else in the company?"

"Well, Marty *was* the director, my dear man. While a play is in rehearsal, *everybody* hates the director. Especially the Actors. Natural enemies, you know. But I've never known of a case where this animosity led to actual homicide."

"What about *you*, Mr. Le Sage? Did you think of Osborn as your natural enemy?"

"Of course I did. He was *directing* me. Which is as good as saying he was trying to control my inner being, violate my individual integrity, stamp on my talent. But that's only at rehearsals. Off the stage he was one of my oldest and dearest chums. Would he have let me stay here with him in this apartment otherwise? Incidentally, it's a vexing question in my mind how long I *can* stay here. Does Marty have any family, any official heirs, somebody who might be ordering me to push along to a hotel?''

"He doesn't seem to, actually. How far back do the two of you go? Where did you first know each other?"

"Oh, we go back to Marty's Hollywood days. I had my fling out there too, in the late fifties, when we were both a good deal younger. Marty and I were featured players together in several notably vile productions. We discovered—excuse me, do you have twenty *of* now? You do? Well—what was I saying? Yes, Marty and I discovered that we both yearned to return to the Theatre so we could feel artistically clean again. I *did* return, shortly afterward. At considerable financial sacrifice, as a matter of fact, but I've never regretted it. And Marty jumped off the Tinsel Town Treadmill through the expedient of marriage."

"You knew his wife?"

"Never had the pleasure of meeting the woman. I gather she was a good deal older than himself, and a good deal richer. I'm afraid I pretty much lost touch during his married years. Only the annual exchange of Christmas cards, and an occasional meeting when he happened to come to New York. They lived in Cleveland, that was his wife's native habitat, I believe. And unless I happened to be on tour, what would ever get *me* to Cleveland?"

He straightened up from his half-reclining position on the half-sofa and took another look at his watch. "I'm sorry, I'll have to ask you to leave now. My damn agent in New York—it could be he told *me* to call *him* back in an hour—"

I stood up, but I didn't start to the door. "Just one more question, Mr. Le Sage. How did you happen to come out here to act in *Macbeth?* You must have a pretty busy schedule back in New York.''

''I certainly do. But I'm between engagements at the moment. The show I was in just closed. Lovely little play, off Broadway, but the critics missed the whole point of it. And I won't be resuming my work on the telly until a month or so from now. I've got a running role on this daily soap opera, 'How Shall I Love Thee?' Maybe you've seen me, I play the heroine's doctor father, they write me in whenever the middle-aged housewives get bored at seeing nothing but teenage muscular development. So when Marty called me a few months ago with this urgent request, I couldn't turn him down, could I? Required some doing with Actors' Equity, of course, had to fill out several hundred forms. But old friendship does have its obligations.''

''And how long did you agree to be out here?''

''My contract says two months, rehearsals and performances included. Equity won't allow me to be with the show any longer.''

''You'll be going home earlier, though, if they close the play now?''

''Possibly. Though I do believe my contract specifies they have to pay me the full amount regardless of unforeseen circumstances. I'm not sure of that. I leave that sort of thing to my agent—''

The phone rang. Le Sage gave a little jump, and his face twitched, the biggest dent I had seen yet in his unflappability. ''You *will* excuse me, won't you?''

He waved me to the door. I could see the bind he was in: he didn't want his caller to hang up, but he didn't want me in the room when he started talking. I decided to let him stew, you never know what might come out of that. So I just stood where I was.

Finally, after the third ring, he grabbed the phone. "Le Sage here! Hold on a moment, will you, Max!"

He put the receiver down and strode up to me. "You'll have to *leave!*" he said between his teeth. "You can find the lift by yourself, can't you?"

I wasn't even out the door before he was back at the phone, snatching up the receiver.

I shut the door, but lingered outside long enough to hear his next words: "What do you mean, they're not interested?"

BACK IN MY CAR, I consulted Grantley's list again. It might be a good idea, I decided, if I left Laurie Franz to Roger. That left Lloyd Cunningham for me. But it was three o'clock already, and I was losing steam. I told myself I'd get stale if I didn't take a break.

The truth is, what was bothering me had nothing to do with Martin Osborn's murder.

I went back to the office and called Mom's number. If she wasn't busy tonight, maybe I could drop in after dinner and have coffee with her, and finally tell her what was on my mind about her and Roger. But instead of Mom, I got her answering machine, with her voice announcing brightly, "This is me. So wait till the buzz and tell me who *you* are."

Since coming to Mesa Grande, Mom had been moving into the second half of the twentieth century with a vengeance. In addition to driving a Japanese car, she had filled her house with all the newest electronic miracles: she had a VCR, a television with remote control, a little CD player, and she was beginning to make noises about how nice it would be to have a word processor.

"But you don't do any writing, Mom, except letters," I said to her once.

"And don't I turn out plenty of those?" she answered me. "Believe me, there are professional novelists don't produce as many words per year as me."

I told her answering machine that I had called, and just as I was hanging up I heard Mabel Gibson greeting Roger in the outer office.

He had come to deliver his official report on his afternoon's activities. He had managed to talk to Greenwald and Imperio, the first and second murderers. Their description of what had happened on the stage last night pretty much jibed with what Assistant DA Grantley had already told us. They had the definite impression that the Third Murderer was taller than he had been in rehearsals; they had found themselves looking into his eyes during their scene instead of looking down at him. Neither of them had found this particularly queer while the scene was going on. "I figured old Harold had gone out and bought himself a pair of elevator shoes," said Greenwald, the high school student. "You know, he gets kind of self-conscious about his height, like a lot of short guys do." Greenwald and Imperio laughed. They were both pretty short guys.

I told Roger about Grantley's list and was about to give him his orders for tomorrow when my phone rang.

It was Mom, and of course she was delighted that I wanted to have coffee with her after dinner. "I'll make some nice schnecken," she said. "But it has to be early, because it's the Sabbath and I'm going to services at the temple. And you'll ask Roger, if he isn't busy, maybe he'll come too?"

This was annoying. With Roger right there in the room with me, I couldn't exactly tell her he was busy or that I wanted to talk to her in private. What's more, in that tiny office of mine you can't stand far away from anything or anybody, so the chances are he had heard her voice over the phone.

He had. "Oh, that's very nice of her," he said. "Thank your mother for me, will you, Dave, but I'm afraid I've got a date tonight. I'm having dinner with Laurie—Laurie Franz." A faint tinge of pink was spreading over his cheeks. He went on quickly. "She's on your list of people who don't have alibis, so by going out with her I'll be able to kill two birds with one stone."

Which fit in perfectly with my plans.

Ann returned from court with the news that the judge had set a reasonable bail for our client and she was out of jail. Her ex-husband Bernie had picked her up in his car and was taking her out to a restaurant to cheer her up.

I fixed myself a quick snack that night in my house. I'm not much of a cook, but since Shirley's death I've gotten pretty good at heating up frozen dinners. Then, around six-thirty, I drove to Mom's place.

THE DELICIOUS SMELL of schnecken and coffee enfolded me as soon as I opened the front door. It made me feel less nervous about the task ahead of me. How could a woman who was capable of concocting such ambrosia possibly slap me down with sarcasm?

She made me comfortable in my favorite easy chair and settled into the sofa across from me. While I sipped and munched, I also talked. "The reason I wanted to come over tonight, Mom, I've got something important to tell you. About Roger."

A look of concern came over her face. "You said he's doing a good job in the office. You said Ann Swenson is happy with him too. So is it something about his health maybe? He don't eat the right food, that schlemiel—"

"He's still doing a good job, and his health is fine, as far as I know. The point is, I want him to go *on* doing a good job."

"So why shouldn't he?"

I took a deep breath and came out with it. How Roger, though he was certainly a nice kid, was also my assistant at the office. How it's always a mistake to mix business with social pleasures. How you can't run an operation efficiently if the respect of the people who are working under you is undermined.

"Roger isn't showing respect for you?" Mom said. "I'm surprised. He always talks polite to you whenever I'm with you together. Is he putting on a show for my benefit?"

"No, I've got no complaints about his politeness. But the point is, he could change in the future if you keep on doing things, Mom, that could...that could...compromise my dignity."

"What things are you talking about?"

"Well... you know the way, sometimes, I talk over my cases with you. And sometimes you make suggestions. Well, you've been doing that in front of the kid. Today at lunch, for instance, you asked all those questions about this Osborn killing. And you made some deductions about how somebody is trying to frame Sally Michaels. Well, don't you see, Mom, how easily Roger could misunderstand what's going on? He could come to the conclusion that... well, the point is, I don't think you should see him as often as you've been doing. I think you should stop having him over for dinner. Except on special occasions."

And now, I thought, would come the explosion. Now, in her sharpest, most sarcastic voice, Mom would let me know what a baby I was.

"Davie, Davie," she said.

Her voice was low; there was no sharpness or sarcasm in it at all. She came around the table and put her hand on my shoulder.

"You're a good boy," she said. "And I give you my solemn promise. I wouldn't talk about your cases with you no more if Roger is in the room. You're right, I enjoy his company. At my age, when people usually have some grandchildren to act foolish over... But you're my son, my flesh and blood, so I'll stop having him so much for dinner."

She gave me a kiss on the cheek, and then she was back in her seat at the other side of the table.

Neither of us said anything for a while. If I had tried to speak up, I think I might have done something crazy, like shed a tear or something. Which is all right for men to do nowadays, so I'm told, but I was born a few years too early.

Finally Mom broke the silence. "Of course," she said, just as cheerfully as if the previous conversation hadn't occurred, "Roger *isn't* in the room with us now, so what *did* you find out this afternoon about the murder?"

Naturally I told her everything. I repeated verbatim my talks with Harold Hapgood and Randolph Le Sage, Roger's report of his interviews with the two murderers, Ann's news about bail for Sally Michaels.

"So who's next on your list for the third degree?"

"I keep telling you, Mom, I don't *give* the third degree. Next on my list is Lloyd Cunningham. I'll go over there first thing in the morning."

"You think he's a good suspect, you could throw him to the police in Mrs. Michaels's place?"

"Don't *you* think so, Mom? Osborn insulted Cunningham in front of the whole cast. Hurt his pride so badly that Cunningham lost his temper and gave up the part of

Banquo. He not only must've been mad at Osborn, he must've resented the whole production."

"So he kills a man to make sure a play don't go on?"

"I know it doesn't sound rational. But they're a funny breed, actors. Their motives aren't the same as ordinary people's."

Mom was nodding her head, frowning. "This I agree with. The problem is, nobody tells you ahead of time who are the actors and who are the ordinary people."

"Meaning what, Mom?"

"Meaning it's like William Shakespeare said. You remember? 'All the world is a stage, and all the men and women are playing around on it.' This comes from a play of his called 'The Way You Like It.' This Cunningham, when you see him tomorrow morning, ask him a question for me, will you."

"What do you want to know?"

"When he got into that fight the other day and quit the play, it's because he got mad at what the big Hollywood director, Allan Franz, said about his performance. He was too nice and sympathetic, Franz said. He wasn't making his character tough enough. Am I remembering this right?"

"Yes, you are. But what's the question you want me to ask Cunningham?"

"As him if he agrees with the criticism. *Was* he making the character too nice and sympathetic?"

"Why should that be important, Mom?" was what I felt like saying. But I knew she wouldn't explain it to me, so I said, "I'll make a note of it."

Then I finished my schnecken, and Mom asked me if I'd like to go to the Friday-night service with her. I told her I couldn't because I had a date. "Naturally," she said. "Your little secretary."

"A paralegal isn't a secretary. It takes several years of training—"

"You've got a good heart, Davie," Mom said, patting me on the cheek. Then, as she showed me to the door, "Give my love to Roger. Let him know I'm very busy these days, with the High Holidays coming along, so that's why I'm not inviting him for dinner for a while. I wouldn't want he should think it's anything personal."

So I left her house feeling guilty as hell. And what else is new?

EIGHT

Roger's Narrative

IN MESA GRANDE, when you go out on a date with a so-phisticated girl who's used to big-city excitement and cul-ture, where do you take her anyway? Nightclubs and bars are strictly for the proletariat—country music and topless chorus girls wearing sombreros. Occasionally some kind of concert or poetry reading is going on at the college, but most of the time you're pretty much limited to the mov-ies.

Not that that's really a limit, in my opinion. What bet-ter way could a couple of civilized human beings find to pass the time?

Laurie Franz was used to Mesa Grande, of course, she'd been going to the college for a year. Still, this was the first time I'd officially asked her out (I don't count informal coffees after rehearsals), so I wanted to do it right. Luck-ily, the Richelieu Hotel has four or five restaurants, each one designed to appeal to a different taste and mood, and one of them, the Cardinal Rouge, is French and elegant. I took Laurie there, and she picked her own live lobster from the tank (the most expensive item on the menu), and I or-dered the broiled sole (the cheapest item on the menu).

You may ask how I could afford to take her to Le Car-dinal Rouge at all, on what the city pays me, and the an-swer is I couldn't. But I had to consider the competition, all those rich men's sons who were her fellow students at her expensive little liberal arts college in the Rockies, and all those swinging types who swarmed around her swimming pool back in Beverly Hills.

During dinner we talked about a lot of things. Like her ambition to be an actress someday. "I mean, a *good* actress," she said. "Not just a pretty face and a good body, like most of them in the movies these days. I want to learn my craft and really get in touch with my inner nature. I want to go to New York and study with one of the great teachers they've got there. Stella or Uta or Sanford. And then I'll act on Broadway for a while, or off Broadway where you can do the whole repertoire—Shakespeare, Chekhov, Tennessee Williams. And *then* I'll go into the movies, when I'm ready to make a real contribution. When I can raise the standards, like Meryl's done."

She talked about the famous people who came to her house for dinner while she was growing up. "Daddy knew them all, they were his close friends, and they all made a fuss over me. They wanted him to put them in his movies, that's why. Oh, it was horrible. The hypocrisy! If you want to see *real* hypocrisy, you have to go to Beverly Hills."

She talked about her mother, who had divorced her father when Laurie was just two years old. "She ran away with this actor, he was French, and they went to France together. That's why Daddy got custody of me. She acted in a couple of French movies, and then she and her husband got killed in an auto accident. Daddy went through a terrible time when he heard the news. He hadn't ever stopped loving her. He married twice after the divorce, but neither of those women lasted long; they moved into the house for a while and then they moved out again. I don't remember my mother at all. I've seen pictures of her, but I just don't remember."

She crinkled up her face, a mixture of sadness and puzzlement. I thought it was one of the most touching and at the same time sexiest expressions I'd ever seen. Carole Lombard, only up-to-date.

She talked about the big house in Beverly Hills where her father still lived by himself ("though occasionally he'll have a friend in, if you know what I mean"). She still called it home, though it was more like a palace really. Dozens of rooms, with a TV set, a telephone extension, and a bar built into the wall of almost every one of them. She talked about the high school she'd gone to, where practically everybody had a father or a mother or both in the movie business.

She'd done a lot of acting in high school, she said, and also in her first year at college. She hoped to do even better parts with the Mesa Grande Players. "Do you know what Lloyd Cunningham told me? Only a few days after rehearsals began, he told me he liked my work so much he wants to cast me later this winter in the big production *he's* directing. Eugene O'Neill's *Ah, Wilderness!* But the most exciting thing about it is he wants me to play the mother. I've never played an older woman before, but Lloyd says he has complete confidence that my talent is up to it."

"Are you going to do it?"

"You just bet I am! I told him definitely yes, and I'll *kill* him if he backs out of that promise!"

Then she talked about Mesa Grande College, and her mixed feelings about going there. "It's an awfully nice place, I have a lot of good friends, and I like my classes pretty much. And of course I love the mountains. But on the other hand, I just don't know if I should be going to college right now at *all*. I'd really like to quit school and go right to New York and get started with my career. But Daddy won't let me quit. He says I'll be a better actress in the long run if I get a good liberal arts education. Meryl

did go to Vassar, after all. What do *you* think? You don't
think Daddy is right, do you?''

What I thought was, she was nineteen years old and a
baby, and I found her almost unbearably attractive, and
what interested me about her *least,* I'm ashamed to say,
was her future as an actress. What I said to her was, ''I
have to agree with your father, don't I? If you went to New
York, when would I ever get to see you again?''

She laughed and blushed a little, and on the whole I decided that my first little step at intimacy had gone down
very well. It would be worthwhile trying a few more steps.

After dinner, I tried them. That is, I took her to the
movies. But even being the movie nut that I am, I didn't
pay much attention to the screen. She didn't either. I'm
surprised they didn't kick us out of the theatre.

When the lights went up at the end of the main feature,
we had to get out of there. Here in Mesa Grande the movie
houses don't run one show straight into the next one;
there's always a long break, and they send you out of the
theatre so they can clear some of the candy wrappers off
the floor.

We were both in something of a state by then. Expecta-
tions had been aroused, and they demanded to be ful-
filled pretty soon. She had an apartment, actually the
whole first floor, of a nice little white clapboard house a
few blocks from the campus. A lot of Mesa Grande students live in this kind of house, but mostly they share a
floor with two or three other people; their allowances from
their parents don't usually stretch to paying for the whole
thing by themselves.

Laurie's living room was furnished a lot better than most
student apartments. The chairs and sofa were new and
comfortable, and on the walls were framed posters of her
father's movies. A door led to a kitchen, and a second

door, I supposed, led to the bedroom. Its furnishings must be new and comfortable too, I thought. But I didn't get a chance to find out. We were too much in a hurry; the couch in her living room had to be good enough for us.

What we did next has nothing to do with the murder, so I'll skip to afterward, when we more or less got ourselves tidied up and she made coffee and brought it in from the kitchen.

While we drank it, I turned the conversation to the murder. I played fair with Laurie, though. I told her I was involved in the investigation and she was one of the people I was supposed to question.

"You don't suspect *me,* do you?" she said, smiling, but I couldn't help noticing it was a pretty weak smile.

"Of course not. But you were backstage at the time of the murder, so maybe you saw something that'll turn out to be significant. Something you hardly even noticed; you've put it out of your mind because you don't think it matters."

"If I've put it out of my mind, how am I going to tell you about it?"

"Well, that's my job. By asking you the right questions, and sort of leading up to it subtly, maybe I can jog your memory. It's no big deal, actually, it's what we're trained to do."

Okay, I felt like a horse's ass even while I was saying it.

As it turned out, she didn't have much to tell me. She had been a waiting woman at Macbeth's court in one of the earlier scenes and had gone down afterward to the dressing room she shared with the Weird Sisters. Suddenly she had started to feel sick.

"My big scene wasn't till the second half," she said, "but I was already beginning to get nervous about it. This always happens to me when I'm in a play. I feel nauseous and feverish, and I'm not all right again until I throw up. The same thing used to happen to Laurence Olivier.''

''Did you throw up last night?''

''Yes, I'm afraid I did. I went to the ladies' room. It's in the basement across from my dressing room, I just barely made it in time. I went into a booth and shut the door, and afterward I sat there for quite a while, because I wasn't sure I wouldn't get sick again.''

''How long was all this before the Banquo murder scene?''

''Oh, it couldn't have been too long before. Because on the way to the ladies' room I saw Martin—Mr. Osborn— standing in the wings.''

''Doing what?''

''Just *standing*. Kind of stiff and erect, you know, the way you do when you're getting ready to make an entrance. And you don't want anybody to say anything to you because you're trying to make sure you remember your first lines. And *you* were standing next to him.''

''Me?''

''Fleance, Banquo's son, I mean. You were waiting to make your entrance too.''

I remembered it myself now. Osborn and me, next to each other but far apart, eyes fastened on the blaze of light beyond the wings.

''You didn't happen to see the Third Murderer, did you? Maybe he was waiting in the wings too, somewhere behind us?''

''I was in such a hurry, I didn't notice anybody else.''

''Was there anybody in the ladies' room with you?''

''I thought I heard the door opening once, and somebody moving around and going out again a few minutes later. But I was in the booth, so I didn't see who it was, and they couldn't have seen me either. When I finally got out of the booth, the ladies' room was empty."

"What did you do after that?"

"Everything was over by the time I went out the door. People were wandering around, and everybody was looking very upset, and I couldn't figure out what was going on. I heard police sirens, and one of the stagehands told me what had happened. Told me that Martin—" She came to a stop, her lips quivering.

This whole business was pretty traumatic for her, I realized with a pang of guilt. I was callous about murders, I'd already seen half a dozen of them, but to her it was new and horrible.

I went over to the couch and sat next to her. I took hold of her hand to comfort her. This time, I thought, we'll use the bed, like civilized people. "Look, if you don't want to go on talking about this—"

"No, it's all right, you have to do your job." She gulped a little air and straightened up, and went on in a steadier voice, "I found out what had happened, as I told you, and then I discovered the back doors were locked and nobody could get out of the theatre—"

"You tried to get out the back?"

"I wanted to go around to the front of the theatre and look for my father. But there was no way to do that. And then Daddy found *me,* he'd gone up on the stage right after the murder. We sat together in the dressing room and waited till the police got around to asking us questions."

"Do you think Sally Michaels killed Osborn?"

"I just can't believe it. Sally has been so nice to me, so sweet and helpful. How could somebody I *know* be a murderer?"

"If it isn't Sally, it'll probably be somebody else you know."

"Why? Why can't it be some stranger who came in from the street, some hoodlum or drug addict or . . . or terrorist or something?"

I didn't bother to go over the reasoning with her. She was so young, and she didn't want the world to be a terrible place just yet.

"From all I heard," I said, "Osborn wasn't a very popular character. He used his money to bulldoze his way into the Players. And he had a reputation as a womanizer. Who knows how many bimbos he's been fooling around with? If one of them has a boyfriend or a husband in the company—"

"Stop it! You've got no right to talk about him that way!"

The words came out of her like whiplashes. I stared at her for a moment, and finally I caught on. I could feel that twist in the pit of my stomach that I usually associate with eating something that makes me sick.

She went on talking, and now she was sobbing as well. "I know what people said about him, and it was awful, just awful. The way they misunderstood him, just because he was trying to raise the level of artistic life in this city. If you'd known him, really *known* him—"

She was out of breath, she came to a stop in a waterfall of sobs.

Then I asked her the most unnecessary question I'd ever asked in my life. "You *did* really know him?"

She nodded between heavings of her shoulders. "We met each other last April just after he moved here. He was at a party that I was at, one of the drama students at the college gave it. We fell in love right away. We saw each other practically every day till school was out. We wrote to each other all summer, and he came out to California to see me a few times. We had to keep our meetings secret, of course."

"Do you know about Sally Michaels and—"

"Yes, of course I knew, there was nothing Martin wouldn't tell me. That silly woman! She completely misunderstood about their relationship. That sort of thing was always happening to him. Was it his fault if women found him attractive and threw themselves at him? He finally had to be quite firm with her, though he knew she'd be vindictive and go around spreading all sorts of lies about him."

I had a little difficulty getting out my next question. "What were you and he...were you planning to..."

She picked up on it without my having to finish. "We were going away together, of course. We decided a long time ago, way back in August. He was going to take me to New York and get me started with Uta or with the Studio. Any school would take me, of course, on account of Daddy, but Martin wanted to make sure I went to the one that would be best for me. He had to guide me and advise me, because he felt I had a very special kind of talent. We were going to leave as soon as *Macbeth* finished its run. Martin felt he had an obligation to the play. Obligations and responsibilities were very important to him."

"But he was in his fifties! He was old enough to be your father!"

She shuddered away from me as if I had physically struck her. "I thought you at least would have some sympathy!"

That made me feel overwhelmed with guilt. But I had my pride too. I was hurt, I had a right to be angry. I made my voice louder: "I *do* have sympathy. If you knew how close I've been feeling to you these last few weeks... But you never *told* me what was going on between you and

Osborn! All the time I thought we were really becoming friends!''

"We *were*. Honestly, Roger. I think of you as a *good* friend."

"Sure. But that didn't stop you from lying to me all these weeks, hiding what was going on in your life. Friends don't hide things like that from each other. I feel like such a damned fool!"

"I *couldn't* tell anybody about Martin and me. We had to keep our relationship secret until we decided what to do about my father. Daddy and I have been so close to each other all these years, since Mother left. And he would've said just what you did, that Martin was too old for me. Which is ridiculous, nothing but middle-class superstition, but that's what he would've said."

"How could you expect him *not* to find out if you and Osborn had gone to New York together?"

"Then it would've been too late for Daddy to do anything. Martin and I would've been *married,* don't you see? But until then, if Daddy had found out, I think he might've *killed* Martin!"

"Might have? I damn well *would* have."

These words came quietly from the bedroom doorway, where Allan Franz was now standing.

"DADDY!" Laurie's face had started off turning white, but as she recovered from the first shock it turned red. "What are you *doing* here? How could you *spy* on me?"

"Sorry, sweetheart," he said, coming into the room. "I didn't mean to spy. But you gave me a key to this place, you told me to drop in whenever I felt lonely in that hotel room. So I finished working on scripts a couple of hours ago, I felt lonely, and I dropped in. You weren't here, so I stretched out in the bedroom to catch a few winks. I guess I woke up a little too soon."

How soon? I asked myself, feeling a little sick to my stomach.

"Those things I just said aren't true!" Laurie was putting on a great bravado act. It was like her Lady Macduff trying to bluff it out with the thugs who have been sent to kill her. "I said them for Roger's benefit. To make him jealous!"

I had scrambled to my feet a long time ago, and now I was scrambling in the direction of the door. "I think maybe...it's getting pretty late...I've got work tomorrow morning..."

But neither of them had a glance to spare for me. "His age wouldn't have bothered me," Franz was saying, keeping his eyes fixed on Laurie. "But the man was such a loser! Professionally, personally. And the way he treated women his whole life! It was well known in Hollywood, I could tell you plenty of stories about him, I could produce witnesses you'd have to believe! Oh my God, sweetheart, if you'd only confided in me, I could've made you understand—"

"That's why I *didn't* confide in you!" There was a quaver in Laurie's voice, she was close to tears. "You're always so sensible and logical, you've always got facts and witnesses, you can always prove to me I've got no right to be happy!"

"I don't see how you can say such a thing. Your happiness is what I care about more than anything else in life. I'd do anything to keep you from getting hurt."

"You'd do anything to keep me under your thumb, to keep me from leading my own life! That's why you're saying all these things about Martin—"

"Come on, be reasonable!" Franz threw his arms up over his head. "Goddamn it, Laurie, will you stop turning our life into the remake of an old movie! Different cast, same old plot! Your mother walked out on me for a lousy two-bit actor who ruined her life and eventually killed her! Do I have to watch you playing out the same crummy script?"

He broke off, suddenly swiveling his head in my direction. "Excuse me—Roger, is that your name? It isn't fair for us to embarrass you with these private family disagreements."

I was glad to take the hint. I stammered some more apologies and pulled the door open.

In the doorway I hesitated a split second, wondering if it was all right to leave Laurie alone with him. He was pretty agitated all right; under that calm manner he was holding in the fires. But then I decided that you can't get between a father and a daughter. Not if you know what's good for you.

So I LEFT the little white house and drove around for a while in my car. "I think of you as a *good* friend," she had said, but who did she think of as a bedfellow? That conceited old toad, that back-number Casanova! What was wrong with her anyway? An advanced case of a father complex? Or maybe nothing worse than a touch of necrophilia?

I got home a little later. I knew I wouldn't be able to sleep, so I put a movie on my VCR. It was an old Sherlock Holmes, with Basil Rathbone exposing George Zucco as Professor Moriarty, the mastermind who was sabotaging Britain's submarines during World War II. I enjoyed it, as I always do. Especially old Nigel Bruce, spluttering away whenever Rathbone delivers a cutting wisecrack at his expense. But my mind kept wandering away from it. Damn Laurie, damn her father, for spoiling Holmes and Watson for me!

And then, as the movie came to an end, I realized that my frustration over Laurie wasn't the only reason for my distracted state. Something else was upsetting me, something that was kicking around in my subconscious mind.

Suddenly I sat up straight on the couch. That something wasn't subconscious anymore. I knew what it was. My God, I had to tell Dave and Ann about it!

And then, slowly thinking it over, I wondered if I *could* tell them about it.

I woke up early Saturday morning, red-eyed from lack of sleep. I'd go nuts if I didn't talk to somebody about this. I needed a wiser head to do my thinking for me.

So I made a phone call to Dave's mother, and she took pity on me and asked me for lunch.

NINE

Dave's Narrative

ROGER GOT TO the office fifteen minutes late on Saturday morning. Most offices in the city government are closed on Saturdays, but not us, not when we're in the middle of a murder case.

Roger looked pulverized. He'd been out with Laurie Franz last night, and I supposed he'd had an exciting time. At his age, dates are roller-coaster rides: one emotional high after another, and lots of enjoyable wear and tear on the nerves and the stomach. At my age dates are more like the merry-go-round. Round and round you go, you get the illusion of activity, but actually you never move very fast and you never leave the ground.

Take the woman I've been seeing for the last couple of months, the legal paraprofessional I was with Friday night. Actually Mom isn't crazy about her, she thinks I can do better, but she's always nudging me about her anyway. "So what are you waiting for anyway? Why don't you make up your mind already?" Dear God, could I be such a romantic adolescent that I'm actually waiting for a roller coaster to come along?

"Okay, let's get down to business," I said to Roger, and he proceeded to give me a play-by-play account of his date with Laurie Franz, including her father's dramatic entrance from the bedroom. I assumed, of course, that Roger left out certain personal details that weren't relevant to the murder.

"So there's another one without an alibi," I said. "She says she was in the john, throwing up with an attack of stage fright. But nobody saw her there, she admits that herself."

"You can't seriously think Laurie did the killing," Roger said. "Even if she put on a dozen raincoats and black masks, nobody could ever mistake her for Harold Hapgood! She's three inches taller than he is."

"We're proceeding on the theory, in this office, that the murderer *was* taller than Hapgood. He walked around the stage with a stoop, to make himself look shorter."

"That theory is for public consumption, isn't it? We don't really *believe* it. Your mother knocked it down right from the start."

I could feel my stomach tightening a little at that, but I was careful not to let anything show on my face.

"Besides," he went on, "even if the audience didn't see through her disguise right away, *I* sure as hell would have."

"Just exactly how?"

"The moment she grabbed me from behind. If that girl ever held on to me like that—damn it all, I would've *known!*"

He must have noticed I was staring at him, so immediately he made his voice businesslike. "Besides, she has no motive for killing Osborn. In fact, just the opposite. Like I just told you, she was crazy about him, they were planning to go to New York together. You don't kill a man when you're in love with him and the two of you are running off together. And there's also—"

He stopped talking. Something about the look on his face made me give him a hard stare. "There's also what?"

"Nothing."

"Is something on your mind, kid? Something you haven't told me yet?"

"No, of course not." He met my stare without flinching. A pretty good job, only it didn't calm my doubts one bit. But he wasn't going to say anything else right now, so I gave a shrug and dropped it.

Our next step ordinarily would have been to report our progress to Ann, but she wasn't in the office, she was taking a deposition in another case and would be tied up all morning. She had left word with Mabel Gibson that she'd see us at four that afternoon for a full report on the Michaels case.

So I told Roger to read through all of my notes and all of his own and spend the morning typing up a detailed report for Ann. Than I went off to talk to Lloyd Cunningham.

CUNNINGHAM'S STORE, the Audio-Visual Palace, was located in another one of the new malls. Ten miles away from the mall where Harold Hapgood had his insurance office, but identical to it in every respect. I got there just after it had opened for the day, but already three or four customers were browsing around. CDs and VCRs and TVs are big business in Mesa Grande. In culture and politics we may be a wasteland, but when it comes to the latest gadgets, we're right up there with Los Angeles and New York.

I hadn't called to warn my target that I was coming. I was pretty sure he'd be there, though. Cunningham owned the business, he wasn't likely to neglect his interests by taking a day off.

I saw him spot me in the doorway. He didn't look a bit surprised or frightened. He gave me a quick cheerful wave, signaled to another salesman to take over with the customer he'd been shepherding around, then came bustling up to me.

With his broad shoulders, his football center's build, could he possibly have scrunched himself up to look like the Third Murderer? Wouldn't he have burst through that raincoat of Sally's and given the game away?

"So here you are," he said, shaking my hand, grinning that slightly crooked sarcastic grin at me. "Actually I was expecting you yesterday. I hope you didn't put me off till last because I'm such an unimportant witness."

"Maybe we've been saving the best till last," I said. "You got any place around here where we can talk?"

"We'll go to the office in back." He led me across the salesroom, pausing on the way to flash big smiles at customers or shake their hands or ask after the last piece of equipment they had bought from him. "How's that Harman-Kardon woofer holding up, Mac? God, that's a sweet little job! I wish *I* could afford one. Are you happy with the new stereo TV, Sid? Curling up at night with that wraparound sound, are you? Not quite as good as a good woman, I'll give you that, but the chances are it'll last you longer. And the woman doesn't come with a two-year warranty, right?"

His laugh was loud and hearty while he ushered me into the little glass-enclosed office in back, but he cut it off sharp as soon as he shut the door.

"The name of this sitcom is 'Cunningham, Super-Salesman,'" he said, waving me to a chair and sprawling behind the desk. "It's my longest-running role. To tell you the truth, I wish the author could come up with some better jokes. All right, all right, let's get down to business. Was I in the theatre Thursday night to see the opening? I damn well was. Since a couple of hundred people saw me there, including yourself, Dave, there's not much point denying it. And I already told it to the cops, incidentally."

"Were you still in the audience when the murder took place?"

"That's the *second* question the cops asked me. The answer is no. I hung around long enough for Banquo's first big scene, then I walked out."

"Why did you do that? If you were curious enough to come to the play at all—"

"How come I wasn't curious enough to stay all the way through? Well, let's just say I satisfied my curiosity with that first scene. I wanted to see if Osborn was going to fall on his ass playing *my* part and make a fucking fool of himself. Okay, I was *hoping* that's what he'd do."

"And what *did* he do?"

"He played the guts out of the part! The son of a bitch was great! He acted everybody else off the stage, including that pathetic old ham he shipped in from New York. I couldn't stand it any longer, so I got the hell out of there."

"Did you make a lot of noise when you left?"

"I sure as hell hope not. I slipped out of my seat as quietly as I could and practically tiptoed out. What was I going to do, call attention to myself, make people think I was a sorehead? Which, in fact, I *am,* but I didn't want people thinking it."

"Where did you go after you got out of the theatre?"

"To the Watering Hole on Rocky Mountain Avenue. It's a couple of blocks away from the theatre, a lot of the actors and the crew drop in there when we're rehearsing."

I knew the place. It was a working stiff's saloon, clean enough, no hookers or topless waitresses, but not in any way elegant.

"How come you didn't go home?"

"First, because I didn't feel like making domestic chatter to Lucille and the kids. The mood I was in, I would've snapped their heads off, and felt rotten about it in the morning. What I had to do was digest a few stiff ones till I calmed down and got back my cool."

"And second?"

"Excuse me?"

"You implied there's more than one reason why you stopped for a drink at the Watering Hole."

"Right. The second reason was, I wanted to get back to the theatre in time for intermission and mingle with the crowd to listen to what people were saying about the show." He gave another laugh. "Okay, okay, pretty childish, right? I'm hoping the audience doesn't like it, I'm hoping it's going to be a big flop. Right, I admit it. You see, it's honesty time."

"Did anybody see you while you were at the Watering Hole?"

"Frankie, the bartender. He saw me when I came in. And Agnes, the waitress. I sat in one of the back booths, and she brought me my gin and soda. Maybe some of the regulars noticed me too, I'm pretty well known in there."

I made a mental note that this was something Roger would have to check. There had to be some weakness in Cunningham's alibi, or Grantley wouldn't have included him on the list.

"And when did you leave the Watering Hole?"

"Well, the first half of the play usually took about an hour and a half in rehearsals, and they started on time, around seven, so when my watch said eight thirty I left the saloon and headed back to the theatre. I was half a block away when I saw the police cars lined up at the curb, and a crowd was forming. I asked somebody what was up, and he told me he heard somebody got killed. So I hotfooted it in the other direction, picked up my car from where I'd parked it down the bock, and went straight home. Lucille can tell you what time I got there, and my oldest kid, my boy Lloyd, Junior, was still up too.''

Another piece of information for Roger to check. ''You weren't curious to find out who got killed in the theatre? You've been working with those people for years, some of them must be your friends—''

''I figured I'd find out fast enough from the late news on TV. I didn't want any cops picking me up.''

''Why not?''

''Because a lot of people knew I'd got into a fight with Osborn and wasn't on such good terms with the Players. If there was some kind of trouble at the theatre, and if the cops caught me hanging around, they might jump to some wrong conclusions.''

''It never occurred to you that they might jump to those conclusions even quicker if you ran away?''

''I was mixed up. Maybe I had too much to drink.''

''Fair enough,'' I said. ''So what do you think about all this, Lloyd? Does it make any sense to you that Sally should've killed him?''

Cunningham scratched his chin. ''That's a tough one. Poor Sally, the perennial sucker, right? Wiggle your little finger at her, and she's so grateful she'll jump right into bed with you. Lucille says she's a whore, it's a disgrace they've let her teach in the public schools all these years. Lucille won't be happy till they strap her into that chair in the gas chamber. Even if she didn't commit a murder.''

''You don't share Lucille's opinion, I take it?''

''It's been a long time since Lucille and I shared an opinion. Or much of anything else, for that matter.'' He gave his head a shake. ''I think of Sally as being into love, not murder. On the other hand, a woman scorned, and so forth and so on?''

''You know about her affair with Osborn, do you?''

"For Christ's sake, who *didn't* know? Well, maybe Roger Meyer, the boy investigator, didn't. He's living in a dreamworld, with all those old Hollywood movies where women are pure and noble. But the rest of us knew exactly what was going on. And knew exactly when Marty dumped her too. And knew who he dumped her *for.* That Franz kid, she's another one with stars in her eyes, she could've got herself real hurt if it had gone on for a while.

"But we're talking about Sally, right? And what I'm saying is, she may have reached the point these days where sex is a bigger issue for her than acting.'

"I don't know exactly what you mean by that."

"What I mean is, since the acting is slipping further and further away from her all the time—"

"What makes you say that?"

"My God, just look at what she did in this little Shakespearean turkey! The first Lady Macbeth in history who plays every damn scene as if she were sleepwalking! Take the scene where she tries to get Macbeth to commit murder, for instance. She builds up to this big speech where she whips him into it—the one that ends with 'the poor cat i' the adage'—and what happens? That cat, and everything leading up to him, goes out of her head completely! She jumps forward to the next speech, so that poor sap Randy Le Sage never gets to look noble and talk about how manly he is. The point I'm making is, if she can't act any more, she has to latch on to *something* for emotional kicks and ego building. So suddenly all that male flesh she's been rolling around in for years starts to get important." Cunningham sighed, and a touch of seriousness came into his voice. "That's always the worst mistake an actor can make."

"What mistake?"

"To mix up his outside with his inside. To let himself get carried away by his emotions. That's where I and the Studio part company. All that Stanislavsky bullshit about getting in touch with your feelings, using the memory of what you've personally been through. An actor can't use his personal feelings, all they'll do for him is make him sloppy. An actor has to *project* feelings, not *feel* them."

"Meaning that a good actor can look you straight in the eye and tell you something and make you believe it, even though he's feeling exactly the opposite underneath?"

"Sure he can. A good actor does it every day."

"*You're* a good actor. You could tell me you didn't kill Osborn and I'd never believe for a minute that you were lying."

"Thanks for the compliment. Being accused of murder is a small price to pay for a rave review. But I have to disappoint you, Dave. I'd like to help you get Sally off the hook, but I didn't kill that goddamned thief."

"Why do you call him a thief?"

"That's what he was. First he stole the Players from me, then he stole Macbeth from me, then he topped it off by stealing Banquo from me."

"You felt like killing him for that, right?" I put this in very gently. I'm not the browbeating type of questioner, at least not when I don't have to be. Usually I put my paw on the mouse as gently as any cat, in or out of the adage.

Cunningham threw back his head and gave his booming laugh. "Pretty good, Dave. Tricky. Yeah, I felt like killing him for those things. I could've killed him for the first one all by itself. Suppose somebody was trying to steal your home and family away from you, don't you think you'd feel like committing murder if that was the only way you could keep from losing them? And for me the Players... Come on, you know my situation. What other home and family have I got?''

Cunningham lowered his head suddenly. For a second or two neither of us broke the silence.

Then Cunningham's head was up, and he was laughing again. "Strike that, will you. I didn't mean it the way it came out. Trashing Lucille, after all she's done for me! The guys she could've married. Rich, successful guys, who haven't wasted their lives dreaming about things that are long gone and you never could've had anyway. Her father was always telling me how grateful I should be to her, and he was fucking right.

"So anyway, where were we? Did I feel like killing Osborn because he robbed me? Sure I did—right afterward. But a few hours later it's over with, I've cooled down. What do you think, I'm a fucking psycho? People don't kill people because they lost a part in a play."

Agreed, I thought. But on the other hand, were actors like people?

"No offense intended, Lloyd," I said. "Just doing my job."

"No offense taken," he said with a grin. "Now, if you're finished with me, the customers are muttering restlessly out there."

He started to move to the door, then turned back to me. "Oh, by the way, I have to ask you a favor. In a week or two, especially if the charges get dropped against Sally, I'm going to open *Macbeth* again. I'll have to redirect a little, work on some of the spots where Marty missed his opportunities, but with all this free publicity we're getting, everybody in town will rush down to see it. The Murder Play! We'll pack them in. So I hope you'll still let that assistant of yours take his nights off for the performances."

"I'll let him if he wants to," I said.

Cunningham's grin broadened, then he started to the door again.

In the nick of time, I remembered the question Mom had told me to ask him. "Just one more thing, Lloyd," I said. "Last week you walked out on the show because Allan Franz told you your Banquo was too soft and sympathetic—"

"*That* wasn't why I walked out, for Christ's sake. It was because Marty *agreed* with Franz. That cowardly asslicking son of a bitch couldn't stand up to the great Hollywood director—"

"But my question is, was Franz right or wrong? Do you think you weren't making Banquo tough enough?"

"That's a crock," Cunningham said. "My Banquo has this nice-guy manner, butter wouldn't melt in his mouth, but underneath he's as ambitious and hardheaded as his buddy Macbeth. That's how I was playing him, and Franz should've seen it. Makes me wonder how he's been getting such great performances out of his actors all these years."

Cunningham gave me a quick nod and went back to his customers.

I left his store and headed for the nearest phone booth and told Roger, back at the office, that after he finished typing his report he should do some checking up on Cunningham: talk to his family and find out when he got home Thursday night, talk to the people at the Watering Hole and find out what time he got there and what time he left. I also asked the kid if he'd wait for me, and we could have a quick lunch together.

"Oh, I'm sorry, Dave," he said. "I've already got a lunch date."

And that was it. Not a word about with whom. What the hell was up with him today?

TEN

Roger's Narrative

WHEN I GOT OUT of my car in front of Dave's mother's house, I looked in both directions before I walked up to the front door. As if I was worrying that Dave had tailed me there! Pure paranoia.

I rang the bell, and a few seconds later she was grabbing me by the hand, kissing me on the cheek, and leading me inside. "We'll go straight to the kitchen, I've got matzo-ball soup," she said.

I followed her, thinking that she was looking kind of tired. There were shadows under her eyes, and it occurred to me for the first time that she must have problems of her own on her mind. It was selfish of me to assume she'd stop everything to take care of mine.

She sat me down at the kitchen table and put a bowl of total deliciousness in front of me. Her matzo balls were exactly the way such things ought to be: firm to your lips, but tender and juicy as they went down your throat. I can't say they were just like mother used to make, because frankly my mother has never been much of a cook and her matzo-ball soup comes strictly from the can.

"It's really nice of you to have me for lunch," I started in. "I wasn't angling for an invitation when I called."

"Naturally not. It's my pleasure to feed people. What I'm always saying is, eating alone is like making love alone. And since making love is a pleasure I don't have no more . . . not so often anyway."

She cleared away the soup and brought in some chopped liver with crackers. The chopped liver had the usual hard-boiled egg and onions in it, but also another flavor I couldn't identify that put it in the category of heavenly.

"I feel funny bothering you," I said. "I just couldn't think of anybody else to talk this over with. If it's inconvenient for you, if you aren't feeling up to it today—"

"I'm feeling fine," she said. "I just didn't sleep so good last night, I'm having a touch of insomnia, but you'll wake me up when you start telling me what's bothering you."

I took a deep breath and jumped in. "You remember, the last time we talked about this Osborn murder, you tried to get me to come up with something that I'd forgotten, you almost pulled it up from my subconscious mind."

"Certainly I remember. So?"

"Well, last night it suddenly came to me. I couldn't believe I'd ever forgotten it."

"And what was it?"

"A ring! The Third Murderer, when he grabbed hold of me, was wearing a ring!"

"And you can also say who that ring belonged to, isn't that right?"

I blinked at her. "How did you know that?"

"You'd go to Davie if you wanted only to describe it. You came here to me because you recognized that ring, and your problem is, should you tell somebody or should you keep your mouth shut?"

"I suppose you'll be telling me next who the ring *does* belong to."

The old lady gave a little shrug. "This is obvious. It can only be one person, otherwise you wouldn't be here."

"I don't understand."

"You came here today because, whoever it is that owns the ring, it's somebody you care about, somebody you got a reason for being interested in, and you don't want you should be responsible for getting this somebody executed for murder. So I'm asking myself, who could this somebody be? In the collection of people who could've done the murder, who is it you care about enough so it gives you a problem to admit the murderer was wearing her ring?

"My first thought was, it's the little Franz girl. She's attractive to you, so you're trying to protect her—"

"I never said I was attracted to Laurie Franz!"

"Does the cat say he's attracted to the mouse? All you need is one look at his face when somebody mentions that mouse's name. But this we don't have to argue about, because the Franz girl isn't the one you're protecting."

"That's true. But I don't see—"

"If you thought she was the murderer, you wouldn't be asking for advice now, not even from me. You'd be suffering inside yourself, your conscience would be doing flip-flips in your stomach, but you wouldn't take the risk she should get arrested. With young people love is bigger than obeying the law."

It made me fidget, all this talk about love, but I couldn't find anything wrong with the old lady's reasoning, so I kept quiet.

"So I'm asking myself," she went on, "who else could you care about so much you'd have a problem telling the truth about this ring? And there's one answer only. Sally Michaels. Am I right or wrong?"

"You're right. It's a big red stone in the shape of a grinning face. She picked it out especially for Lady Macbeth, and she wore it at all the rehearsals. I couldn't be wrong about whose it is."

"So let me get this straight, why you're coming to me for advice. Now that you've remembered seeing this ring on the murderer's finger, you're afraid to tell Davie and Ann

Swenson about it. You're afraid this ring could be a piece evidence against Sally Michaels. Davie and Ann Swenson will have to send you to the district attorney—that's the law, what else could they do?—and you'll have to testify for the prosecution. So you're thinking maybe it's better if you keep your mouth shut."

She had it all figured out, there was no way I could be cagey about it anymore. So I let my feelings come pouring out, just like a little kid when he finally confesses some terrible crime to his mother. "I'd be responsible for ruining our client's defense! How could Dave and Ann keep me around after that? I wouldn't blame them at all if they fired me!"

The old lady looked at me for a while, a soft smile on her face. She didn't seem to be condemning me or even feeling sorry for me. If anything, she seemed sort of amused. "And what happens if you *don't* come out with the truth about this ring?"

"Nobody finds out about it, I won't have to give evidence against Sally."

"And if she gets off free, you'll feel good about what you did?"

She had me there. It's difficult talking to people who see things you don't want them to see. I was reduced to taking sips of coffee, though there was practically nothing left in the cup.

"You want my advice?" she said. "Is it your fault you recognized that ring on the murderer's finger? No. So are Davie and Ann Swenson going to get mad at you for it? Positively not. What it all boils away to is, do you think they're people without any fairness?"

"Of course they're not."

"So if you're sure of that, you've got only one thing you can do. You'll tell them about this ring as soon as you see them, and you'll let *them* decide what happens next."

"But if they decide to keep quiet about it, I'd still have this on my conscience, wouldn't I?"

"Naturally you would. The question is, what are you willing to have on your conscience and what not? You think you can get through life with *nothing* on your conscience? Believe me, it never worked that way. Read the Bible already. Look at all those holy people, what *they* had on their conscience. Like King David sleeping in the bath with the Queen of Sheba. And Moses burning up bushes. And Abraham, he was the worst one of all, he was going to stick a knife into his own son. Every father *feels* like doing it from time to time, this is only natural, but if the angel didn't come along, Abraham would've *done* it. So the point I'm making is, nobody's perfect. And you don't have to be the exception."

I didn't even need to do much thinking about this. I said I'd turn my evidence over to Dave and Ann, and after that I'd just let things take their course. Already I felt a lot better.

Then I saw the time and got to my feet, not too enthusiastically because there was still a piece of schnecken left on the plate. But I had a lot of work to do before Dave and I met with Ann at four o'clock. I had to check out when Lloyd Cunningham got home on the night of the murder, talk to the people at the Watering Hole saloon, and take care of a few items pertaining to other cases. I thanked the old lady for the food and the advice. I didn't know which I was more grateful for.

At her front door I said, "The way you figured out whose ring it was—that was a terrific piece of deduction. It reminded me of the way Dave deduces things. If I didn't know better, I'd think maybe *he* comes to you for advice too."

I let the words slip out as if they had suddenly popped into my head, right out of the blue. But of course, even as I heard myself saying them, I knew this was exactly what I'd been wondering about for weeks now. This was my crazy suspicion, and all along I had been intending to confront her with it.

She looked at me in silence. And with her eyes so steady that pretty soon I couldn't meet them anymore.

"Everybody's a detective" was what she finally said. Then she put her hand on my arm and gave a squeeze. Her expression wasn't harsh or angry, but it was very serious. "This is something you don't ever say to Davie, you follow me? This is something you don't ever let on that you know. If you like him at all, and care a little bit for his feelings, you keep quiet about even *thinking* such a thing."

I nodded hard and gave her my solemn promise.

Then I said, "Good-bye, Mrs.—"

But she didn't let me finish. "Mrs. is what I am to the butcher and the baker and the rabbi. You'll call me Mom, wouldn't you, like Davie does? Unless this makes you feel uncomfortable."

"No, it's all right. I'd *like* to call you Mom."

"You're a nice boy," she said. Then she was pecking at my cheek again. An old lady's kiss, dry and quick, like something fluttering against my face. "And you're a good eater. One thing I like in this world, it's a good eater. Davie was a good eater too, at your age."

I HAD Lloyd Cunningham's home address in my notebook, so I drove in that direction, hoping to find his wife and kids at home. And while I drove, and subliminally enjoyed the streaks of autumn red and yellow that were beginning to take over the trees on all the streets, I thought about what I had just learned. Of course I would never tell Dave. I could understand how embarrassed he would feel. But I wish I *could* tell him somehow, so that I could let him know that it didn't make me think less of him in any way.

In fact—and this thought came to me as a big surprise—I had never felt so close to him before.

ELEVEN

Dave's Narrative

I GRABBED A BITE of nothing at the courthouse cafeteria, and put in an afternoon clearing up the paperwork on four or five earlier cases. This is how District Attorney Marvin McBride hopes eventually to sink the public defender's office: he can't be more efficient than we are, but maybe he can tie us up day and night with forms to fill out.

I finished the forms at three, naturally in a lousy mood, so I took out the bottle of whiskey that I kept in my desk drawer and gulped down one shot. This isn't a remedy I turn to very often; in fact, in the couple of years that I've had this job, I've replaced the bottle only once. My persistent vice, as Mom always reminds me, isn't drinking, it's complaining about my life. "You're a kvetsh," she often told me. "Kvetshes don't kill themselves at a young age, like drinkers and dope-takers. They lead long lives, full of misery."

A few minutes before four Roger arrived, and then Ann buzzed from her office and said she was ready for us.

So we reported our latest activities to her. I gave her the details of the interview with Cunningham, and Roger told her about his date last night with Laurie Franz. Then he told her what he had been doing this afternoon after lunch, how he had checked with Cunningham's wife and family and with the bartender and waiters at the Watering Hole. All this had accomplished was to confirm what Cunningham had told us already: he did get home around eight-forty on the night of the murder, he did arrive at the Watering Hole around seven-thirty and leave around eight-thirty. But he had occupied a booth way in the back, near the fire door to the alley, and nobody could say he hadn't slipped out before the time of the murder and slipped in again afterward.

Ann seldom expressed enthusiasm, even for good news. For non-news like we had to offer—a few motives, a few opportunities, but nothing substantial to put up against Sally's button—she just gave a poker-faced grunt. "Okay, if that's it," she said. "I'm trying for a preliminary hearing, two weeks from today. It would be nice if we had something definite by then, we might be able to keep her from going to trial at all. How's the chances, do you think?"

I shrugged, my normal defense when Ann tries to pin me down to a promise or even a cautious note of optimism. "Give me tonight to look over my notes and think about what we've got, then I'll tell you tomorrow morning where we go from here."

"I don't see what else we can do," Ann said. She turned to Roger. "You have any ideas?"

I expected him to shake his head no, but instead he got this terribly serious, nervous look on his face. "There's something I didn't tell you yet," he said.

He stopped, while we stared at him, waiting. So he started in again. "The reason I didn't tell you, I wasn't sure if it's something you'd *want* to know. I mean, if I never told you about it, nobody could ever say you should've done something about it."

"Roger, what is it?" Ann said quietly.

So he finally came out with it, and when he was finished I couldn't keep myself from giving a groan. "Great! Just great!"

"I *shouldn't* have told you! Now you'll have to report it to the DA, and it'll make the case against Mrs. Michaels even worse!"

The expression on Ann's face had hardly changed at all. One of the best things about her is the way she takes bad news. In her usual businesslike voice she said, "Did Sally wear that ring onstage on opening night?"

She addressed the question to Roger and me, and we both paused for a while before answering. I was racking my brains over it, trying to bring back an image of what Sally Michaels had looked like during that opening-night performance. I tried to visualize her hands, but nothing came to me at all. And Roger was looking just as blank and frustrated.

"What about when we interviewed her in the jail yesterday morning?" Ann said. "Was she wearing the ring? No, don't bother to torture yourself, Dave, I can tell you the answer. She was."

"That doesn't necessarily mean she's the person who grabbed hold of me," Roger said. "The murderer could've stolen the ring from her, worn it during the murder, and slipped back to her dressing room afterward. Like with the raincoat. All part of the frame-up."

"It wouldn't be easy to do," I said. "If she wore that ring onstage, if she never took it off her finger all night."

"It *has* to have happened that way." Roger's voice was getting louder. "You can't tell me she'd be crazy enough to keep that ring on her finger while she was committing the murder! A dead giveaway to who she was?"

"She'd be crazy enough if the thought just didn't occur to her," I said. "She's so used to wearing that ring that she forgot all about it when she dressed up like the Third Murderer. After all, she had something more important on her mind."

"It's pointless speculating about it." Ann got to her feet. "Obviously the next step is to hear what *she* has to say about the ring. Get her on the phone, will you, Roger. If she's home, tell her the three of us will be right over."

"And after we talk to her," Roger said, "is that when I turn over this information to the district attorney?"

Ann said nothing for a while, her face absolutely without expression. Then, in a neutral tone of voice, she said, "It goes without saying that you have to report this to the district attorney. This office has a legal duty not to suppress evidence in a criminal case. You have the same duty as any citizen."

She paused, stared into space, then went on, "The only question is when. As an employee of the public defender's office, your first obligation is to report important information to your immediate superior. Meaning Dave. And *his* first obligation is to report it to *his* immediate superior, meaning me. That could be a long-drawn-out process, there has to be time for locating people, working your way into their schedules, et cetera. And even when you finally *do* get the information to me, *my* first obligation is to evaluate how important it is, with the ultimate purpose of determining who *I* should report it to.

"I might then decide that I should report it directly to the district attorney himself. Well, that could be easier said than done. By this time in the afternoon, if past experience is any guide, District Attorney McBride is at least three cocktails on the way to his nightly celebration of the rites of Dionysus. Is he in any condition to receive important information that might require high-level policy decisions? Will he be in such a condition tomorrow morning, as he struggles to recover from the effects of those rites? Frankly, I doubt it. In fact, my offhand estimate is that it won't be feasible to get this information to him until noon tomorrow at the earliest. Which gives us plenty of time to have a nice leisurely conference with our client. Roger, didn't I tell you ten minutes ago to get her on the phone? What's holding you up?''

Roger scurried out of there, and Ann gave a grunt and settled back into her chair.

Sally Michaels lived in an old stone house on the north end of Mesa Grande, the oldest and one of the most expensive parts of town. Sally didn't have much money, but she had inherited this house from her parents thirty years ago, so all it cost her was the upkeep and the property taxes. When she was married to Bernie, I'm told, she used to rent it out, and they lived in his little house in a much less fancy neighborhood. After the divorce, Sally moved back to the old homestead.

Ann had called first to make sure she'd be expecting us, but her front door was opened by Bernie. His smile flickered, friendly but nervous, as he let the three of us in.

''Sally called me after she talked to you,'' he said. ''She got the feeling something bad was up. She thought she'd be needing moral support.''

''I hope not,'' Ann said. We went into the living room, furnished with faded overstuffed furniture that belonged to an earlier and uglier era.

''She's in the kitchen making coffee,'' Bernie said.

''That isn't necessary,'' Ann said, and we all sat down on a large sofa printed with big red and yellow sunflowers.

''It's necessary for *her*.''

I could understand how intimidating we must be. Three grim-faced officers of the court, sitting stiffly in a row.

A few minutes later, accompanied by the faint aroma of Magnolia Blossoms, Sally came in with the coffee. She bustled around, pouring for us, asking who took sugar and cream. Finally she settled into an armchair across from us, leaned forward, and squeezed her hands together as if she were doing her Lady Macbeth sleepwalking-washing act. "All right, get it over with, tell me the bad news."

Ann took a few beats, then said, "That's an interesting ring you're wearing."

Sally looked down at it, and so did the rest of us. I couldn't take my eyes away from the large stone shaped like a grinning face.

"Oh, yes, isn't it lovely?" Sally said. "It has deep sentimental value for me."

"I understand," Ann said, "that you and Martin Osborn got into a fight about that ring at one of the rehearsals. He didn't want you to wear it during the performance—"

"Oh, certainly not a *fight*. I don't *fight* with people. We had a disagreement on artistic grounds."

"And you won the disagreement, did you?"

"If you mean did I wear the ring on opening night, I certainly did. Imagine that *vulgar* man telling *me* about beauty and good taste!"

"Nobody blames you for wearing the ring, Sally," Bernie put in. "Everybody understand that artists have more refined tastes than ordinary people."

"My white knight," she said, leaning over to pat his hand. "Always defending me, always rescuing me from the dragons. Why didn't I have the sense to hold on to this sweet man while I had him?"

"You could have him again, anytime you want," Bernie said, blushing very deeply.

Sally laughed. "Luckily for you, darling, I won't take you up on that offer. I'm too fond of you to make your life miserable all over again."

"So you *were* wearing the ring when you went onstage opening night?" Ann said.

"I wore it all that day; I was wearing it when I got to the theatre."

"And you never took it off, not even when you were in your dressing room resting up before the banquet scene?"

"Why should I have? It's such a nuisance to take it off, it's so tight on my finger these days. I *have* put on just a tiny little bit of weight since my twenty-first birthday, you know."

"It never occurred to you that Osborn might be right, about the ring being unsuitable for Lady Macbeth?"

"He *wasn't* right. He was trying to frighten me, telling me the audience would laugh at me for wearing it, pretending he thought it was just some cheap vulgar piece of trash. That was his way of making me jump when he snapped his fingers. Marty loved to make people jump. Well, I was damned if I'd give him that satisfaction! I wore the ring all that night, on my finger, in plain sight. I never took it off, from the time I got to the theatre to the time I left. And I'll make you a bet right now: nobody in the audience even *noticed* I was wearing it!"

She came to a stop, shaking a little. Saint Joan standing up to her inquisitors, refusing to be intimidated even in the shadow of the stake.

Ann gave a little sigh and turned to Roger. "Why don't you tell Sally what you've remembered."

Roger looked positively wretched; I couldn't help feeling sorry for the kid. He brought out his story in an apologetic voice, as if *he* were the one who had something to feel guilty about.

After he was finished, the room was silent for a long time.

"Now look." Bernie finally broke the silence. "It was dark up on that stage, you admit that yourself. And this murderer, his hand was on your chest, so you could only see his ring out of the corner of your eye—"

"It wasn't that dark," Roger said, "and the hand was pretty close to my face. I'm not lying about this, believe me."

"I never said you were lying!" Bernie's voice was high and strained. "But look, you *couldn't* have seen the same— Wait, wait, hey, isn't *this* possible? Somebody bought a ring that looked exactly like Sally's, found it in a store somewhere, and put it on deliberately when he was committing the murder, so Sally would be implicated!"

"That's a pretty unusual stone," I said. "And the whole style of it is old-fashioned. We'll check every store in town, but I'd be surprised if there's any place that carries anything like this."

"Then the murderer didn't pick up the duplicate ring here in town," Bernie cried, "he went to some other city for it, maybe some other part of the country!"

"Cunningham quit the play and Osborn took over the part of Banquo," I said, "just four days before the opening night. That wouldn't give your murderer much time to travel any distance and rummage through secondhand stores."

"All right, Sally." Ann directed her gaze straight at her now. "Let's hear what you have to say about Roger's story."

None of us had looked at Sally since Roger finished talking. Bernie's interruptions had distracted us. We all looked at her now.

Her face was very white. Her voice came very low. "I swear to you, I never took this ring off all night. And I didn't kill Marty. I swear it."

"Then how do you account for Roger seeing the ring on the murderer's finger?" Ann said.

She shook her head. "How can you expect me to account for things? I've never been any good at accounting for things!" A long low wail came out of her, and the tears burst from her eyes.

Bernie was over to her in a split second, putting his arms around her, letting her sob into his chest. And over her head his eyes were fixed on us with a look of deep reproach.

But reproachful looks have never been known to stop Ann when she had something to say. So she waited for Sally's tears to subside, and then she said, "One more question. A few days before the murder, did you and Martin Osborn have an argument in your dressing room? Did he tell you he didn't like the way you were playing Lady Macbeth's sleepwalking scene, and did you tell him you could kill him for that?"

Sally's head snapped up. She wasn't sobbing at all now. Her eyes weren't even wet. "Who told you such a ridiculous thing?" she said, facing Ann directly. "Marty and I couldn't possibly have had such an argument. He *loved* my sleepwalking scene. He complimented me on it many times. Whatever you say about Marty, he *was* a superb judge of acting."

"Who's been telling lies about Sally?" Bernie put in. "Just tell me who!"

But Ann just kept her eyes on Sally. And finally she gave a grunt and got to her feet, and we left the house.

IT WAS AFTER FIVE, no point going back to the office. Ann told Roger and me to have a restful Sunday and went off in her car. Roger said good night too. The look on his face was positively pitiful. A small animal that somebody had kicked, and he was coming back for more because he thought he deserved it.

"Listen, I'm going to my mother's for dinner," I said. "She'd love it if you came too."

"But she isn't expecting—"

"She'll have plenty of food, believe me. Today's the Sabbath, so she did all her shopping for the week yesterday. And she's always got twice as much as she and I can possibly eat."

He brightened up a little. So I got into my car, and he followed me in his. On the way I asked myself why the hell I was doing this. After the long lecture I'd given to Mom about how she should stop paying so much attention to this kid!

When she opened the door to us and I muttered my explanation, I was expecting a certain look to appear on her face. That look that gave new meaning to the word "ironic."

It didn't appear. She smiled and hugged us both, and assured us, as she led us into the living room, that there was enough pot roast to fill up half a dozen growing boys.

During the pot roast, she asked offhandedly how our investigation of Osborn's murder was going. I brought her up to date, fully expecting her to hammer out two or three brilliant deductions that I hadn't begun to think of and to issue two or three orders as to what steps I was to take next. But instead, when I got to the end of my report, she blinked her eyes and looked completely bewildered.

"What a mishmash it sounds like," she said. "The more you find out, the more it looks like you've got a client that could spend the rest of her life in jail. Believe me, Davie, for a million dollars I wouldn't want your job. Such complicated thinking you have to do, so many facts and ideas you have to keep sorting out in your head. Only to think about it makes me dizzy!''

I swallowed a piece of pot roast the wrong way and coughed for a while. Mom as the poor helpless female who couldn't keep her balance in the face of complicated problems was a concept I had trouble digesting. Then I realized what she was doing. She was following through on our talk yesterday, she was protecting my dignity and self-respect in front of my assistant. For a moment I felt like going over to her and hugging her.

"So I've got an extra-special dessert tonight," Mom was saying, "on account of it's the Sabbath. Mrs. Gilhooly from down the street just gave me her recipe for Black Forest cake. It's about time I learned how to cook some of the native dishes out here. If you're in Rome, you should eat what the Romans eat. Naturally I added a little more sour cream, and also some chopped walnuts—"

We finished dinner and helped Mom with the dishes, and suddenly the phone rang. It was for me.

The voice was hoarse and hurried, and spoke in a whisper. I couldn't be sure if it was a man or a woman. It said my name, and when I agreed to my identity it said, "I've got information, vital information."

"How did you know I'd be at this number?"

With a touch of impatience, the voice said. "You put it on your answering machine." The voice was right. When I went to Mom's for the evening, I always left her number on my machine. "Do you want this information or not?"

"About what?"

"The Osborn murder, of course. I could always change my mind and give my information to the police."

"All right, I'm listening."

"I won't give it to *you*. To your assistant. Young Roger Meyer. He's the only one I'll talk to."

"Is there any reason—"

"I trust him. I won't argue with you about it. You can contact him, can't you?"

"Yes, I can."

"You tell him this. I'll be at the theatre at eight tonight. The Ramon Novarro Theatre, eight sharp. That's curtain time. Tell him to be there."

"In front of the theatre?"

"*In* the theatre. I'll meet him on the stage. Don't tell me he hasn't got a key, because I know everybody in the *Macbeth* cast was given one. And he's to come alone! If you're with him, if anybody's with him, you won't get a thing out of me!"

I heard the phone ringing up at the other end.

I waited a few seconds, thinking things over. Anonymous calls are usually a waste. They come from nuts, they don't lead to a damn thing. But once in a dozen times maybe, they're *not* a waste, you actually learn something from them. Which means you have to check them all out, regardless of the odds. Even if they sometimes lead to real trouble, real danger.

So far, since Roger came to work for me, it hadn't happened, but I guess I knew all along that I'd have to face it eventually. Police work is mostly tramping from place to place, talking to people, writing endless reports. But occasionally somebody shoots at you, and somebody even gets killed.

I had told all of this to Roger when I hired him. It was nothing for me to feel guilty about.

So I turned to him now and told him about the call. And he looked at his watch and said, "I've only got twenty minutes."

Meanwhile, neither of us was looking at Mom.

We all went to the front door, and Roger and I thanked Mom for the delicious dinner.

Her answer was "I'll be home all night. There's a play on television, about this girl that lost both her legs but she still won the Olympics skiing championship. So give me a call. It don't matter how late, I'm not sleeping so much these days anyway."

Her expression couldn't have been calmer and more cheerful. In a murder case full of actors, Mom was completely at home.

TWELVE

Roger's Narrative

"I'LL FOLLOW YOU down in my car," Dave said, after his mother shut the front door.

"You can't do that, can you? This character wants me to be alone. He won't talk to me if you're with me."

"Who's going to be with you? I'll park around the corner, and I'll stand across the street. In case you don't come out again in a reasonable amount of time.'

"That's taking too much of a chance. Suppose he spots you?"

"How's he going to spot me? You think you're working for an amateur?" He hesitated, then he said, "You've got your gun, I suppose?"

I didn't know one end of a gun from the other when I came to work for Dave last summer. In the family and the world I come from, guns belong to Mafia types from *The Godfather* or to those Mexican bandits in *The Treasure of the Sierra Madre,* never to real human beings. The biggest shock I got when I first came to Mesa Grande was from seeing the inordinate number of gun stores in the downtown shopping section. Dave arranged for me to take a quick course at the local police training school, but I didn't enjoy it very much, and I never strapped that uncomfortable holster around my waist unless I had specific instructions to do so.

"No, I don't actually have it with me," I said. "It never occurred to me I'd be working tonight."

"I'd give you mine, only I don't happen to be carrying it tonight either." He gave a sigh. "Okay, you probably won't need it. This way, at least, there's no danger you'll shoot yourself in the foot."

He took another pause, and then he said, "You don't do anything stupid, you understand? You don't try to show off what a big hero you are. You're not Bogart, and you're not trying to bring in the Maltese Falcon."

He sounded as if he was actually worried about me. It gave me a very nice feeling. I didn't have the heart to tell him that the Maltese Falcon was a thing, not a fugitive.

Driving downtown, I was conscious all the time of the lights from his car shining through my rear window. Then I turned onto the street where the theatre is, and those lights couldn't be seen anymore. I parked the car near the theatre and started toward the little glass door with the small sign above it. As I walked, I wondered why I had never realized before how dark and deserted this street was.

I took out my key to the theatre entrance and put it in the lock, and then I realized I didn't need it. The door was unlocked already. My whispering host must have got here before me.

I went through the door and into the empty lobby.

THE LOBBY, really just a hallway, wasn't completely dark. Some light was seeping through from somewhere, enough so I could see the shapes of tables and chairs and the two large doors leading into the auditorium.

I went to the nearest of these doors, and as soon as I opened it I saw where the light was coming from. Across the empty auditorium, with its rows of deserted seats, was the stage. The curtain was open, and a single light bulb was hanging about a third of the way down from the ceiling. It was turned on, a large splash of yellow cutting through the black. Even from the back of the auditorium, it hurt my eyes to stare at that bulb.

Then I saw that the stage wasn't empty. Underneath the bulb was an armless wooden chair, the kind the backstage area was full of. And somebody was sitting in that chair.

I could feel my heart giving a little jump. Not that I was actually scared. As I had been telling myself ever since that phone call came, this was strictly a routine assignment. We had dealt with anonymous informers before, and mostly they were lame pathetic types more likely to feel fear than to arouse it. This informer *had* asked to talk to me personally, but that didn't mean he was planning to hurt me. Nobody could possibly be out to hurt *me*. I'm a nice guy, I never did anybody any harm in my life. Getting beaten up or killed was what happened in movies.

"Is that you, Roger?" A voice came across the auditorium at me, high and quavery, but still carrying perfectly. I recognized the slight lisp immediately.

I don't mind saying I felt a little rush of relief. If there was anybody in the world nobody had to be afraid of, it was poor inoffensive ineffectual Harold Hapgood.

"Harold, what are you doing here? Are you the one that made that phone call?"

"Yes, that was me." He was leaning forward in his chair, and as my eyes got used to the strange light I could see his hands squeezed together in his lap and the pale intense look on his face.

"You don't have to stand back there," he said. "I'm not going to hurt you, for heaven's sake. Come up here where we can talk."

I started down the aisle to the stage. Harold got up suddenly and moved toward the wings. I thought for a second he had got cold feet and was going to beat it out of there, but all he did was reach into the area to the left, hidden from the front, and pull out another one of those wooden chairs. He placed it next to his on the stage, and when I got down the aisle he motioned for me to climb up and join him.

So I did, and for a few moments we sat next to each other, neither of us saying anything. A couple of easygoing rural types sitting on the front porch, enjoying the night air and the stars, with all the time in the world. Like one of those old Will Rogers movies.

Pretty soon I began to feel silly. "So what's this all about, Harold?"

He gave a little start. "Oh, sorry," he said. "I guess my mind was wandering. I've been under such a strain."

"What kind of strain?"

"The play, to begin with. *Macbeth* is such a— Oh my God, I said it, didn't I? I said that name—inside the theatre!" He crossed himself quickly three times and mumbled something in a prayerful tone. Then he looked up at me a little sheepishly. "Where were we? Yes, the strain I've been under. I know I haven't got the biggest parts in the play. But that doesn't mean I'm not serious about them. I throw myself into them as if I was playing the leading role. There are no small parts, only—"

"Everybody knows how conscientious and hardworking you are," I said.

"I certainly try. And it was truly gratifying to have somebody like Allan Franz, a real authority, tell me that he understood what I was trying to do. So if Lloyd *is* able to get the show started again—" He broke off, the excitement fading from his face. "I shouldn't be talking this way, it's terrible of me. How could I forget what's happened? There's been a *murder,* a fellow human being got *killed.* And the murderer actually attacked me; I might've been killed too!"

"Probably not, Harold. All he wanted was your mask, and to keep you from going on the stage."

"But what if I had happened to turn around and see the murderer's face? If she didn't stop at killing Marty Osborn, why would she stop at killing *me*?"

"So you've decided Sally *is* the guilty party, have you?"

He moved to the edge of his chair and peered at me very hard. "I didn't believe it at first. I *couldn't* believe it. I've known Sally for such a long time. I mean, not socially or anything like that. I've heard the rumors about that sort of thing, but there's certainly never been anything like that between Sally and *me*."

"Why have you changed your mind about her, Harold? Why do you believe she's guilty now?"

He wet his lips. "I remembered something, that's why. Late this afternoon, while I was at my desk in the office, it suddenly came back to me. I don't know why I didn't think of it sooner—"

"What did you remember?"

"When the murderer hit me over the head the other night, I told you I couldn't see who it was. And that was true, I didn't *see* anything. But what I remembered this afternoon is that I *smelled* something. Just before I blacked out, I got a strong whiff of perfume. And when I woke up in the broom closet, that same perfume was still in my nose. Magnolia Blossoms, Roger! The perfume Sally always uses."

"You couldn't be mistaken?" I said. "You only had a second or two to get a whiff, and a lot of perfumes have pretty much the same smell."

"Not Sally's brand. It's terribly strong. If you get too close to her when she's wearing it, you feel as if you're *drowning* in the Old South."

"All right, but why are you coming to the public defender with this? Why don't you go to the police?"

He frowned a little. "I thought about doing that. That would be my duty as a citizen, I guess. But like I told you, I've known Sally a long time, I'd like to help her if I could. And Martin Osborn—he wasn't a *nice* man, was he? The way he used to speak to me sometimes. And when all's said and done, Sally and I are both artists, and we of the profession ought to stick together."

"But why *me,* Harold? Why didn't you bring this to the public defender directly? Or to Dave, my boss?"

He blinked, sort of bewildered. "I don't know. I just felt I could say it all easier to you. Maybe it's because we're close to the same age. I mean, I'm still in my twenties. Almost. And Mrs. Swenson and your boss—don't you get the feeling sometimes that you can't really trust people that old?"

"Another thing I don't understand," I said. "Why are we here? Why didn't you come to the courthouse to give me your information, or to my house, or ask me to your house or your office? I don't see the point of meeting in this empty theatre."

At this the look on his face was suddenly confused, with maybe a touch of fear mixed in. "This afternoon, when I remembered about the perfume, I wasn't alone. Somebody was in my office with me, somebody had dropped in to discuss insurance problems with me. And then this memory came to me, and I blurted it out. Out loud. Just a couple of words, and then I realized who was in the room with me, so I shut up fast. But it seemed to me—what I blurted out might have made this person suspicious. So I didn't think you and I ought to meet publicly. And my own place may not be safe anymore, and your house may be watched too."

It all sounded pretty farfetched and melodramatic to me. I decided that Harold was acting and thinking pretty much like a teenager. Indulging in adolescent fantasies, making his dreary life dramatic. You couldn't exactly blame him for that. Shut up for this whole life with Teddy Hillary and his wheelchair—

"Okay, Harold," I said, as we both got to our feet. "I'll pass this on to the public defender first thing in the morning. She'll be in touch with you and tell you what to do next." I held out my hand to him. "I'm grateful to you, believe me. Well, we shouldn't be seen leaving here together, should we? So suppose you go first."

"Yes, that's a good idea." He looked pleased that I was joining in on his game. He reached out to take my hand.

Our fingers touched, and it was as if the contact suddenly set off a switch somewhere. The bulb above our head went out. Absolute darkness exploded on us.

A second later the explosion wasn't outside me. It was inside my head, turning me into a living fireworks display. And then a lot of blackness came and snuffed the fireworks out....

I DON'T KNOW how long it was before I woke up again. The process was slow and painful. It involved a certain amount of gagging and coughing, which luckily didn't lead to actually throwing up. At last, my eyes managed to pull themselves open, and I noticed that I was on the floor somewhere, in the dark. I couldn't see a thing, but I could sure as hell smell something: it was the smell of smoke.

The end of Alfred Hitchcock's *Rebecca* flashed into my mind. Judith Anderson, as Mrs. Danvers, standing at the window with the flames licking around her. And I couldn't help remembering that Mrs. Danvers didn't get out alive.

THIRTEEN

Dave's Narrative

I PARKED MY CAR on the side street around the corner from the theatre. Whoever the mystery caller was, he might be peeking out a window or hovering in a doorway to make sure Roger wasn't bringing any company with him.

Then I got out of my car and walked to the end of the street where I had a good view of the entrance to the theatre. There was a street lamp on this corner, but it didn't give out much light. Every year the local newspaper runs half a dozen letters from citizens complaining about the inadequacy of street lighting in Mesa Grande, demanding an end to penny-pinching with people's safety, and every year the City Council goes on ignoring the problem.

I was just in time to see Roger go through the door into the theatre. He was alone. X must be waiting for him inside.

I flattened myself into the doorway of a hardware store on the corner, where the streetlight couldn't reach me, and settled in for a long wait.

When I first got into police work, all those many years ago, this was the part of the job I really hated. Surveillance, stakeouts, whatever fancy name you gave it, it amounted to standing around and doing nothing for hours at a stretch. It was hard enough on your feet, but the real strain was on your psyche. What the hell do you think about when you have to stay in one place for hours and do nothing? Especially if you're the type that hates to be alone with your thoughts.

So I stood and waited now, watching the dark doorway of the Ramon Novarro Theatre, keeping myself numb but not exactly unconscious.

When the disturbance occurred, I came to life instantly.

A thick black cloud of smoke was suddenly coughing out from a window close to the sidewalk on the side of the building. I started running as fast as I could across the street. I'm not in as good a shape as I'd like to be. I jog on the weekends, and do some exercising every morning, only on some weekends I'm too busy and on some mornings I oversleep. So I could feel the aching in my legs and thighs and my breath coming in heavy, painful snorts. But the question pounding through my head was louder and stronger than all that: What kind of trouble had that kid got himself into?

I got to the front door and grabbed the handle, expecting it to be hot to the touch, considering all the smoke that was now belching out from the window. But the handle wasn't even lukewarm, and as soon as I turned it, the door opened easily. Inside, in the outer corridor where my ticket had been taken on opening night, the smell of smoke was stronger than ever. But still no sign of any fire.

I went through one of the doors to the auditorium. It was very dimly lit. After blinking a little I could just about make out the rows of seats stretched out before me, and nobody was in any of them.

Then I looked up at the stage and saw where both the smoke and the light were coming from. A lightbulb was hanging down by its wire from the ceiling. It was lit, but obscured by the smoke curling around it. The smoke, thick black billows of it, seemed to be coming up from the floor.

I put a handkerchief over my mouth and climbed up on the stage. Then I lowered my head and charged through the wall of smoke like a fullback pushing those last few inches for a touchdown. It was a crazy thing to do, but my luck held beautifully. I found myself on the other side of the smoke cloud, standing in the wings. I started yelling Roger's name and running through the backstage area. The light didn't reach there, and I stumbled around until my eyes got used to the darkness. Still no sign of Roger. I clumped down the stairs to the basement like a meshugene lunatic—to use Mom's phrase when anybody behaves in a more than normally irrational way—and as soon as I got to the basement corridor I was engulfed again by smoke. It made me cough, but it didn't seem to be searing my throat, the way smoke from a raging fire was supposed to do. It wasn't killing me, it was just being a damned nuisance.

Then I saw where it was coming from. Some kind of box or bag or something, hard to tell its exact color or shape or size in the darkness. It was fastened to one of the walls in an alcove that jutted off from the corridor. This alcove was located, as Roger had explained to me on the night of the murder, just under the trapdoor that opened onto the stage. Actors, before they made an entrance through the trapdoor, waited in this alcove for their cue. A row of steps was built into the wall so they could climb up to the stage.

At that moment I heard this muffled but steady banging noise. Somebody was banging on a door somewhere. I ran along the corridor until I found it, the door to that same broom closet where Harold Hapgood had been stowed on the night of the murder.

And there was Hapgood himself. Lying on the floor in front of this door. He had the kind of expression on his face that living human beings just can't seem to manage.

That's why actors are hardly ever convincing when they play dead.

I tried the broom closet door. It wasn't locked. It came open with one yank, and the first thing I saw was Roger on his knees. His face was smudged, his hair was a mess, one side of his shirt collar was torn, it looked as if somebody had thrown him in here none too gently.

"God damn it," I shouted at him, "I can't leave you alone for five minutes, can I?"

He looked up at me, grinning feebly, a little gray around the eyes and mouth. "Did you see him?" he said, in a hoarse voice, and then the words trailed off in a fit of coughing.

"Who?"

"The one who clobbered me. The one who killed Harold."

"I've been watching the front entrance since you came in here," I said. "I would've seen anybody who—son of a bitch!"

I left Roger right there on the floor—he didn't look as if he was in very good shape, but what else could I do?— and made my famous short dash up the basement steps again. And then to the backstage doors that led to the alley.

Sure enough, one of those doors was swinging wide open.

I went back downstairs to Roger, who had managed by this time to get to his feet. He was staring down at Hapgood's body, and steadying himself against the inside of the door. "My God, he killed—he—" He choked a little.

"Whoever it was got away," I said. "While I was running around in circles looking for you—"

"I'm sorry," Roger said.

I peered into his face, and I could see he wasn't making a joke. He was looking genuinely ashamed as if I'd been accusing him of screwing up on the job.

I told myself I should say some words of encouragement to him. Something to let him know that I didn't blame him for the bad luck, that his life was more important to me than catching any criminal.

"If you're okay," I said, "I'll call the cops and the fire department. And before any of them get here, you're giving me your report. Start from the beginning, and don't leave anything out, no matter how trivial. By this time you know how to give a report, don't you?"

WHILE WE WAITED for the cops, I helped Roger up the stairs and eased him into one of the chairs in the wings.

He was safe, all right, but he was looking positively awful. I told him he was within his rights to claim he was feeling too rotten to be questioned, but he said he'd rather get the third degree over with. He might be suffering from the great granddaddy of all headaches, but he still didn't want to miss any of the action.

The first wave was uniformed cops. They took us through our story, making us repeat parts of it three or four times. I could see Roger getting paler. With the second wave, the plainclothesmen, came the medical examiner. He was there to look at Hapgood's body, but I got him to check Roger out first and make sure he had no concussions or broken bones. If I hadn't done this, Mom would have killed me.

The third and last wave was led by Assistant District Attorney Leland Grantley, who showed up in a tuxedo. He'd heard the news of the murder at a fund-raising dinner for District Attorney Marvin McBride's re-election campaign next year, and he'd rushed right off, in the middle of the baron of beef, to do his duty. I could imagine how eager McBride had been to grab this opportunity to impress potential givers with the efficiency and dedication of his staff. Selfless servants of the people who gladly put their duty above baron of beef and probably wouldn't get back in time for the strawberry shortcake.

From Grantley, though *he* thought he was pumping *us,* I found out a lot of things I was glad to know.

Hapgood had been stabbed in the back two or three times with the same kind of heavy-duty kitchen knife that had been used to kill Osborn. The knife had been left on the floor of the broom closet right next to the dead body, and it had a rubber handle that wouldn't take fingerprints.

Also, Hapgood had been killed up on the stage, after which the dead body, along with Roger's unconscious one, had been lowered down to the basement through the trapdoor and stowed away in the broom closet. A bloody trail showed pretty clearly what had happened.

Also, the smoke hadn't been caused by a fire at all. It had been caused by something known as Smokey the Bomb, a device you could buy in a hundred toy- or novelty stores. It looked like a plain black box; a tube came out of it that connected to a door or a piece of furniture; if that door was opened or that piece of furniture moved, Smokey would be activated and cough out an impressive quantity of black crap. Harmless enough, but definitely frightening. This one had been placed on the wall of the basement alcove and hooked up to the trapdoor right above.

Also, the police forensic experts, having picked up fingerprints from every conceivable surface around the theatre, hadn't come up with any that gave them a lead to the killer. Not surprising, since dozens of people, including all

our hottest suspects, had been in and out of the place dozens of times in the last four weeks.

And there was one final piece of information that
Grantley obligingly passed on to Roger and me. For the
last half hour police officers had been putting in phone
calls to everybody more or less connected to the Martin
Osborn murder, trying to establish who was where while
Hapgood was getting killed. The results, as I would have
predicted, were inconclusive: every phone call got answered, all the suspects had stories that didn't clear them
but didn't incriminate them either.

Lloyd Cunningham had been out at the movies; he'd
just got back to his apartment when the phone rang. And
no, his wife had a headache tonight, so he'd gone to the
movies by himself.

Laurie Franz had been alone in her off-campus house;
her father, in his room at the Richelieu Hotel. Room service had brought him his dinner on a wheeled tray, with
instructions not to pick it up again until he rang, which he
hadn't yet done by the time the police called. He had been
working on scripts, he said.

Randolph Le Sage had been alone in Osborn's apartment, watching TV. He hadn't vacated it yet, though it did
make him feel rather odd, he said, as if he were rooming
with a ghost. He offered to describe the TV shows he had
seen in detail, but nobody bothered to listen, since Osborn had a VCR, and Le Sage could have taped those
shows and looked at them when he got back from committing murder.

Finally, putting on an earnest Ivy-League look, Grantley said, "It's my duty to tell you fellows something. I'll
call Ann in the morning, and make it official. Subject to
Marvin's permission, of course, I intend to ask the judge

to cancel your client's bail and remand her to jail until the trial."

"Why would you do that, for God's sake?" I said.

"I've got no alternative. It's obvious she killed Hapgood, isn't it? He let it drop that he remembered about her perfume. He said it himself, didn't he, that he'd been careless and blurted it out to the wrong person? Maybe to her ex-husband Bernie Michaels, who then passed it on to Sally. Anyway, she knew his testimony would clinch the case against her, so she followed him down here—"

"You're saying she doesn't have an alibi for tonight?"

Grantley's little smile was polite but pleased with itself. "She's one of the people we phoned, of course. She answered the phone and told me she was just finishing her dinner. She said she'd been there with Bernie for a few hours."

"Well, there you are!"

The polite little smile turned into a polite little laugh. "Come on, Dave. You know as well as I do how Bernie Michaels feels about that woman. He wouldn't hesitate for a moment about perjuring himself to save her skin."

In other words, Hapgood's murder made the case against Sally Michaels stronger than ever. So it may seem strange that I picked that moment to tell Roger to come out with his information about Sally's ring. It was a close decision, but it seemed to me that it was too risky for Roger to keep this to himself any longer. If he waited till tomorrow, Grantley would come down on him hard for not mentioning it tonight.

"Excuse me," said Grantley, after Roger had told his story, "but why didn't you see fit to share this evidence with the district attorney's office much earlier?"

"I didn't remember it until a few hours ago," Roger said. "And I didn't want to disturb you in your home on a Saturday."

Roger said all this without the smallest crack in his voice or blinking of his eyes. I was proud of him. Slowly but surely he was learning his trade.

"Now how about letting us go," I said to Grantley. "You've heard all we have to say, and Roger has had a rough time. I don't want him collapsing on me."

"Very well," Grantley said, "the two of you are excused. For now."

We hurried out to the street in front of the theatre, and I saw Roger swaying a little. "You're in no condition to drive a car," I said. "Also you're in no condition to take care of yourself tonight. I'm taking you in my car, we'll pick up yours in the morning. We're driving to Mom's house, and you'll stay the night with her."

"I don't want to impose—"

"Don't be stupid. You'll be doing her a big favor. You know how long it's been since she had a helpless boy in her clutches? Your job is to keep her from drowning you in chicken soup."

WE DROVE across town together, neither of us having much to say. Mesa Grande, as it flashed by me through the windshield, somehow didn't look real tonight. I looked at the storefronts, dark and deserted, or with dim yellow lights in their windows; at the houses plunged in blackness except for the glow of their front-porch bulbs; and I found myself feeling the absolute conviction that behind these storefronts and these lighted porches was nothing. Nothing at all. They were stage sets. They had no depth to them. If you opened the doors and walked through, you'd find yourself on the street at the other side.

My life wasn't real either, I thought. I was frittering it away on things that didn't exist. Dignity, respect, professional pride, God knows what other foolishness! Only in plays and movies did anybody give a damn about such things.

I stole a glance at the haggard-looking, white-faced boy at my side. I've never had a son—or any other children of my own. I don't actually know what it feels like when you're faced with the possibility of losing one. But I couldn't imagine it feeling any worse than I had felt that moment when I looked down at this kid lying on the floor, with blood all around him.

In the real world, I thought, in this world of liars and thieves and murderers, what matters is friendship, family, love. People who care for each other. Things that don't fade away or change shape on you in the blink of an eye.

I pulled the car up at Mom's house. I wasn't worried that I'd be disturbing her at this late hour. I knew she wouldn't go to bed until she heard all about Roger's expedition.

Sure enough, all the lights were on, and she greeted us at the door with a big warm smile. Then she saw what Roger looked like, and while I told her everything that had happened since we left her, she fussed over him, felt his forehead for a fever, and plunked hot tea in front of him and ordered him to swallow it down.

He sipped, and some of the color came back to his cheeks. I watched from across the kitchen table and I suddenly felt the urge to do something crazy. I spoke up quickly, before I could back off from that urge.

"Mom and I are going to talk about the case now," I said, facing the kid, keeping my voice calm and steady. "You probably figured out already that I talk about all my tough cases with Mom. She solves them for me, she sees things I could never see for myself."

So it was out. I leaned back in my chair. I was sweating a little, but also feeling lighter and more comfortable than I had felt in weeks.

"I didn't know that," Roger said. "I sure would like to hear what the two of you have to say about *this* case."

For a moment I had a twinge of disappointment. Where was his look of amazement? Where was the astonished gasp, the embarrassed stammering? I should've been glad, I suppose, that he wasn't making a big deal out of my revelation. But at least he might have made *some* kind of deal out of it.

Then I saw Mom giving me one of her most approving beams, and my disappointment went away.

"All right, we'll talk a little bit," Mom said. "But as soon as I give the word, this boy is going upstairs to bed. And believe me, I don't take no for answers."

Roger agreed to these conditions, and Mom turned to me. "So how about a nice cup of tea for you too, Davie? And also a piece schnecken?"

"I can take it or leave it, Mom."

"You better take it. You'll need your strength and your brainpower. We got a lot to talk about tonight."

I recognized the glitter in her eyes, and I felt my heart beating a little faster. "You know who the murderer is? You've got the answer?"

In spite of his exhaustion, I could tell that Roger's heart was beating faster too.

"I've got the question. Sometimes that's more important."

"What question? You're deliberately being mysterious, you know how that drives me up the wall."

"Excuse me. I don't want you driving up walls, you could have a bad accident. All I'm trying to say to you is, think about what happened in the theatre tonight. Don't it jump right out at you, the big question? For some reason this murderer wants to kill Harold Hapgood. Maybe so he won't testify about the perfume, maybe for some other reason. Whatever it is, this no-good creeps up behind you, Roger, hits you on the head so you won't see who it is, and stabs this Hapgood in the back. Then he takes the unconscious body and the dead body, and lowers them into the basement through the trapdoor and locks up the live one in the broom closet."

"The big question being," I broke in, "why would the murderer go to so much trouble and risk? Why not just leave them on the stage and get the hell out of there?"

"No, no." Mom's head was shaking hard. "The answer to why the bodies had to be taken down to the basement is no mystery at all. The murderer expected that Roger told somebody he was going to the theatre, and this somebody could show up any minute. If this somebody sees bodies on the stage, the alarm is given right away, and the murderer didn't want this should happen. He—or she—needs time to get out of the neighborhood and go back to wherever he—or she—is living."

"Then what *is* the big question?"

"The smoke bomb, what else? If the murderer's idea is that the discovery of the bodies should be delayed as long as possible, why set off a smoke bomb in the basement? The smoke is going to attract attention, no? People will think the building is on fire, they'll rush inside and go to the basement where the smoke is coming from, and naturally they'll find the bodies there. What kind of meshugene murderer goes to all that trouble hiding two bodies so they won't be found fast, and then goes to more trouble setting off a smoke bomb so they *will* be found fast?''

"All right, Mom, what's the answer to the question?"

"What I *think* is the answer I couldn't prove yet."

She turned suddenly to Roger. ''You look like you could fall asleep sitting in that chair! Bedtime already! Go upstairs right away!''

Roger made some feeble protests, but of course he was no match for Mom. She gestured at me to give her the benefit of my strong right arm, and together we more or less walked Roger up the stairs and into the spare bedroom.

From the dresser Mom took an old pair of pajamas, which I recognized as an old pair of mine before I got married and moved into an apartment of my own. Then we left the kid alone in the bedroom. I'm sure he was flat on his back on the bed, snoring away if he snores, before we got down the stairs and back to the living room. "I guess it's time for me to be turning in too," I said.

"Sit," Mom said. "I didn't finish with the murder yet. I'm coming to the part I don't want the boy should hear about."

I sat down slowly. It was a solemn moment, and I felt it in the depths of my soul. Mom was letting me know that when the chips were down, I was the one she really trusted.

"Like I mentioned to you," she went on talking, "I've got an idea what's behind these murders. I've also got an idea how you can prove it. Tomorrow is Sunday, when a lot of people don't work. So you and Ann Swenson should get in touch with the people from *Macbeth*—the ones that don't give alibis to each other, and the ones that were on the stage during the murder—and you should tell them to come to the theatre tomorrow in the afternoon. And make sure the assistant district attorney lets Sally Michaels come.

In fact, the assistant district attorney and some of his policemen should be there also.''

"What are we supposed to do with these people once we get them into the theatre?''

"What else is a theatre for? They'll act.''

Then Mom leaned forward and made a speech that I couldn't understand at first. "Sometimes,'' she said, "murders just flare up, like out of nowhere, like when somebody goes crazy and starts shooting at people in the street. But most of the time murders happen the same way a lot of plays are put together. You've got a big happy family, where everybody is close to everybody, and life goes along in the same way for years. Maybe there's hatred and envy and greed underneath, but it don't lead to murder—until one day the door suddenly opens, something or somebody new comes in from outside, and everything blows up. Like in *Macbeth*. It's the witches that come in from outside. They don't *make* Macbeth and his wife ambitious. They wake up in them the ambition that's there already.''

"What are you saying, Mom? That the Mesa Grande Players are like a big happy family? But what's the something new that came in to stir them up? Doing Shakespeare for the first time? Osborn taking over as director?''

"Neither of those,'' Mom said. "Listen to me careful, all right? And what I'm about to tell you, you'll promise me you wouldn't repeat any of it to Roger. He's a lovely boy, and very bright, but he's twenty-two years old, which by me is a baby. And babies aren't so good about keeping their mouths shut.''

I gave her my promise gladly. Then she went through the whole thing with me, down to the last detail, and there was no way I could pretend that it didn't sound right.

FOURTEEN

Roger's Narrative

GOD, DID I sleep late that Sunday morning! It was way after ten o'clock before I woke up, and blinked around and wondered whose bed I was in. Then I picked up the gorgeous smell of pancakes and coffee, and I remembered.

I was up and dressed in ten minutes, and wolfing down the breakfast Dave's mother shoveled into me. I felt like a twelve-year-old kid again. I wasn't a bit ashamed of myself for the feeling.

I was finishing up my second cup of coffee when Dave arrived. "I'm driving you downtown to pick up your car," he said, "and then we're both going to the office. We've got a lot of phoning to do."

"Who're we phoning?"

Dave didn't answer this. He hustled me out of the house and into the car; I barely had a chance to thank his mother for her hospitality. Outside the Ramon Novarro Theatre I transferred into my own car, and then we were in the public defender's office, making ourselves at home at Ann's desk.

"Who're we *phoning?*" I asked.

"Our guests for the party we're throwing at two this afternoon," Dave said. "In the theatre, with the assistant DA in attendance and all the suspects and a few others. Here's the list, get on the phone and invite these people."

"Do I tell them what it's all about?" Which was my sneaky way of asking Dave to tell *me* what it was all about.

"All you tell them is, it's important, we'd appreciate their cooperation. If they give you a hard time, put me on the line."

His caginess really pissed me off. Why wouldn't he let me in on his plans? Was I a member of the team, or wasn't I?

"You've got Sally's name on this list," I said. "Leland Grantley will never go along with it. He's planning to have her bail revoked this morning."

"Ann spoke to Grantley an hour ago. It's all fixed up with him. Are you going to make those calls, or aren't you?"

I sat down at Ann's desk and started dialing. Not in the spirit of graciousness, though.

The two Murderers were easy. They both said they'd be at the theatre at two, and I could hear the excitement in their voices. If you're young and your health is good and you're not a serious suspect, there might be some pleasure in being involved with a murder.

Randolph Le Sage, apparently awakened from his Sunday morning beauty sleep, also raised no objections. Time must have been hanging on his hands in Mesa Grande. No Sardi's or Players club for him to lounge around in, swapping stories with cronies at the bar.

I reached Laurie at her off-campus house. I was nervous about taking an official tone with her; I didn't want her getting sore at me. The result was I stammered and blushed as I put my request to her. But she didn't seem to mind. She told me how glad she was to hear from me, and she started to say how much she looked forward to seeing me at the theatre this afternoon, but then the phone was pulled away from her.

Her father's voice barked into it. "What the hell is this all about?" The authentic bark, I guess, that struck terror into the hearts of his slaves on the set.

Dave took the receiver from me and explained to Franz, in his most deferential voice, that the public defender had requested this gathering in order to clear up the two murders.

"Laurie had nothing to do with either of them!" I could hear every word Franz was saying, even though the phone was three feet away from me.

"Of course not," Dave said. "But she was backstage at opening night, and she may have seen something that's slipped her mind or is kicking around in her subconscious."

"I very much doubt it."

"It's a longshot, Mr. Franz, we know that. But I'm sure you're the sort of person who wants to see justice done, especially if it means that innocent people don't have to suffer for crimes they didn't commit. I've been to your movies. I know they had to be made by somebody with liberal humane ideals."

There was no way Franz could hold out against that particular line. What they all yearn for out in Hollywood is for people to tell them how liberal and humane they are. That's why Academy Awards go to dull movies about race relations instead of to entertaining movies about sex relations.

"All right, I'll let Laurie come to your meeting," Franz said. "But on one condition only: I'm coming with her. And if anybody says one word to her that's out of line, I'm taking her the hell out of there."

Dave thanked him and promised that none of our words would be out of line. He replaced the receiver, then handed the phone back to me.

Next on my list was Lloyd Cunningham. He made trouble at first. Since he had left the theatre before the murder, he didn't see why he had to show up for any gathering of suspects. At Dave's prompting, I told him this was exactly why his presence would be so vital to us. We needed somebody who knew the staging for Banquo, who could tell us what Osborn would have been doing and where he would have been standing at each moment. Cunningham sniffed a little, but he was softened up. He said he'd be glad to do us a favor.

My next call was to Sally Michaels at her house. Bernie's name was right under hers on my list, but he answered Sally's phone. It was eleven-thirty in the morning; I didn't ask him if he'd been there all night. He said Sally was still asleep, he was in the process of making breakfast for her. If her attorney told her to come to this meeting, she would certainly come. And he'd be glad to come too.

So I hung up the phone, feeling as if I'd done a good morning's work. And wondering what the hell I was working *at*.

FIFTEEN

Dave's Narrative

THERE'S SOMETHING ABOUT a theatre. It can be empty and badly lit, as the Ramon Novarro Theatre was when Roger and I got there at a quarter to two that Sunday afternoon. There can be no audience, and the curtain can be up, and the scenery on the stage can look like what it is, flimsy canvas-and-wood flats with paint smeared on them, dilapidated sticks of furniture from Goodwill. Even so, a theatre makes your heart beat a little faster in spite of yourself. It makes you take a deep breath and wait for those beautiful people, who are bigger and smarter and more alive than you are, to start hugging and kissing, or making witty remarks, or scratching each other's eyes out, or crying into each other's shoulders.

And if a theatre has this effect on me—who, as I've mentioned, am definitely no theatre nut—what could it do to a bunch of actors, to people who already halfway see their lives as a series of big scenes playing themselves out behind lights? It could make such people dizzy with excitement, it could cut whatever ties they might still have to reality. Flying up into a dreamworld, posing and making faces in the clouds, they could say things they wouldn't say if they had their feet on the ground.

So I understood why Mom wanted me to put them through this little charade, and in the same theatre, on the same stage, where murder had been done twice. The only thing that worried me was that the person we were aiming all this at might get *too* carried away and try to do murder for the third time. All I could hope was that the presence of Assistant District Attorney Leland Grantley, sitting in the best seat, third row center, and of three or four uniformed cops stationed at strategic points around the hall, would take care of that little problem.

By two-fifteen some of them still weren't there. Then Allan Franz and his daughter Laurie arrived—fifteen minutes late, which seemed only proper; you can't expect great directors to arrive at their sets earlier than the actors. But Sally Michaels and Bernie still hadn't shown. That definitely made me nervous, and I knew it was having the same effect on Ann Swenson. She sat in a front-row seat next to me, stiff as a ramrod, glaring into space. Suppose our client had lost her head and decided to jump bail, confirming her guilt just as we were about to prove her innocence! Sally was spacey enough that I could imagine her doing such an idiotic thing.

But at two-twenty she came sailing in, with Bernie trailing after her at the distance that bridesmaids trail after brides whose trains they're holding. An invisible train stretched from Sally to Bernie as she greeted everybody with smiles, handshakes, hugs and kisses where appropriate, and apologies to Ann and me.

"I didn't oversleep, I really didn't," she said. "Bernie can tell you, if you don't believe me. Tell them, Bernie. I was wide awake *hours* ago, wasn't I? Because I fully intended to get here not only on time but *ahead* of time, to show you how seriously I take this meeting. I haven't got the slightest idea what it's all about, of course, but if dear Ann and Dave—and you too, my darling little Roger— think it's important for me to be here... I've got complete faith in the three of you, and I fully intended to show you that by being a good girl and getting here on time. But you see, that's exactly why I'm late. I was so sure this was going to be an important occasion that I became horribly nervous and self-conscious and, in fact, positively *pan-icky* about what I was going to wear. I had to look *exactly* right for such an occasion, but no matter what I tried on, somehow it didn't seem *exactly* right, and finally I just threw on whatever old thing was closest to my hand, as you can see."

The old thing that had been closest to her hand was a frilly little gown in pinks and blues, with sweater and beads and hair ornaments to match.

Sally took a seat next to Lloyd Cunningham, patting his hand and saying in a loud whisper, "Lloyd, darling, I didn't see you! How *nice* that you're back with us again! It's the way it *should* be, isn't it? Everything the way it was before—" She stumbled on the "before," gave a little cough, blushed rather prettily, and went on with a giggle, "Well, you know what I mean, don't you?"

Bernie, looking just as flustered as Sally, though he hadn't spoken a word, sat down next to her. Silence fell heavily.

I got up, climbed onto the stage, and faced them. I felt a little funny about this at first. I've never gone in much for acting, even when I was a kid in school. Standing up there like that, looking across the end of the stage at all those people, I felt for a second like in one of those dreams where you're in a play and you get out in front of the au-dience and suddenly realize that you don't know your lines.

But I pushed aside my stage fright by reminding myself that I *did* know my lines, I'd been coached in them by Mom, how could I do better than that? What's more, this had to be done. As Mom had said to me—her final words before I went home last night—"Most murders you solve because the murderer is lying and everybody else is telling the truth. In this murder they're all lying. Why not? They're actors. So you have to clear away the little lies that don't matter before you can crack open the big lie that does."

"Ladies and gentlemen," I started in, "the public defender and the district attorney's office asked you to come here this afternoon for a very simple reason. As you know, there's been another murder. Harold Hapgood, who was a member of your cast, was killed last night, right here on this stage. That's the second time somebody was killed on this stage. We're here today to find out who's responsible. And we're going to do that by going through, as accurately and thoroughly as we can, all the events leading up to and including Martin Osborn's death last Thursday night."

"Wait a second," Allan Franz broke in, "you mean this is going to be some kind of reconstruction? Everybody doing what they did on the night of the murder? And the killer is supposed to lose his head and make a full confession? My God, that brand of corn went out with the old Thin Man movies!"

"Bear with us for a while, Mr. Franz," Ann Swenson said, in the easygoing, unruffled voice that had succeeded in calming some pretty wild beasts in the past. "If it turns out we're making fools of ourselves, you can say you told us so."

Franz heaved a deep sigh. "Okay, okay," he said, and subsided into his seat. His daughter took him by the arm and whispered something to him. Her face was very pale, and I could see that Roger had noticed this too: he was staring at her from his seat across the aisle.

"First of all," I said, "in the course of this reconstruction, I'm going to have to use the forbidden word, and more than once too. It's the name of the play, so there's no way I can avoid it. If you believe in that old superstition, I apologize to you. Chances are, when I say the word—Macbeth—the bad luck will come down on *my* head, not yours. Though I'd better warn you, a lot of bad luck is going to come down on one of *you* before I'm through this afternoon."

I paused to let this sink in, then I went on, "Twenty minutes before the scene where Banquo gets killed, Harold Hapgood finished his scene as the Old Man who reports that Scotland is suffering from a lot of agitated birdlife. Then he went down to his dressing room to change into his Third Murderer costume. He put on the black mask and the poncho, and stepped out to the corridor. He never made it to the stairs. Somebody came up behind him and hit him on the head, and dragged him into the broom closet. Then this somebody took the mask off his face and went upstairs to take Hapgood's place as Third Murderer. All this had to be done fifteen minutes or less before the murder.

"So, those of you who were on or near the stage, suppose you go to where you were located during that time."

PEOPLE STOOD UP and started talking all at once, but gradually sorted themselves out and made their way to different parts of the theatre. Allan Franz moved away from Laurie and took the aisle seat in the fifth row, where he'd been sitting on opening night. Roger went to the wings backstage right, and Murderers Number One and Two took their places in the center of the stage. "After the Old Man exits," said Jeff Greenwald, the high school student, "Macbeth has this scene with his wife—Mr. Osborn moved it up from later in the play—and then *we've* got this scene with Macbeth. This is when he hires us to kill Banquo."

Le Sage got up onstage with them. "Quite so. You can see, then, that I had no opportunity to attack poor Hapgood. I was playing this scene at the very time—"

"No sorry, Mr. Le Sage," said Danny Imperio, the waiter. "You actually leave the stage before the end of this scene, and Jeff and I have this business where we sharpen our knives for a few minutes. It's not in Shakespeare, but Mr. Osborn added it. Don't you remember?"

"Oh, yes, that's true," said Le Sage. "I'd quite forgotten about that. So many entrances and exits, one does get confused. I left the stage and went downstairs to my dressing room. Shall I go there now?"

"Not necessary, Mr. Le Sage," I said. "Just pretend you've gone down there, and stay here with us in the auditorium."

Le Sage took a seat in one of the side sections, and Roger stuck his head out from the wings. "Banquo—Osborn, that is—was standing next to me while I waited out here. Fleance and Banquo made their entrance together two or three minutes into the murder scene."

Lloyd Cunningham got to his feet. "I'll be Banquo, okay? Might as well start getting back into the role. You won't be needing me for anything else, because I wasn't even in the theatre at this time on opening night."

I told Lloyd that I very much wanted him to play Banquo, and he vaulted up on the stage and headed for the wings on Roger's side.

"I wasn't in the theatre either," Bernie said. "I was watching the mad killer dispose of his third or fourth teenager around this time. At the Mesa Grande Triplex, that is. If you'd like me to run over there now—"

I told him I'd rather he stayed with us, and he laughed and sank down next to Sally again.

"I was in the ladies' room in the basement," Laurie Franz said. "I wasn't feeling well, because...well, I've already told you all that."

She broke off, reddening. Her father squeezed her hand reassuringly.

"I was in my dressing room, as I've repeatedly told you," Sally said. "My last scene took place right after Harold's appearance as the Old Man. It's the scene where Macbeth hints that he'd like to get rid of Banquo. I don't appear again until the banquet scene, after the intermission, so I stretched out on my couch. That's where I was when Harold got assaulted. *And* when the murder took place."

I turned to Le Sage. "All right, Macbeth exits after his scene with the two murderers, and you went downstairs to your dressing room and that's where you were at the time of the murder?"

"Exactly."

"The other day, when I questioned you, you told me you paused on the way to your dressing room to knock on Sally's door."

"So I did. I wanted to mention to her that she dropped a vital speech in the scene where we plan to kill King Duncan. The speech beginning 'Was the hope drunk wherein you dress'd yourself?'"

"I *couldn't* deliver that speech, Randy dear," Sally said, giving him her sweetest smile, "because you never gave me my cue for it. You're the one who forgot your lines, which meant that I had to skip ahead several speeches to make any sense out of the scene."

"Pardon me, Sally dear, but I've devoted a special amount of effort to that particular scene because I feel that the very lines you accuse me of forgetting are precisely the whole key to my character. Therefore there's no possibility that I left them out—"

"All right, all right," I said, "so Sally didn't answer you when you knocked on her door?"

"That's right. I assumed she wasn't there, and I went on to my own dressing room. Which is where I was when I heard the commotion in the corridor and found out about poor Marty's tragic fate."

"I heard his knock, of course." Sally's smile was serene. "I felt quite sure who was knocking too. But I was exhausted, I simply didn't feel like listening to old theatrical stories. 'When I played the Dauphin opposite Cornell...when I played a season of Chekhov with the Guild.' I simply couldn't let myself be taken out of the necessary mood for the banquet scene. Not to mention that I was rather peeved at him for forgetting my cue—"

I broke in on her. "How cold was the theatre on opening night?"

This was the question Mom had told me to ask Sally, and also Mom had predicted what the result of asking it would be.

"It was an icebox—as usual!" Sally snapped back at me.

"Then how were you able to stretch out in your dressing room and take a rest? Weren't you too cold to be comfortable?"

"Good Heavens, I *covered* myself, of course."

"With what?"

"What I usually cover myself with—my coat."

Exactly what she was supposed to say. Chalk up another one for Mom.

"You weren't in your dressing room at all, were you, Sally?" I said. "That wasn't where you went when you left the stage after your last scene."

A long pause. Then Sally drew herself up—one of her best poses, she had the chest for it. "You're supposed to be on *my* side, aren't you? How can you insinuate—"

"How do you know she wasn't in her dressing room?" Grantley pushed his head forward, very alert, no doubt thinking I was giving him ammunition for his case against her. It was necessary to let him go on thinking so for a while.

"You just told us, Sally," I said, "that you stretched out on the couch and covered yourself with your coat. You had to, or you would've been too cold to take a rest. But what coat? You had only one in the theatre with you, that black raincoat. As you told me yourself the other day, you were afraid to bring any of your better coats to the theatre, because it's so dirty here. The Third Murderer stole your raincoat from your dressing room and wore it up on the stage. How could you stretch out on your couch with that coat covering you, if it was being worn by the murderer onstage at the same time?"

"Because *she's* the murderer!" Grantley cried.

I shook my head. "Because she's a creature of habit, like all of us," I said. "She always covers herself with that coat when she stretches out on the dressing-room couch. So this time, when she wanted to lie about being in her dressing room, she naturally said she covered herself with the coat as usual. She brought the coat into her lie because it *doesn't* have any special significance to her, because she *wasn't* wearing it while she committed a murder. Her mentioning it at all proves that she doesn't have any guilty awareness of it. In other words, there's something else she's trying to hide from us, something that has nothing to do with the coat. What is it, Sally? If you weren't in your dressing room at the time of the murder, where *were* you?''

In a moment all of Sally's beautiful offhandedness seemed to collapse on her, and her face screwed up, and she suddenly looked old and wrinkled. "It's *hateful* of you. Just hateful.'' Her voice was a baby's petulant wail. "I was in the ladies' room, that's where I was! I was in one of the booths. I didn't come out until I heard people screaming about the murder.''

"For twenty minutes, half an hour, you were in the ladies' room?'' Grantley raised his eyebrows. "What were you *doing* in there for so long, Mrs. Michaels?''

Her collapsed face glittered with anger, as she turned it on him. "I was going over my script, if you want to know, you rude man! For the banquet scene—my next scene—I was saying the lines out loud to myself!''

"Why in the ladies' room?'' I said. "Why not do that in your dressing room?'' I knew the answer already, of course. Mom had figured it out.

"Oh, for God's sake,'' Sally practically yelled, "do I have to spell out *everything* for you idiots? Those dressing-room walls are as thin as paper. And Randy's is right next to mine. If I went over my lines out loud in *there*, he'd hear every word, and he'd know exactly what I was doing.''

"Why *shouldn't* he know?'' I said, punching away at her, because it all had to come out before we could move on.

"It's my memory, for God's sake! Don't you see, I just can't hold on to the words the way I used to. It's what happens to you after a while, it's what happens to actors and actresses at the end of their careers—'' She broke off, and the anger washed away. Her face was red and crumpling again. "Only I never even *had* the career, did I?''

Then her hands were in front of her face, and her shoulders were heaving.

Bernie stood up next to her and put his hand on her shoulder. He glared around at the rest of us, as if daring anybody to persecute her any further.

"It's a matter of no importance, of course," muttered Le Sage, "but as I pointed out earlier, *I* wasn't the one who left out a speech."

Nobody seemed to be listening to him.

I waited until the decibel count on Sally's sobs had lowered a bit. Already I could see the outburst was doing her good. A small gleam in her eyes told me that part of her was looking around, judging the effect of her scene on the audience, and finding it satisfactory.

"Just a few more questions, Sally," I said, putting on a much milder voice. "After you left the stage, you didn't go directly to the ladies' room, did you? You must've gone back to your dressing room first."

She nodded, and Grantley peered at me suspiciously. "How did you know that?"

"Before she could go to the ladies' room to study Lady Macbeth's lines, she had to pick up her script, didn't she?" I shrugged off the deduction modestly. As well I might since, as a matter of fact, it was strictly Mom's deduction.

"Yes, I popped into my dressing room very quickly," Sally said. "I grabbed the script from the dressing table and popped out again. I didn't even shut the door behind me. Then I went straight to the ladies' room—"

"You picked out the ladies' room, didn't you, because the walls *aren't* paper thin? If anybody came in, you could hear the door opening and you could immediately stop saying your lines?"

"That's right."

"But you kept on saying your lines all the time you were in there?"

"Yes, I told you that."

"So nobody *did* come in while you were there?"

"Yes, yes. I'd have heard them if—"

I whirled around, in my best Perry Mason manner, and shot a finger at Laurie Franz. "You told us *you* were in the ladies' room for half an hour or more before the murder. How come Sally didn't see you there?"

THE GIRL'S FACE turned very pale. Her father gripped her arm and jumped to his feet. "Now listen, I'm taking Laurie right out of here if you're going to throw around a lot of wild accusations!"

"She'll have to explain it sooner or later, Mr. Franz," I said. "Where were you, Miss Franz, before and during the murder?"

"Don't you say a word, honey!" Franz looked hard into his daughter's face. "He's not allowed to badger you or even talk to you, if you don't want him to. We'll call my lawyer—"

"Oh, Daddy, stop it!" Laurie's face got a little of its color back as she met his gaze. "He's right. I *wasn't* in the ladies' room. I made up that story about getting stage fright and throwing up. I *never* get stage fright, I wouldn't let myself be such a wimp. I *love* being on the stage, and *nothing* makes me throw up. I wasn't prowling around either, hitting people over the head and killing people."

"Then for God's sake, honey, why did you have to invent—"

"I just didn't want to tell you where I *really* was, Daddy. Because it's so embarrassing."

"You don't have to tell me now," Franz said.

She shook her head impatiently. "Of course I do. Or they'll never believe I wasn't up on stage wearing a mask and pretending to be a man!" She turned to me now, facing me squarely. "For the last twenty minutes of the first act, after my scene as a waiting-woman, I was standing in the wings, on the left-hand side, so I could watch the performance."

"I don't get it, sweetie," said her father. "What's embarrassing about that?"

"What's embarrassing is *why* I wanted to watch the performance. It was because—oh, dammit all!" She suddenly turned and faced Roger. "I wanted to watch *you*. When you came on as Fleance in the murder scene. You wear those tight-fitting cowboy jeans, and the top button of your shirt is open—well, you obviously don't know it, but you look terrifically sexy! And when the Third Murderer grabbed you around the neck and pulled you back, and the lower part of your body kind of shoved itself forward—I *loved* to watch that part, I just couldn't get enough of it!" She broke off with another sigh and turned back to me. "There you are, and if you think it's stupid, that's *your* problem."

I sneaked a look at Roger. His face was red, and he couldn't bring himself to look straight into anybody's eyes. I was sorry to put him through this, but as Mom had said, "All right, it'll make him blush a little and feel self-conscious. But in the long run, is a boy his age going to be too upset when a beautiful girl lets him know she loves to eat him up with her eyes?"

"If you were standing in the wings on the left-hand side, Miss Franz," I said, "how come Roger didn't run into you there when he left the stage during the murder scene?"

"Because there's a flat there; I hid myself behind it when he made his exit. I certainly didn't want him to know what I was doing!"

"Did *anyone* see you while you were standing there?"

"I don't think so. Nobody came up to me and spoke to me. Unless Mr. Michaels happened to see me."

"Me?" said Bernie. "How could *I* possibly have seen you? I wasn't even in the theatre then, I was taking in this slasher movie at the Mesa Grande Triplex."

"No, you weren't," Laurie said. "You were standing in the wings at the other side of the stage."

"Miss Franz," Ann said, a bit sternly, "you should've told us this sooner."

"How could I? If I told you I saw *him* there, that would be like admitting *I* was there."

But nobody was listening to her by this time. All eyes had turned to Bernie.

"THAT'S CRAZY," Bernie said. "I left the theatre long before—"

"No, you didn't, Bernie," I said. "I was pretty sure of that already. It's nice to have it confirmed by a witness."

"How the hell could you ever have figured—"

"You told me the other day that you got into the movie in the middle, saw it to the end, and then saw the first part of it, after which you left the movie house and came back here for the *Macbeth* curtain call. Just in time to find the police here and push your way in to see if Sally was all right."

"That's absolutely the truth! You can check the schedule at that movie—"

"Oh, the schedule checks out all right. That's not where you slipped up. You don't go to the movies very much, you told me. It's been ten years since you went to one here in town. But back in Newark, when you were a boy, you used to go to the movies all the time. You remembered what it was like back then—the double features, the packed houses, one show following immediately after another without any break. But that's not how the movie houses operate anymore, either here in Mesa Grande or almost anywhere. Nowadays, when a show is over, the lights go up, and everybody who's in the house gets ushered out, and there's some attempt to clean up the floors before the next batch of customers are let in.

"Now what are you asking us to believe, Bernie? That you paid to see the second part of the movie, and then paid all over again to see the first part?"

"I might have. Why not? Since I had time on my hands—"

"The truth is, once your role as Duncan was finished, you never even left this theatre. You stayed right here, backstage, not letting yourself be seen."

"But I didn't get here till after the police came. You know that—at first they didn't want to let me inside, I had to get special permission."

"Sure you did. As soon as the murder took place, you sneaked out the back doors into the alley. A couple of minutes went by before Roger got those doors locked, and that's when you managed to get through them. You hid out for an hour or so, maybe you sat in your car in the parking lot, and when your watch showed you that enough time had gone by for the movie to get out, you showed up in front of the theatre, pretending you didn't know what was going on, and pushed your way inside. Come on, Bernie, that's the way it happened, isn't it?"

Bernie had never been any good as a liar. That's why he always played upright old men, never weasels or villains.

He couldn't tell a convincing lie in real life any more than he could on the stage.

"Okay, Dave, okay." He threw up his hands. "I *was* in this theatre all the time. I lied about it because—I just didn't want to say *why*." His mouth turned down now. "I guess I *have* to say it, don't I?"

"I can say it for you," I said. With Mom's words echoing in my head, it wasn't hard. "You like to watch Sally act, don't you?"

An agonized grin twitched at Bernie's lips. "I like to watch Sally, period," he said. "And when she's acting...everybody knows how terrific she is! It gets to me every time!"

Sally looked up at him, and their eyes met for a moment. She had a puzzled expression on her face. Then he quickly turned his eyes away.

"Why, Bernie darling," Sally said, "that's just too sweet for words."

She read the line with a slight tremor in her voice. Not too loud, and perfectly timed. Poor Bernie, I thought, he didn't have a prayer of getting what he really wanted from her. The best he could hope for was to go on forever being a sympathetic secondary character in Sally's play, the devoted old friend whose function is to pat the heroine's shoulder and squeeze her hand supportively.

On the other hand, as Mom had said, "Maybe he prefers having a small part, it's better than he shouldn't be in the play it all."

But there wasn't any time for psychological doodling. I had a lot more business to do.

I turned the spotlight away from Bernie. "Mr. Le Sage," I said, "let's take another look at *your* story."

THE ACTOR NODDED at me and ran his hand over his shock of long white hair. The king graciously giving the commoner permission to address him.

"Mrs. Michaels just told us that she wasn't in her dressing room during that period fifteen minutes before the murder."

"Well, doesn't that fit in with my testimony?" Le Sage said. "I couldn't get her to answer my knock."

"Why did you have to knock when her dressing room door was wide open?"

"What's that? Excuse me—"

"She just told us that she looked into her dressing room long enough to pick up her script, then she ran down the corridor into the ladies' room, not even bothering to shut her dressing-room door behind her. Even if she hadn't told us that, we could've guessed it. She's well known for her offhand way of not closing doors behind her. So why did you have to knock on her door, when it was wide open and you could've *seen* she wasn't inside?"

"Well, now..." Le Sage stroked his chin, then opened his mouth, and his eyes grew wide, almost a cartoon of the light dawning. "Of course! Now that you mention it, the door *was* wide open! Extraordinary the tricks that memory plays on one!"

"It's not your memory that's being tricky, Mr. Le Sage. You *didn't* go to her door and knock on it, did you?"

"You *didn't*?" Sally was staring at him, her eyes flashing. "Randolph Le Sage, you *invented* that story about knocking on my door and getting no answer! You were deliberately trying to incriminate me!"

"No, no, believe me, Sally darling, there was no such intention! He was asking me what I did when I got down to the basement, he was demanding a detailed itinerary from me—and I was flustered, I had to come up with some details on the spur of the moment. The idea of knocking on your door was simply the first thing that came into my head. Merely a touch of verisimilitude, no ulterior motive whatever!"

"What *did* you do down in the basement?" I said.

Le Sage's mouth worked silently for a second or two. He hadn't decided yet what line he was going to take—piteous breast-beating, righteous indignation, dignified refusal to be bullied? You could almost see the different expressions trying themselves out on his face, until he finally decided on easy amused laughter.

"All right, you've caught me in the act, as it were. Marvelous detective work. I bow to you, sir. Sherlock Holmes—who incidentally I played in summer stock early in my career—couldn't have managed it better."

"So what were you doing, Mr. Le Sage?"

"What *was* I doing? Well, everybody else is coming clean, aren't they? 'Coming Clean,' that seems to be the name of this little piece you're staging this afternoon. Very well, I'll get into the spirit of the game. I wasn't in my dressing room. I wasn't in the wings looking at the play. Nor was I in the men's room, either throwing up or struggling over my lines. My memory happens to be just about perfect, as a matter of fact, it's the marvel of everybody in the profession who knows me. To beat around the bush no longer, my dear sir, I was—"

"Let me tell you. You were on the phone."

He raised his eyebrows at me. "Amazing! Yes, there's a pay phone at the end of the basement corridor. I went to that phone immediately after I left the stage, and at the time of the murder I was engaged in an important long-distance conversation. With my agent in New York, to be exact. He can confirm my story, if you care to get in touch with him. So can his wife, for that matter. Since it was late at night in New York when I called, I got him at his home rather than his office.''

"Wait a second," Grantley said. "You've got an alibi for the time of the murder?''

"So it would seem," Le Sage said, smiling benignly.

"Why didn't you give it to us in the first place?" said Grantley. "Why tell us you were alone in your dressing room, when you could've taken suspicion off yourself from the beginning?"

"Interesting question," said Le Sage. "Suppose we just chalk it up to a perverse streak in my nature. It comes over me sometimes to do things that make no logical sense by the standards of a mundane unimaginative world.''

I could have destroyed his self-possession easily enough. All I had to do was repeat what Mom had said to me about him. "Don't you see it, from every word that comes out of his mouth? He's a frightened little man. He don't know where his next job is coming from. The only person in the world that can give him any hope is his agent. So he's on the telephone a dozen times every day, and at night too, trying to find out if anything is coming through for him. Didn't you watch it happening yourself, the day you went to question him?''

"But why wouldn't he admit he was on the phone, Mom? Why would he throw away a perfectly good alibi?''

"Davie, Davie, put yourself inside his shoes. Who is he out here in Mesa Grande? He's the successful actor from New York, the big professional who's doing his old friend a favor and giving the benefit of his experience to these poor no-talent amateurs. Can he admit he's so desperate to get work that he has to call up his agent late at night? What an alibi compared to being humiliated in front of your audience?''

So now, remembering Mom's words, I decided not to puncture Le Sage's balloon. He spent most of his life being kicked in the face by people who held his fate in their hands. In other words, he was an actor. Why should I add to his troubles?

Instead, I asked him the question that Mom had especially instructed me to ask him. "When you went down the basement corridor on the way to the phone, did you trip over anything?"

He frowned, "People or objects? Well, either way the answer is no. There was nothing for me to trip over, and there were no other human beings in sight. Why on earth should you ask such a question?"

I'd be telling him in due time. Meanwhile, I had to clear away another one of the small lies, so we could get closer to the big one.

I TURNED TO Lloyd Cunningham. "You were sitting in the back booth of the Watering Hole during the time of the murder, is that right?"

"Absolutely."

"Witnesses saw you come into the place around seven-thirty, and they saw you go out again an hour or so later, which was after the murder. But nobody, if I follow you, saw you for most of the time you were in the booth. The waitress gave you a bottle and left you alone, and your booth wasn't in sight of the bar in front. You could've ducked out the back door, been gone for half an hour, then ducked in again the same way, with nobody noticing you ever left."

Cunningham shrugged. "I suppose I could've, but I didn't."

"You stayed in that booth the whole time?"

"Right."

"Then tell us how you knew Lady Macbeth left out an important speech in the scene where she and Macbeth plan to kill the king?"

"Come again?"

"It's a simple question. When I talked to you the other day, you mentioned that Sally forgets her lines a lot, and the example you gave was a particular speech from that scene. You even identified the speech by quoting its last line, about the cat in the adage. Now Sally never skipped that speech during rehearsals. Le Sage told me she never did, and you can bet he would've complained about it if she had. It was only on opening night that she skipped it— which you couldn't have known unless you were in the theatre at the time, listening to her do it."

Now it was Cunningham's turn to be the target of everybody's stares. The attention made him fidget a little, but less, it seemed, out of fear or worry than out of annoyance. After a while he produced one of his sharp sarcastic laughs and spread his hands in a gesture of defeat. "Okay, I ducked out the back of the Watering Hole. I went to the theatre, I got backstage through the alley door. That scene was going on up on the stage, and that's when I heard Sally fumbling her lines. But that was a lot earlier than the murder. By the time of the murder I was back in my booth at the Watering Hole."

"Why did you lie about it?" Grantley said.

"Why do you think? Because I knew everybody'd jump to the wrong conclusions. Everybody would think I was killing Marty Osborn instead of—what I was really doing."

"Which was what?"

"I don't think I'd care to say." Cunningham pressed his lips together and gazed up at the ceiling.

"So I'll say it for you." I hope my smug tone of voice wasn't too obnoxious. "You were setting up the smoke bomb under the trapdoor."

There was a lot of gasping at this. But Cunningham didn't seem to be letting it faze him a bit. In fact, he suppressed a little yawn. "You want to know the truth, I'm getting fed up with this Sherlock Holmes crap. What gave you the idea I set up that smoke bomb?"

"It's obvious," Mom had said to me last night. "You should only look at this smoke from the correct angle. You should remember what we noticed already, the peculiar way the murderer behaved after the second murder. He carried Hapgood's dead body and Roger's unconscious one off the stage and into the basement, because it was important to him that the discovery of these bodies should be delayed. At the same time, he set off a smoke bomb in the theatre, which looks like a good way of getting the police earlier to the scene of the crime. What is it with this mixed-up murderer? He can't make up his mind what he wants? He's one of these splitting personalities, two people inside one head?

"Or maybe it really *is* two people we're talking about. Maybe the two murders are from one person, and the smoke bomb is from somebody else. Maybe it wasn't set up under the trap door on the night Hapgood got killed but two nights earlier, on the opening night of the play. Banquo's ghost was supposed to rise up through this trapdoor in the second act of the play—so maybe, when this happened, the bomb was supposed to go off and the stage and the auditorium would fill up with black smoke. And this would ruin the opening night.

"But this isn't what happened. On opening night the bomb *didn't* go off. Why not? Because the murder happened instead, strictly a separate operation. It happened at the end of the first act, so the actors never got around to the scene with the ghost. So the trapdoor never got used on opening night. Which leaves this smoke bomb all set and ready to go, sticking to the wall under the stage, waiting till the trapdoor *does* get used. And when is this? Not till last night, when Hapgood is killed and Roger is knocked out and the murderer drops them into the basement through the trapdoor. The smoke bomb goes off, pretty soon it looks like the theatre is on fire! A big shock for the murderer, no? He barely has time to hide Roger in the broom closet—then he gets out of the theatre as fast as he can and runs all the way home.

"But let's drop the murderer for a while and get back to the smoke bomb. I'm asking myself, who has a motive for ruining the opening night of *Macbeth*? Who knows all about the trapdoor and exactly when it was scheduled to be used during the production? Who could come up with such an idea, that disaster should strike the play exactly when the Ghost of Banquo appears? Who has such a sarcastic sense of humor? You could even imagine this person thinking to himself *he's* the Ghost of Banquo—not the one that gets killed by Macbeth but the one that got maneuvered by Martin Osborn into quitting the play. So he'll spoil Martin Osborn's play the same way Banquo's Ghost spoils Macbeth's dinner party!"

"In other words, Lloyd," I finished my explanation, which naturally had been in my words, not Mom's, "once we separate the smoke bomb from the murders, it smells exactly like you."

Cunningham shrugged, and his voice and expression couldn't have been less perturbed. "It *was* pretty childish, wasn't it? All I can say about that is, I was mad as hell. I wanted to get back at the son of a bitch. He made a fool out of me, so why shouldn't I do the same to him? It's one of Shakespeare's best plots. Shylock's pound of flesh. Iago screwing Othello for doing him out of his promotion. Hamlet putting his sword through his father's killer. What I told myself was, if it's good enough for the Bard, it's sure as hell good enough for *me*!''

For a moment Cunningham twisted his features into a look of triumphant evil that was positively Iago-like. Then he broke off and gave a pleasant easygoing laugh. "Okay, everybody, I apologize. If I'm back on this stage as Banquo in a few weeks, I give you permission to make an asshole out of me with the stupidest practical jokes you can think up.''

Hesitantly a few people started laughing. Then Sally's laugh rang out, louder and heartier than the rest. "You're an asshole already, Lloyd, no way we can improve on that!''

This released the laughter in all the others, and it was a while before Sally's next words could be heard. "One thing I'll *never* forgive you for, Lloyd darling. I wear my most beautiful gown in that ghost scene. If that smoke had ruined it ... !'' She shuddered, then she laughed louder than before. "Oh, well! You're a baby—but such a *talented* one, it's just not possible to stay mad at you!''

Then Sally was on her feet, sailing up to Cunningham, planting a big kiss on both his cheeks.

At that point there was a real danger of the proceedings degenerating into an orgy of hugging and kissing, actor-style, so I spoke up fast. "Hold it, ladies and gentlemen! Sorry to break up the love-in, but it's time for us to get to the murder.''

USING ALL the new information that had come out, we now established where everybody *really* was just before the murder scene, and I sent them there. Laurie Franz in the wings left; Bernie Michaels in the wings right; Allan Franz in the audience, sitting next to me: Roger as Fleance in the wings waiting for his entrance with Banquo (for purposes of convenience we had Cunningham play Banquo again); the two murderers skulking in the shadows on the stage.

People who hadn't been on or near the stage took seats in the audience, but first had to announce where, on opening night, they had actually been: Le Sage talking on the pay phone in the basement; Sally holed up in a ladies'-room booth, reciting her lines; Cunningham lurking in the back booth at the Watering Hole.

I played the Third Murderer, Mom having coached me exactly how I was to do it. I waited in the shadows along with Murderers One and Two, then I gave the signal for the scene to begin.

The first two murderers said a few lines, then I said Third Murderer's line in a hoarse croaking whisper, as he had done on opening night. Then I stopped the scene and asked the two murderers if Third Murderer had seemed to be stooping when he talked to them, pretending to be shorter than he actually was.

They said pretty much what they had said a few days ago. Ordinarily, when they carried on their dialogue with Harold Hapgood, they found themselves talking down to him slightly, even though they weren't very tall themselves. On the night of the murder they seemed to be at eye level with him. This had seemed perfectly natural to them at the time; only later, when they found out Harold hadn't been onstage with them that night, they began to wonder if the Third Murderer had been stooping.

Then Banquo and Fleance appeared, at the other side of the stage. They had some lines, too; Cunningham spoke his with great feeling. Then they came toward the center of the stage, and Third Murderer (me) sneaked along the sides until I was planted behind Fleance. Then the cue was given, one of Banquo's lines, and we cutthroats pounced on our victims.

From the corner of my eye I could see the first two murderers grabbing hold of Banquo, pinning his arms while he struggled. But most of my attention was on Fleance. I flung one arm around his waist, and the other one I flung around his neck in a chokehold.

"Wait, wait!" Roger was crying out, half strangled.

I relaxed my hold a little so his voice could be heard. "That's not how he did it on opening night! He put his arm on my chest!"

"What's the difference?" I said.

"The difference is . . ." Roger stopped in mid-sentence. Then he shook his head. "With your arm around my neck, I can't see your hand, I can't see the ring!"

I could feel him hopping up and down in my grip. "Dave, that's why the murderer used a different hold on me than Harold ever did. I was *supposed* to see the ring! I was *supposed* to identify it as Sally's!"

Bernie Michaels came charging toward me from his place in the wings right. "I've said it all along, Sally's been deliberately framed! The murderer stole her coat, the murderer stole her ring and made sure Roger would see it—"

"Hold your horses here!" Grantley rose up from his seat in the audience. "If the murderer was wearing Mrs. Michaels's ring, then *she* must be the murderer. She's told us a dozen times already that she never took that ring off her finger on opening night."

"Yes . . ." Sally shook her head, looking a little dazed. "That's true, of course. . . ."

"All right." Grantley turned to me with a smirk on his face. "How do you expect to get around *that* one?"

"It's simple," I said.

Sure it was. When I presented the same question to Mom last night, she had answered it without a blink of her eye. "You heard about the fight that Sally Michaels had with Martin Osborn over this ring, a few days before the opening? The same day, in fact, that Lloyd Cunningham quit the play? Osborn told her the ring was too vulgar for Lady Macbeth, it would make her look like a woman with no class. Sally said she would never take off the ring, it was in perfect taste, and she didn't care from Osborn's opinion.

"In other words, Sally made up her mind she wouldn't look like she was taking orders from Osborn or admitting there was even a possibility he could be right. But to herself, in her private thoughts, could she be so sure about this? Could she stop herself from thinking maybe he *was* right? People like Sally Michaels, what worries them more than anything in the world is somebody should think they're vulgar, somebody should accuse them they don't have good taste.

"So you tell a woman like Sally the world's going to look down its nose at her she should wear a certain ring, believe me you're tearing her into two pieces. One piece is saying to her, 'You wear this ring on opening night, and everybody sees your dirty secret that you're a vulgar person.' The other piece is saying to her, 'You *don't* wear this ring on opening night, and Martin Osborn has the last laugh on you, he gets the satisfaction you obeyed his orders.' Vanity on one side, pride on the other—what a megillah!"

"So how did Sally resolve it?" I asked Mom.

"Like my niece Estelle that was married to Horowitz, the foot doctor."

"I'm sorry, Mom, I never knew till this moment that you had any such niece."

"Who says so? Many times I talked to you about her. What a stingy man this husband of hers was! He wouldn't give her anything outside her monthly allowance, no matter what emergencies came up or how nice she asked him. One day she asked him for a pair of new shoes that her allowance wouldn't cover. You'd think, being a foot doctor, he'd want his wife should have decent footwear, it's a matter from professional pride. But no, he told her she couldn't have one penny more than usual.

"And then, all of a sudden, like a voice from the heavens, it came to her how to handle him. She went down to the market for the weekly groceries, and she called up Horowitz at his office and told him a crook just snatched her purse, and she didn't have any money for buying their food for the week. So Horowitz sent his office receptionist down with a credit card, and Estelle charged the groceries. And with the cash she still had in her pocket, because naturally there wasn't any purse-snatcher, she went to the shoe store and bought the nice pair she wanted."

"Didn't it spoil her pleasure, Mom, that she could never wear those nice shoes in her husband's presence?"

"Certainly not. She wore them all the time in his presence. He even asked her once if they were new, and she said, 'These old things, I've had them for years, I'm thinking of giving them to the United Jewish Appeal.' This is the whole point why I'm telling you the story. Women expect other women to notice what they're wearing, but from men they don't expect. On such subjects, in the opinion of women, men are blind, or even if they see something you can always talk them into thinking it's not what they saw.

"So you follow what Sally Michaels did? She decided she couldn't wear the ring onstage; every woman in the audience would notice it. She also decided, if she didn't wear it, Martin Osborn wouldn't notice at all. Unless she waved her hand in his face and said, 'Look, no ring!' he'd be absolutely blind. Even if it occurred to him later, in the back of his mind, that he didn't see this ring on her finger during the performance, straight in the eye she'd look him and tell him it *was* there.''

''And that's what you did, didn't you, Sally?'' I said— after going through Mom's reasoning, but leaving out her niece Estelle and the foot doctor.

Sally blushed, one of her ''pretty'' blushes, and giggled a little. ''As a matter of fact, it is. I took the ring off as soon as I got to my dressing room on opening night. *I* wasn't going to make a spectacle of myself in front of those old biddies I teach school with! I put it on my dressing table and didn't think about it again until it was time to go home, after the murder and the police coming and all. When I finally remembered it, there it was, on my dressing table. And all through the first act Martin never said a word about it. I'm sure he never even noticed I wasn't wearing it!''

''The murderer stole it from Sally's room early in the evening,'' I said, ''and wore it during the murder, making sure Roger saw it. Though it must've been a major shock that Roger didn't mention the ring when he first told his story. Then the murderer slipped it back into Sally's room after the murder. Along with her raincoat, which he dropped on the floor. But why do I keep on saying 'the murderer'? You all know who it was by now, don't you?''

There was a very gratifying silence at this. Mom would have approved.

''Suppose we run through all the things we know about this character,'' I said. ''Put the separate details together, and maybe we'll see a face. First...''

"First," Mom had said, raising her index finger, a gesture I could remember from childhood, "why did this Third Murderer go on the stage with Sally Michaels's raincoat and her ring?"

"Because she was the perfect person to frame for this murder," I said. "She has a good motive to kill Osborn. She isn't so tall she *couldn't* disguise herself to look like Harold Hapgood. Everybody knew she liked to be alone in her dressing room while the murder scene was happening on the stage. She's a natural."

"Maybe so. But why does this murderer *need* such a natural? Stealing those things from her dressing room was a big risk, no? Somebody happens to see somebody who don't belong there, and right away the murderer is in trouble. Wouldn't it be easier, if you're the murderer, you knock out Harold Hapgood, you take from him not only his mask but also his poncho, which he was supposed to wear on the stage anyway, so the other actors wouldn't be surprised to see it on you? And after you finish the murder, you don't have to go back to Sally Michaels's dressing room and return her raincoat and her ring? An extra risk. Why bother with them in the first place? What does the murderer *gain* from this already?"

"Isn't it obvious? If Sally gets arrested for the crime, the real murderer will go free."

"He'll go free anyway, won't he? As long as nobody recognizes who he is while he's up on the stage, as long as it could be practically anybody, what's the point making a frame-up?"

"Maybe the murderer hates Sally?"

"Enough to run such unnecessary risks? You talked to everybody that's involved in the play, some of them don't like Sally Michaels very much, but did you run across anybody yet that has a reason to hate her? To hate her so much it's worth getting caught as a murderer so you could do her some damage?'' Mom shook her head. ''This Sally Michaels is a silly woman that means well. It isn't hate and revenge that she stirs up in people, it's pains in the neck. She's a nuisance, a nudnik, she isn't an Adolf Hitler.''

''All right, the point is well taken, Mom. But what's the answer? The murderer *did* try to frame Sally, after all.''

''Certainly,'' Mom said. ''Not because the murderer hated her but because by this murderer it's *necessary* to have a frame-up. Why? Because otherwise this murderer is the first person everybody's going to suspect, the person that right away will look like the guilty party. As a matter of fact, at the beginning of the case, until the evidence started coming in against Sally Michaels, the police *did* think he was the guilty party.''

''Mom, there's only one person that applies to. And he couldn't possibly—''

''When Harold Hapgood got knocked out,'' Mom went on, ''he was put inside the broom closet. And the murderer was in a hurry, so some of the brooms got pulled out and didn't get put back when the closet door was closed. You found those brooms yourself, Davie, on the floor outside the closet, just before you opened the door and Harold Hapgood came out.''

''I don't see what's suspicious about that—''

''When this New York actor, this Le Sage, came off the stage and went to the pay phone in the basement, he passed the broom closet to get there. This has to be only a few minutes, five minutes or even less, before the murder scene begins up on the stage. Harold Hapgood has to be knocked out and inside that closet already by the time Le Sage walks by it. How come, when you asked him if he tripped over anything on his way to the phone, he said there wasn't anything to trip over? How come he didn't notice the three brooms and the mop that were on the floor?''

"You think Le Sage was lying about that?''

"Why should he? If he was the murderer, wouldn't he tell you he *noticed* those brooms on the floor, only he was worrying too hard about his long-distance call so he didn't give them a second thought? The answer is, he's telling the truth. Those brooms and that mop were positively *not* on the floor when Le Sage walked by. They weren't on the floor while the murder was happening up on the stage. They weren't on the floor until *after* the murder—''

"When Harold Hapgood ran down to the basement, locked himself in the closet—pulling out some of the brooms to make room—and pretended he'd been knocked out and dragged in there!''

"Wonderful.'' Mom beamed. "You see how clear it is, if you only open your eyes and take a look? And this explains a couple more things that were bothering me. First, the argument this Harold Hapgood overheard a few days before the murder. It was in Sally Michaels's dressing room, and Osborn was telling her, '*Macbeth* is a play about royalty. Lady Macbeth is a queen. She and Macbeth have feelings of guilt.' Am I quoting the words right?''

"Yes, that's what Hapgood heard Osborn say.''

"Only he didn't. Osborn wouldn't say such words. There's an old superstition with theatre people—how many times did I hear about it in the last few days!—that you don't say the name Macbeth in the theatre, this will bring you bad luck. On the first day of rehearsal Osborn had made a speech to his actors, telling them about this superstition, saying he wasn't superstitious himself—naturally, who admits such a thing?—but just to be on the safe side, nobody should ever say the name out loud. So all of a sudden, in Sally Michaels's dressing room—which is certainly inside the theatre—Osborn comes out with the name Macbeth. Not only once, but three times in only a few minutes! I wouldn't believe it, Davie. There *was* no such argument, just like Sally Michaels told you. Hapgood made it up to throw in another piece evidence against her.

"And second, don't forget about the perfume. Magnolia Blossoms, Sally Michaels's perfume from *Gone With the Wind*. Harold Hapgood calls Roger to the theatre last night and tells him he just remembered smelling it on the person who knocked him out. This has to be a lie. If Sally Michaels was wearing this perfume when she knocked out Harold Hapgood, and if she went up on the stage right after and acted the part of the Third Murderer and killed Martin Osborn—tell me, please, why the other actors on the stage didn't smell her perfume too? How come the first two murderers didn't mention any *Gone with the Wind*? How come Roger didn't notice it when she grabbed him from behind? So Harold Hapgood made this up about the perfume, it was one more part of his framing-up against Sally Michaels."

"No, it won't work, Mom. Greenwald and Imperio—the other two murderers—they both testified that the Third Murderer was standing on eye level with them. He was *taller* than Harold Hapgood."

"Why not? Isn't this something everybody's been saying all along? It isn't easy to go up on a stage and pretend you're shorter than you really are. But to pretend you're taller, this isn't much of a trick. All it takes is you should put on a pair of shoes with the bottoms built up. 'Elevators' is what they're called, am I right?''.

I was pretty excited by now, the way I get when the truth finally comes out of Mom's mouth. But I was also confused. "But Mom, if Hapgood was the Third Murderer, that seems to raise more questions than it answers. Why did he kill Osborn? And for God's sake, who killed Hapgood?''

"The two questions are connected," Mom said. "Have another bite schnecken, and I'll answer them."

I did as I was told.

Mom leaned back, smiled gently and said. "The person that killed Harold Hapgood is the same person that put him up to killing Martin Osborn."

A COLLECTIVE SIGH of relief—I could almost feel it on my skin, as well as hear it—had come out of the group as soon as I told them Harold Hapgood was the murderer. It's nice to know that the murderer is somebody who's safely dead, and therefore not the person who's sitting next to you at the moment.

But when I moved on to Mom's suggestion, expressed now in my language instead of hers, that Hapgood had just been a pawn in somebody else's hands, tension filled the theatre again. Suddenly that person sitting next to you wasn't safe anymore.

"We'll go back to our reconstruction now," I said. "What we still haven't gone through is the murder itself. Okay, Roger—Fleance—you've broken away from the Third Murderer and run offstage. I'll go on being the Third Murderer. I turn my attention to Banquo now. If I can't kill the son, I can at least polish off the father. Lloyd, will you go on being Banquo? Murderers One and Two, grab hold of Banquo again, the way you did on opening night."

They did it, each holding one of Cunningham's arms from behind, and I moved toward them and pulled out my dagger. Only I didn't have one, it had to be invisible, like Macbeth's "dagger of the mind" earlier in the play.

"Tell me if I'm doing it right," I said to the first two murderers. "Be sure and correct me if I make any moves that this character didn't make on opening night."

They nodded, and I moved closer to Cunningham, till my face was only a few inches from his.

"No, that's a little too close," said the Second Murderer, that is, Danny Imperio. "They weren't eyeball to eyeball, there was about a foot of space between them."

The First Murderer confirmed that, so I took a few steps back. Then I lunged, hard enough so that Cunningham let out a loud "Shit!" when my fist pushed into his chest. If I'd had a real knife in my hand, I certainly would have killed him.

I pulled my fist back from Cunningham's chest, then pushed it forward again, because Osborn had been stabbed twice. Then I threw my invisible knife to the floor. At this point, on opening night, the murderer had run to the wings, but I stayed where I was and said, "So what did Banquo do after he got stabbed?"

"He fell forward," said the First Murderer. Cunningham started to do that, but the two murderers were still holding him by the arms, so his fall was broken before it got started.

"What now?" I said.

"Third Murderer was offstage already," the First Murderer said. "We let go of Banquo and ran out the other direction."

They let go of Cunningham, who did a very good imitation of a dead weight hitting the floor.

"After that, how long was Osborn lying on the stage by himself? It seemed to me like at least twenty to thirty seconds."

"That sounds about right to me," said Allan Franz, from his seat in the audience. "Then I went down the aisle and jumped up on the stage."

I urged him to do it instead of talking about it. He got up from his seat, ran down the aisle, and hoisted himself up on the stage. There he got down on his knees next to Cunningham.

"I picked up his wrist and realized that there was no pulse. Then I yelled out for a doctor."

"Who showed up a few seconds later," I said. I took a pause and went on, "Thank you, ladies and gentlemen. I think that's all the reconstruction we need to do." I moved center stage again. "Everybody take a seat. In the audience or on the stage, it doesn't matter. Just make yourselves comfortable, please."

I made my voice more serious then before. They picked up on my tone, as I wanted them to, and it sobered them. Cunningham got to his feet, and he and Franz went back to their seats in the audience. The two murderers took the chairs nearest to them on the stage. Everybody was looking at me.

God, it *is* one hell of a high! Being the center of attention, holding an audience in the palm of your hand! I can see why people are willing to devote their lives to it, even if they have to suffer humiliation and discouragement along the way.

"Ladies and gentlemen," I said, "did you notice something about this murder that doesn't make any sense? It's very simple, really, once you catch on to it. The Third Murderer, Harold Hapgood, was more than a foot away from Osborn when he stabbed him. And Osborn didn't fall more than an inch forward, because the other two murderers were holding his arms behind him. A few seconds later they let go of him, and he sank to the floor, by which

time the man who killed him was long gone. In other
words, Osborn never touched his murderer, he never even
had a chance to reach out to him, much less grab hold of
his coat. So how did that button get off the murderer's
coat and into Osborn's hand?''

I let them think about that for a moment, just like Mom
had done for me. ''The point is,'' I went on, as soon as
they started looking as if they were in pain, ''Osborn
couldn't have pulled that button off the murderer's coat.
But the button *was* in his hand. Which means it must've
been put there later, planted in Osborn's hand after he was
dead. But when? Osborn's body was in plain sight of hundreds of people from the moment Hapgood ran him
through. And a few minutes later the doctor who first examined him found him clutching that button. A lot of
witnesses can swear that nobody had a chance to plant
anything in Osborn's hand during those few minutes.

''Only, that's not strictly true, is it?''

I paused, looking around at their blank expressions.
Laurie Franz's was as blank as everybody else's and the
edge was suddenly off my exhilaration. If I expected to go
on with this I'd better look away from the girl's face.

''One person *did* approach Osborn's body after the
murder,'' I went on. ''That's you, Mr. Franz. Before I
could make a move, before a doctor could be called, you
ran down the aisle, jumped up on the stage, and knelt
down by the body. Will you tell us why you did that,
please?''

ALLAN FRANZ got to his feet slowly.

His eyes were fixed on me, and he was smiling a little.
He wasn't much to look at—a bald man with thick
glasses—but somehow he dominated the room. ''Let me

get this straight, Dave," he said. "You're saying I shoved a button into the dead man's hand?"

"Why did you jump on the stage?" I repeated my question without raising my voice.

"Why? Isn't it obvious? I had this strong feeling that something was wrong. Osborn was lying there, but the curtain wasn't going down—"

"You went to a rehearsal of *Macbeth,* Mr. Franz, you saw the cast run through the play. So you knew that the curtain wasn't *supposed* to come down right after Banquo got killed. He was supposed to be alone on the stage for a while, so he could say a few words before he died."

"That's it," Franz said. "When he didn't say those words, when he just lay there without speaking, that's how I knew—"

"Sorry. He didn't lie there long enough for you to be sure he wasn't going to speak. He couldn't have been lying there more than twenty or thirty seconds when you jumped to the conclusion he was dead and ran up on the stage. Nobody else in the audience thought there was anything wrong. I've been looking at dead bodies on a regular basis for thirty years, and *I* didn't think anything was wrong. Why should *you* have such a quick reaction? Unless you already knew for sure that the Third Murderer had killed him, and your job was to put that button in his hand."

"Don't be ridiculous! I saw the blood, the position of his body made it seem he was really dead—"

"Sure it did," I said. "As members of the audience we *want* things to look real on the stage. If a body is contorted in a way that suggests death, we don't scream and shudder and believe somebody really has died. We praise the actor for doing such a realistic job. That's the whole point about a theatre."

And Mom's words from last night were still ringing in my ears. "A theatre is a funny place," she had said to me. "Here's the audience, there's the stage, and nothing is keeping the two of them apart from each other. No iron bars, no invisible glass shield like in the toothpaste commercials on television. Nothing stops you from getting up from your seat during the play and walking onto the stage. So why don't you do it?

"Because there *is* something that separates the actors up there from the audience down here. It's inside your mind, which makes it even harder to break through than iron bars. You sit in your seat, you look at what's happening on the stage, and you don't ask yourself if it's real. You *know* it isn't real, but you say to yourself, 'So what? This is how it's supposed to be.' What happens up there on the stage, it has to be a very big mess before you decide it shouldn't be happening."

"Wait a second, Mom," I had said. "That might be true for *ordinary* audiences, but Allan Franz is an experienced professional, he's directed hundreds of actors, he's in a better position than anybody to know the difference between what's real and what's playacting."

"He's in a *worse* position to know such a difference. Who is it looks at a play or a movie and takes it all for real, and sometimes even jumps up on the stage to stop the actors from doing something? It's people from primitive tribes that never saw a play or a movie before. People with experience *know* nothing on the stage is real. They *know* the actors are only pretending. There's *nothing* they wouldn't take for granted. They see somebody getting his head chopped off on the stage. 'Look at that,' they say, 'I wonder how they did it!'

"What I'm saying, Davie, this Allan Franz didn't behave like an experienced member from the audience. He behaved like an actor that was doing his part in a play. Only the play wasn't *Macbeth* by William Shakespeare, it was 'Killing Martin Osborn' by Allan Franz.''

I finished making this point, and Franz didn't have anything to say to it. He turned away from me to his daughter, putting a heavy dose of bewildered innocence into his voice. "Laurie, honey, don't listen to this man, for Christ's sake. Everybody knows what's going on. They're desperate to get their client off, so they grab at straws. They pick on *me*, because I'm a well-known personage, because they know the public is always willing to believe the worst about successful people."

Laurie was staring at him as he talked. She wasn't saying a word, but her eyes were bulging.

"Look, Laurie, sweetie, I swear to you I didn't kill that Hapgood fellow. And I didn't kill Marty Osborn either." Franz swiveled around, waving his arm to include everybody else in the theatre. "I had dinner last night at the Richelieu. I had it sent up to my room at six-thirty, because I was expecting some important phone calls from the coast. They didn't come, actually, but I passed the time reading scripts. I never travel without half a dozen scripts to read. I was still in my room at nine or so when the DA's office called to tell me about Hapgood's murder. So if I'd been in the theatre killing Hapgood at eight-thirty, how did I get back to the Richelieu by nine? I don't have a car with me here in town. My daughter's been chauffeuring me around, and she stayed home last night."

"There's a car-rental agency in the Richelieu lobby," I said.

"I didn't rent any car at the Richelieu. Ask them if you don't believe me."

There was something about his tone of voice as he rapped this out, something about the gleam in his eyes too.

I stared at him for a moment, and then I knew the answer. He had overplayed his hand; it's amazing how often they do. People who kill other people have a way of being arrogant bastards.

"Mesa Grande is full of car-rental agencies," I said. "Maybe you used one of the others. Just so it wouldn't be easy to check. But you know, Mr. Franz, it *will* be easy. All it takes is a little patience."

The gleam stayed in Franz's eyes, but it seemed to freeze there, and no words came out of his mouth. His daughter was looking at him, her eyes wider than ever.

Roger had been heading in her direction ever since I began hammering at Franz. I had seen him edging toward her out of the corner of my eye. Now he was right next to her. He reached his hand out to her, then thought better of it and didn't touch her. He turned and looked at me, and there was nothing ambiguous about that look. You son of a bitch, it said.

"Now just a minute, Dave," Leland Grantley was saying. "Mr. Franz is a distinguished visitor to our town. You can't just make a lot of unsubstantial accusations. What *reason* could he have to kill Osborn? How could he possibly talk Harold Hapgood into doing the job for him? And how do you explain that scene Hapgood made in this theatre last night? Telling Roger here that he smelled Sally's perfume on the person who hit him. *That* sure doesn't sound as if he was about to finger Mr. Franz as the murderer."

I had put the same questions to Mom, so I was ready with the answers. "I'll explain about last night first," I said. "Franz got Hapgood to kill Osborn—I'll go into their motives in a minute—but Hapgood made conditions. He was a nervous little man, and he wasn't about to do a murder without protecting himself. There had to be a good scapegoat to take the blame for him. Sally was the best prospect, so he insisted that the murder be pinned on her. That's why he stole her coat and her ring and wore them on stage. That's why he grabbed Roger around the chest instead of the neck, making sure he'd see the ring. That's why he wanted the police to find one of Sally's buttons in the dead man's hand; he thought that would clinch the case against her. And since he wouldn't have a chance to put the button in Osborn's hand himself, he made Franz do it for him. Hapgood pulled the button off Sally's coat right after she hung it up in her dressing room on opening night, then he slipped it to Franz out in the street, before Franz officially showed up in the lobby—isn't that the way it happened, Mr. Franz? And you had to agree to jump up on the stage and plant the button in Osborn's hand, whether you wanted to or not. You had no choice. If you didn't go along with Hapgood's precautions, he'd pull out of the murder.

"But you didn't much like it, did you, Mr. Franz? Hapgood was carrying his frame-up of Sally too far. Too many details, too much evidence. It was overkill. The man made you very nervous.

"Even after Sally got arrested, Hapgood wasn't satisfied. Roger and I started poking around, asking dangerous questions. We weren't on to Hapgood, far from it, but he didn't know that. Just being questioned at all threw him into a panic. First he told us a farfetched story about Sally threatening to kill Osborn. Then he came up with the idea of meeting Roger in the theatre, pretending he'd just remembered about Sally's perfume, and acting as if he was afraid Sally or Bernie or both of them would try to kill him.

"It was a crazy scheme, of course. And my guess is, Mr. Franz, that this was about the time you decided you'd have to get rid of Hapgood. He wasn't acting rationally anymore, he was getting hysterical. How long could it be before he broke down and confessed the whole thing, including your part in it? So you encouraged him to meet Roger at the theatre, and you followed him there. And when he had told Roger just enough to incriminate Sally, but not enough to give away the truth, you knocked Roger out, and killed Hapgood. Then you stowed them away in the basement because you didn't want any janitor or passing patrolman or whoever wandering into the theatre and finding them too soon. You had to get back to the Richelieu and be in your room before the police could check up on your whereabouts.

"How about it, Mr. Franz? I haven't been so far off up to now, have I?"

On Franz's face was a soft smile, a little bit amused. Also, I thought, a little bit condescending.

"And what was my motive in all this?" he said. "Why did I want Martin Osborn dead?"

"I'll make an educated guess about that one," I said. "I'd say the key to the whole thing was Osborn's relationship with your daughter. He made her fall in love with him. She was about to quit college to go to New York with him. But from what I've been hearing about Martin Osborn, a nice quick affair with a pretty young girl wasn't what he really had in mind. I think he came to Mesa Grande last April specifically because he'd heard your daughter was going to school here. I think he took up with her and made her fall in love with him specifically because he knew you'd blow your top when you found out about it. You'd hate the idea of your little girl throwing herself and her future away on this second-rater, this has-been who never made it as an actor in Hollywood. You said it yourself the other night, when you overheard your daughter telling Roger about her plans to run away with Osborn. What you said was, if you'd known about it you'd have killed him.''

"Yes, and I meant it. But I *didn't* know about it. I didn't find out anything about it until that night. And Osborn, I'd like to point out to you, was dead by then.''

"I don't think you found out about it for the first time that night. I think Osborn called you at home in Hollywood at least six weeks ago, in August, when he got your daughter to agree to go to New York with him. I think he told you he'd break up with her, he'd promise never to see her again, if you'd do something for him in return.''

"Blackmail?" said Grantley. "It won't hold up, Dave. Osborn had plenty of money, a lot more than he ever spent.''

"It wasn't money that Osborn wanted from Allan Franz," I said. "He wanted something else a lot more. To get back into movies. And he wanted good parts, for once in his life. That's what he asked you for, wasn't it, Mr. Franz? Your daughter in return for a good part in your next picture.''

Franz still said nothing, with that quiet unruffled little smile on his face.

"But you didn't like that deal,'' I went on. "You were damned if you'd compromise your picture for this creepy little nobody. You let Osborn believe you'd close the deal with him during your visit to Mesa Grande. Maybe you told him you'd have some scripts for him to choose from. But actually you were looking for your chance to kill him. And you thought you had it when Lloyd Cunningham quit the play and Osborn took over the part of Banquo.

"As a matter of fact, you pretty much egged Cunningham on during that argument. You're a first-rate judge of acting, you must have known that Cunningham was giving a good performance as Banquo. Yet he was the only one in the cast you actually tore to pieces. You needled him about his performance because you knew Osborn would go along with you. And because your assessment of Cunningham's character made you pretty sure he'd blow up at this and quit the show. And like everybody else, of course, you'd heard Osborn boast about how he played Banquo on Broadway when he was a young man.''

"The bastard *didn't* think I was giving a lousy performance?'' Cunningham burst out. "He was *manipulating* me all along?'' His voice appeared to be trembling with rage, but on his face there was relief and satisfaction.

"And how did I manipulate poor little Harold Hapgood?'' Franz said. "It would take quite a manipulator, don't you think, to finagle a man into committing a murder?''

"It wasn't too hard for you, I'm afraid,'' I said. "You took a leaf from Osborn's book. You saw that what Hapgood wanted more than anything else in life was to be an actor, to give up the insurance business that he hated and join the profession. You started softening him up on the day Cunningham quit the play. You told him what a nice performance he was giving in his two or three small roles, and you followed that up, I'd guess, by telling him there was a part for him in your new movie.''

"You've got some evidence for that absurd theory, I assume?''

"Hapgood dropped hints about it to his partner, Ted Hillary. That's why Hillary kept kidding at him while I was questioning Hapgood, making cracks about Hapgood wanting to be a Hollywood star and how he couldn't believe the big shots out there were totally crazy. Anyway, when you had poor Harold salivating over that prospect, you dropped the bomb on him. I think you admitted to him-very frankly, very openly, like you really trusted him—that Osborn had something on you, and was black-mailing you into giving *him* the part you were hoping to give Hapgood. You said you didn't *want* to give in to Os-born's blackmail, you knew Osborn would go on bleeding you for the rest of your life. And besides, Hapgood would be much better in the part—but what else could you do? If only Osborn could be got out of the way. Some lucky accident maybe. But how could you expect a stroke of luck like that to happen? And then, bit by bit, you came up with your plan for Hapgood to kill Osborn, and you fed it to him, and he was all primed for it by opening night. And that's pretty much the whole story."

I paused a moment, then went on. "What you're think-ing now, Mr. Franz, is that I don't have any evidence, the kind that'll stand up in court. But you know something, I don't expect to have much trouble finding it. If Hapgood was wearing elevator shoes on the stage during the mur-der, I'll bet we'll find those shoes somewhere in his dress-ing room or in his home. I'll bet there's somebody out at the Richelieu, a guest or a doorman or a parking-lot at-tendant, who saw you driving away in your rented car around eight o'clock last night or driving back again around nine. The phone company's records will certainly show calls that you made from your number in Holly-wood to Osborn's number here in Mesa Grande. Once the police really start combing this theatre for fingerprints, you can't tell me they won't find a few of yours—on the trap-door, on the doorknob of the broom closet, some other places where they have no business being.

"And one more thing I'm taking bets on. Hapgood told his friend Ted Hillary a lot more about your dealings with him than he ever let on about. With Hapgood dead, Hil-lary may just be eager to testify against his killer."

"No!" A cry of pain and fury suddenly broke out of Laurie Franz. "He didn't do it! I was with my father all last night, I was in his hotel room with him! I'll testify to it under oath!"

Everybody turned to look at her. Franz turned too, and looked at her harder than anyone. Then he reached out to her, pulled her to him, and patted her shoulder while she sobbed into his. "Thank you kindly, sweetheart," he said. "Don't waste your sacrificial gestures, though. No point playing Hamlet's mama and swallowing the poison that was meant for me."

He disentangled himself from her gently and turned to face me. "Congratulations, Dave, you did a first-rate job. But let me save you a little sweat on one point, okay? You won't find any records of phone calls from me to Osborn. There was only one phone call, back in August, and *he* made it to *me,* from Mesa Grande to Hollywood. And after midnight too! The son of a bitch wanted to get the cheap rates! That's when he told me I had to give him a part in my next picture, and I told him I'd need a few weeks to work out the arrangements. By that time, you understand, there was no other course I could take. He was trying to take my daughter away from me. He was trying to take my picture away from me. The bastard was asking for it, right?"

Then suddenly Franz gave a chuckle, as if some terribly amusing story had just popped into his head. "It was a really terrific plot, wasn't it? Beautifully constructed, ingenious complications, all those people to manipulate! Take my word for it, I never shot a better script!" Then he sighed, a little sadly. "Where did it go wrong?"

"Your second biggest mistake," I said "was thinking you could depend on Harold Hapgood. That pitiful, little shlump, he was bound to cave in under the pressure."

"Sure he was. Do you think I didn't know that ahead of time? I was prepared for it, for God's sake. Once he'd established my alibi, I was watching him like a hawk, ready to shut him up if he looked like he was going to do me any damage. It's like actors, you know what I mean? All actors are imperfect. None of them ever gives you the performance you really want. But you have to use them anyway, there's no getting along without them. So you use them, you pull whatever you *can* out of them. You turn their limitations into advantages. All right, all right, what was my *biggest* mistake?"

"Why did Osborn have to be killed when he was onstage, in front of a couple of hundred people?"

"I told you, it was necessary so I'd have an airtight alibi."

"Why was it necessary? As long as you were going to use an accomplice, why not arrange for Osborn to be killed in a dark alley somewhere, while you were miles away playing poker with half a dozen reliable witnesses?"

Franz gave a shudder. "That stinks. Excuse me, Dave, but you could never be a movie director. No dramatic imagination. A dark alley somewhere! Don't you see, Osborn getting killed onstage, in front of an audience, was the most beautiful touch in the whole scenario. He was an actor. He lived like an actor—when he made love to my daughter, he was giving a performance—so he had to die like an actor."

"But the risks you—"

Franz laughed. "Risks, for God's sake! I take them all the time in my business. Do you think I could ever make a movie if I was afraid of a few risks?"

So I shut up. The questions I had just asked Franz were the same questions I had asked Mom when she first spelled

out her theory to me. And his answers were pretty much
what she had predicted.

"Absolutely, it was a crazy way to commit a murder,"
Mom had said. "But this murder *was* committed this way.
This is a fact. So you should ask yourself, 'Out of what
type person could such a cockamamy murder come?'
Every murder has its own peculiar individual personality.
Like fingerprints. You told me this many times yourself,
Davie, when you were on the Homicide Squad. This is why
I had my suspicions from Allan Franz right at the start,
even before you started talking to people and digging up
clues. You remember what he said to you the first time you
met him? How directors go about making movies? 'The
script gives you a general outline,' he said, 'but the details
along the way keep changing, so you have to improvise,
you have to take crazy chances. And if you want to survive, you have to *enjoy* fear and uncertainty.'

"To me this murder right away had such a feeling to it.
It was put together like a scene from a movie. Plenty action, plenty twists and turns, plenty opportunities for everything to go wrong, all building up to a big climax.
Definitely a movie director's murder."

I used this phrase to Franz now, and he grinned and
made me a small bow. "Thank you, Dave. You couldn't
pay me a nicer compliment."

He rose to his feet and turned his smile on Grantley.
"You'll want to book me now, I suppose? Book—is that
the word you people use? It's what we always use in the
movies. Well, let's get it over with, and then I'll be on the
blower to my lawyers. I've got some very good lawyers,
incidentally. This won't be an easy one for you."

He held his wrists out, as the two uniformed cops who
had come along with Grantley approached him. In a movie
Grantley would have motioned them away; no handcuffs

would be necessary for this gallant gentleman murderer. I could almost see the idea forming behind Grantley's eyes. But it never got through to the surface, and the cops put the cuffs on Franz just as they would have put them on any other criminal.

"Oh, there *are* a couple of last words I want to deliver," Franz said, as they were nudging him toward the front entrance. "Mrs. Michaels, I'm truly sorry for what Hapgood and I put you through. I don't suppose it'll be any consolation to you, but there was nothing personal in it at all. As a matter of fact, I kind of enjoy your acting. You've got a real quality of your own. You're going to be a very entertaining Lady Macbeth."

Sally's mouth was wide open. Never before had I seen her at a loss for words.

Franz was led down the aisle, Laurie marching by his side. He kept telling her he didn't need her, and she kept saying he wasn't going to get rid of her that easily. At the door he stopped, and for the first time I could hear the strain in his voice. "Okay, sweetheart, you do what you want. What does it matter? It's all a bad movie anyway. Lots of publicity today, nobody'll even remember the title tomorrow. A grade-C stinker directed by some idiot. Meaning absolutely nothing."

Then they were gone, and after a long pause Ann said, "Thank you, everybody. I think the performance is over now."

I felt a sudden impulse to break into applause.

I didn't give in to it, of course, but silently, inside myself, I murmured a "Bravo!" to Mom.

SIXTEEN

Roger's Narrative

A LOT OF THINGS happened that Sunday. I think I'm still trying to sort them out.

After we left the theatre, Dave and I went to his mother's house, and she gave us an early dinner. I wasn't much of a guest. I kept thinking about Laurie, and that interfered with my concentration on the food and the conversation. And I was on the phone every half hour, calling Laurie's apartment. No answer, which didn't exactly surprise me. She would stay with her father at headquarters until the cops kicked her out. Or maybe his high-priced lawyers had flown in from Los Angeles already, no doubt they chartered their own plane, and he was out on bail, and she was holding his hand and giving him moral support in his hotel room.

Still, I wanted to talk to her if I possibly could, so I kept phoning.

I didn't tell Dave and his mother who I was trying to reach, but I didn't have any delusions that they hadn't figured it out for themselves. A couple of sharp cookies like those two, you can't have any secrets from either of them. They're good friends, but don't go to them if you're looking for privacy.

Especially that old lady. All the time we were in that theatre Sunday afternoon, all the time Dave was coming out with those fancy deductions, I knew it was really the old lady talking. While he peeled away one layer of lies after another until he finally got down to the naked truth, I could hear the old lady's voice in my imagination.

And during dinner that night, Dave stopped making any bones about it. He came right out and congratulated her that her deductions had turned out to be true. He said it without any squirming or blushing in my direction. The way you're willing to say anything that comes into your head as long as it's in front of your family.

Between my phone calls, I kept trying to concentrate on the conversation. Mostly it was Dave telling his mother everything that happened in the theatre, and her explaining from time to time how she tumbled on to this or that.

"To tell you the truth," she said, "it's a relief everything's out in the open finally. Like I told you, I had my suspicions about Allan Franz from the beginning."

"Why wouldn't you tell us about them, Mom?"

She fidgeted a little. "There were certain things about him. They made it so I didn't *want* to believe he was a murderer. So I pushed it out of my mind."

She didn't look at me while she said this. But I guess I knew what she was talking about.

"Maybe this is why I wasn't sleeping so good lately," the old lady said. "Telling yourself you *don't* think what you *do* think, this isn't good for your peace of mind."

Then a smile came over her face. "One thing makes me feel better about it, though. He started off spoiling my sleep—but I ended up spoiling *his* even worse!"

She laughed. It was the laugh that comes out of Blanche Yurka, in *A Tale of Two Cities* (the 1930's Ronald Colman version), while she's knitting under the guillotine.

Then she brought out a chocolate cake, a big rich one she had baked herself. Ordinarily it's the type of dessert I can jump into, like a fish jumps into the water, and really swim around in. But that night I had too much on my mind, my troubles were ruining my appetite. All I could get down was one medium-sized piece, and another half a piece for seconds.

Then I asked her if I could use her phone one more time. I excused myself and went into the living room and dialed Laurie's number, and my God, after a couple of rings I heard her voice. "Hello?"

The crazy thing was, I couldn't say a word for a second or two. As if my throat was paralyzed.

"Hello?" she repeated, a little louder and impatient.

She'll hang up in another second, I thought, so I forced myself to speak, even though what came out sounded like a croaking frog in my ears. "Laurie, it's Roger. I just wanted to find out, are you okay?"

There was a long pause, then her voice came again, very even, very steady, "Yes, I'm okay."

"Can I come by? I want to talk to you, I want to explain—"

"Don't," she said. That was all, just that one word. It exploded in my ear, and then she hung up the phone on me.

I sat for a while. I shook my head a few times. The poor kid, I told myself. She was ashamed. She thought she couldn't face people. All right, we, her friends, had to make her realize that we still cared about her, and it didn't matter to us what her father had done. I'll go down there, I told myself. I'll plant myself at her front door; she'll have to let me in eventually.

I said good-bye to Dave and his mother. Dave told me he'd call me tomorrow, not before eleven. It would be Monday, the office would be open, but he figured I was entitled to at least a morning off.

I got in my car and drove as fast as I could in the direction of Laurie's house. If I got picked up for speeding, it would delight the heart of District Attorney McBride and his elves, but at that particular moment I didn't give a damn. Dave could chew me out until my toes started curling, Ann Swenson could fire me on the spot—nothing mattered except getting to Laurie.

I pulled up in front of her house. It was nearly midnight, nobody was on the street. The streets empty out early in Mesa Grande.

I got out of my car and went up to the front door of the little white clapboard house. I could see there was a light on beyond the door. I paused because I could hear sounds.

Music. Some rock group, I recognized them right away, but I couldn't seem to think of their name. I stared at the doorbell while the music blasted away inside.

She'll hate me if I bust in on her now, I thought. If I lay my big insensitive clodhopper hands on her distress. Just to indulge my own feelings, my own unhappiness.

I'll talk to her tomorrow, I told myself. Or the next day. When it seems right. When the wounds have started to heal.

So I turned away from her house and drove home. I put the Marx brothers on my VCR—*Duck Soup*. It did it for Woody Allen in *Hannah and Her Sisters*, but that night it just didn't do it for me.

SEVENTEEN

Dave's Narrative

WHAT'S LEFT FOR ME now is to tie up some loose ends.

Allan Franz was charged with murder on Monday morning, October 7, just four days after the fateful opening night of *Macbeth*. Right away, and regularly for weeks, *The Republican-American* ran human-interest stories about the accused's suffering in jail, the agonies of remorse and shame that were keeping him from sleeping at night, the bravery of his young daughter in sticking by her father during his ordeal. Along with the lawyers, a battalion of savvy press agents were on Franz's team.

Three weeks later Lloyd Cunningham was true to his word and reopened the Mesa Grande Art Players production of *Macbeth*. Randolph Le Sage had to leave the show, his two-month dispensation from Equity having expired, so Lloyd took over the title role. Sally Michaels returned in her triumphant performance as Lady Macbeth. Danny Imperio moved up to Banquo, and a kid who was going to Mesa Grande College became the Second Murderer, among other parts. Laurie Franz obviously couldn't go on as Lady Macduff, so the youngest of the weird sisters filled in. She did a creditable acting job, once you got used to her looking more like Macduff's mother than his wife. Third Murderer became the local high school soccer coach, who had been playing the Porter at Macbeth's gate and the bloody Sergeant in Duncan's army. Harold Hapgood's other roles were thrown to Jeff Greenwald.

Roger asked my permission to return to the play too. Privately I wasn't sure it was a good idea for one of the investigators who had exposed Banquo's killer to go on the stage night after night playing a part in Banquo's murder scene. Somebody could have accused the public defender's office of using the play to get a little free publicity. But I didn't have the heart to tell Roger he couldn't do it. The kid was going around with such a long face these days. Things weren't working out between him and Laurie Franz, which was obviously no big surprise.

It was clear at opening night that *Macbeth* was going to be a smash hit, the first one the Mesa Grande Art Players had ever had. The house was packed, with standing room. Ovations for the actors' big speeches were frequent.

After the performance, the cast held an opening-night party, to which Ann and I were invited. It was at Lloyd Cunningham's house, but his wife was nowhere to be seen; we were told she had retired with a splitting headache. Her absence didn't dampen anybody's high spirits. The liquor flowed freely—and the joints too, to which Ann and I, as officers of the court, had to shut our eyes diplomatically.

Lloyd grew more and more exuberant as the night wore on. He took every possible opportunity to make toasts—to everybody in the cast, to the public defender's office, to himself. The toast I remember best was the one he made to Sally:

"To our lovely and beloved leading lady, with gratitude and admiration. And here's a piece of advice, Sally my precious. Get yourself arrested for murder before every play you're in, and by God, you'll be a star!"

Everybody roared with laughter, and Sally's giggle rang out above the rest.

I didn't do much drinking myself at that party. I watched quietly, with amazement and growing understanding. It wasn't really the opening of *Macbeth* they were celebrating. What was making them laugh and cry and paw each other and yell their lungs out was, first of all, their relief that none of them had turned out to be the murderer. And second of all, their delight that Allan Franz and Martin Osborn—the intruders, the aliens from another planet—were gone for good. Osborn's money would be missed, financial disaster (*Macbeth* notwithstanding) was probably waiting for them around the corner, but the loss was worth it to get back that fragile something that had temporarily been shattered.

They *were* a big happy family, I thought, and their sense of it was what held them together. It gave some meaning and joy to their knowledge that none of them would ever make it to Broadway or Hollywood, or even get a decent review from the drama critic of *The Republican-American*.

The success of *Macbeth* continued after the opening night. The house was full at every performance, even though Cunningham took a chance and doubled the ticket prices. The run, originally scheduled for four Thursday-through-Saturday weekends, was extended for two more, and for another two after that. By Mesa Grande standards that's practically *A Chorus Line*.

A FEW MONTHS after the last performance of *Macbeth*, Allan Franz's trial began. It promised to be an even bigger hit, though it was on for a limited two-week run. Crowds gathered in front of the courthouse every day to see the famous Hollywood people who made personal appearances as character witnesses for the defendant. Limousines with familiar faces sitting in them drove through town for the duration of the trial, and *The Republican-American* made sure to put every one of those faces on the front page. Newspaper people from big cities on both coasts moved into the Richelieu Hotel and other cheaper establishments, and among them all there seemed to be some confusion as to whether they were covering a murder trial or a major-studio world premiere.

Sally Michaels was a leading witness for the prosecution. A persuasive witness, because she obviously held no grudge against the defendant regardless of what he had tried to do to her. In the course of her testimony, she referred several times to "Mr. Franz's generosity in telling me how much he appreciated my efforts in the role of Lady Macbeth."

Bernie was in the courtroom watching her, of course. He spent most of his free time with Sally nowadays, and it was common knowledge that he had moved into her house, though officially he still kept his own. All you had to do was look at him while he was looking at her, and you knew how much he was dying to marry her again. Personally, though, I don't think she'll ever go that far herself. The role of wronged woman, gallantly protected by her ex-husband whose heart is breaking for her, suits her very nicely.

Another prosecution witness, even more effective than Sally, was Ted Hillary. He was introduced by Grantley as "Mr. Hapgood's business associate and lifelong friend," and he testified from his wheelchair, a hard prop for the defense to operate against. Hillary's face was the color of old cracked paper, he looked ten years older than when I had seen him last, but he gave his testimony firmly and clearly. He described how Harold had told him, almost in so many words, that Allan Franz had promised him a part in his next film. Harold hadn't explained what his own side of the bargain was to be, but Hillary, fixing his bitter grief-stricken gaze straight at the jury, said, "He was in a state of strange excitement for four days before the murder. Like he was hypnotized or drugged. The sweetest, gentlest man in the word. Some devil got into him and corrupted his soul!'' All of the defense counsel's objections couldn't erase that speech from the jury's mind.

Since the trial, incidentally, Hillary has taken a new partner into the insurance agency with him. This young man also shares the apartment above the office.

Franz himself took the stand in his own defense. He didn't make nearly as good a witness as we had expected. His face was chalky, his eyes were pins of light surrounded by black circles; suddenly I could believe the newspaper stories that he wasn't sleeping at night. But somehow his state of physical devastation made him look sinister rather than sympathetic. And his voice was failing him too: it cracked and grated, and the judge kept telling him to speak up so the jury could hear him.

In spite of all these advantages, however, the prosecution was far from a shoo-in. District Attorney Marvin McBride positively surpassed his usual standard of ineptitude in conducting the case. There were moments when the betting around the courthouse was even money that Franz would be acquitted. What tipped the scale was Franz's team of astronomically expensive lawyers, who made it clear, without meaning to—as Easterners in our part of the world so often do—how much contempt they felt for our town full of moronic hayseeds. Even so, when Franz was finally found guilty, the jury reduced the charge to second-degree murder. Ann Swenson would've got him off scot-free.

The judge was good old Harry Van Heulenberger, who's been on the bench in Mesa Grande for thirty-five years and, since there is no mandatory retirement age for local judges, holds on to his job with a grip of steel. He frequently confuses plaintiffs with defendants, and in recent

years has taken to giving suspended sentences to all juve-
nile offenders who can prove to him that they play varsity
sports in their high school. "Varsity sports build character," says Judge Van Heulenberger at every possible opportunity, and especially at sentencing time. "This young
man knows what it is to stride down the playing field as
part of a team. I feel sure that he's learned his lesson and
will never commit armed robbery with violence again."

As it turned out, Judge Van Heulenberger was a movie
fan, and Allan Franz's pictures particularly appealed to
him. He even referred, in his sentencing speech, to the
"salutory effect" they always had "in upholding the moral
standards and traditional values of American life." He
gave Franz ten years, the minimum sentence possible under the law, and specified that his time be served at our
state's country-club prison for white-collar criminals; it's
located up in the mountains near one of our best ski re-
sorts.

With good behavior, Franz will serve four years. His
name will appear in the Hollywood columns at regular in-
tervals, thanks to his press agents. And since four years is
about how long it ordinarily takes him to prepare a picture, he'll be out just in time to start shooting his great
autobiographical epic of crime, punishment, and redemp-
tion. His future looks reasonably bright, unless his insomnia continues to plague him.

NOW HOW do I feel about this case? Was I upset that after
all my efforts Allan Franz got off with such a mild punishment? Frankly, I never let that sort of thing bother me.
I learned a long time ago that what a cop does—catching
criminals—and what the lawyers do after that, are two
entirely separate matters.

And after all, if it hadn't been for this case, my relationship with Roger wouldn't be what it is today. Between friends, even when one of them is old enough to be the other one's father, there should never be any secrets, there should always be nothing but the truth. Roger knows the whole truth about me now, and he couldn't be handling it better. In every case we've worked on since last fall, including a few where Mom got into the act, the kid has gone out of his way to recognize my peculiar contributions to the success of the investigation.

Only one thing about this still bothers me. It has nothing to do with how I look in Roger's eyes. More with how I look in my own eyes. Have I been letting myself depend too much on Mom? I'm capable of solving the tough ones myself, aren't I? So why do I have to take the line of least resistance and run to her? The next time I get a tough one...

ON THE LAST DAY of Franz's trial, in early January, when the jury brought in its verdict, Roger and I were in court.

We sat in the middle of the courtroom, with a decent view of everything that was going on. But Roger's eyes had only one object they wanted to look at. For the whole morning's proceedings—in fact, throughout the whole two weeks of the trial—he'd been looking at Laurie Franz, who sat in the front row just a few feet behind her father. I was pretty sure that Roger never got to see her at any other time.

At noon, the verdict having been announced and the judge having set a date for sentencing, the court was adjourned and Roger and I followed the crowd into the hallway. And suddenly we were face-to-face with Laurie Franz.

"Laurie, thank God!" The words came rushing out of Roger, he didn't seem to give a damn that he was in the middle of a crowd of people and everybody was listening to him. "I've been trying to reach you, I keep leaving my name on your answering machine, but I guess you're not getting the messages. Have lunch with me, will you. We have to talk."

Her face was paler and thinner than it had been a few months ago, when she was Lady Macduff and Roger was Banquo's son Fleance and Macbeth was out to get the pair of them. Her eyes were very bright as she fixed them on Roger.

"What will we talk about?" she said. "Will we talk about how you're a lackey for these small-town redneck politicians who have railroaded my father into prison? Will we talk about how you and the crooks who employ you don't care if you ruin the life of an innocent man, just so you can make your headlines and get votes for the next election? Will we talk about the type of person who tells somebody he cares about her and the next day stabs her in the back?"

"Laurie, that's not what I did!"

"Oh, go to hell!" she said. "I'd rather die than see your face again!"

She turned away and was quickly lost in the faces around her. Most of them were staring in Roger's direction, showing the eager delight people feel when they're watching a good show.

"She'd rather die than see my face again." Roger managed a little laugh. "You know where she got that one, don't you? It's almost word for word from that prison picture her father directed. Natalie Wood says it to Robert Redford."

"Let's get out of here," I said. "I'll stand you a drink."

THAT NIGHT Roger was supposed to have dinner with me at Mom's house. He told me he wouldn't be there. He was feeling sick, he was coming down with the bug that was around, he'd call Mom and apologize to her and ask for a rain check.

Later, while I helped Mom dispose of a roast chicken, I told her what had happened at the courthouse that morning.

She looked thoughtful, but at first she didn't make any comments. Then I told her something Roger had told me about himself a few days ago. He hardly ever went to the movies anymore. And when he stayed home, he hardly ever looked at old movies on his VCR.

Mom lifted her chin and got that familiar look of determination on her face. "All right, enough is enough," she said. "What this boy needs is a big dose of something."

"What something? They don't make a medicine that's good for what's ailing *him*."

"Who says they don't? The name of this medicine is truth."

"What truth are you talking about, Mom?"

She didn't seem to hear my question. "We'll have a quick dessert and coffee," she said, "then maybe I'll send you home. It's late, and I've still got some letters to write."

EPILOGUE

Dear Roger,

GETTING THIS LETTER from me will be a big surprise for you. Especially since I could call you up on the phone and ask you over for a cup of coffee and talk to you straight into your face. But I didn't want to do this because I thought maybe it would be embarrassing for you, talking about such things to another person, especially an old lady. I know how it is at your age, practically everything is embarrassing. Believe it or not, I was twenty-two years old myself once.

So I'm putting all the facts into this letter and personally driving to your house to slide it under your door. And the reason I'm doing this, I have a good idea what's going on inside of you right now. My son Davie told me you spoke to the girl today, and what she said to you. It wouldn't take any Albert Einstein to figure out how this made you feel. My heart goes out to you like I was your own mother. If your mother was here now, instead of a thousand miles away, I'm positive she'd do for you what I'm going to do.

For the last few months already I knew these facts. I kept them locked up inside of me because I was afraid the truth could hurt you. But since you're hurting anyway, what harm can it do if you hear it? Maybe it could even do you some good.

So here it is, the truth about those murders, the whole truth, and nothing but . . .

To begin with, I'm pointing out to you three or four peculiar things that I noticed about those murders.

First of all, Allan Franz decides to kill Martin Osborn because Osborn is blackmailing him, he's saying to him, "Your daughter or your picture!" So how did Allan Franz find out about this affair and about this blackmail? Martin Osborn called him long distance and laid it all out for him. What number did Osborn call? The number of Franz's home in Hollywood. This big mansion that the girl told you about, with more rooms than she and her father can possibly live in, and a phone in practically every room. And when did Osborn make this call? Lake at night, after midnight, six weeks or so before the murder, in other words, in August. Before school began, you'll notice. Exactly the time when this girl was home for the summer vacation.

Once I knew all these facts, could I stop my mind from playing around with a certain possibility? Suppose this girl was home in the mansion when Osborn's long-distance call came. Suppose she picked up the extension in her room when the phone rang, only her father picked it up a little sooner. Suppose she heard Osborn's voice on the line and listened in, without letting them know she was doing it, to what Osborn was telling her father.

All right, you're saying, that's a lot of supposing. Is there any evidence for all these supposes?

First piece evidence: When they were sitting together at the opening night, Allan Franz talked to Davie about his daughter. He said she was a temperamental girl, and lately her moods were changing all the time, suddenly she was going from up to down without any reason. He gave an example of this: how the girl, living with him in Hollywood last summer, went to bed one night as happy as clam chowder and the next morning when she came to the breakfast table she was snapping off everybody's head. He compared her to Juliet from William Shakespeare. One night she's happy because she's in love with Romeo, the next morning she's miserable because he's dead.

For such an overnight change in a girl's mood, even a temperamental girl, there has to be a good reason. Something happened to her. So what was it? What *could* happen to her between going to bed at midnight and waking up the next morning at nine? No visitors came to the house and woke her up from sleeping, or why didn't her father mention them? Nothing upset her in the morning mail, because her mood was already changed when she came down to breakfast. I'm telling myself there's only one thing that could come into her life in the middle of the night—a phone call. And we know already about one phone call that came to Franz after midnight, the call from Martin Osborn where he explained how he was using the girl's feelings to blackmail a movie part out of her father. If the girl *did* happen to overhear her boyfriend saying such a thing to her father, this would be a plenty good reason for her to suddenly act unhappy. Romeo is worse than dead; he's turned suddenly into a schmuck. How much more would a girl need to change her mood overnight?

So how big a coincidence can you swallow? If you don't have a pretty big suspicion she listened in to this phone call, you're the type never has any suspicion about anything, and I'd like to sell you my old car.

Second piece evidence: The night after the murder, when you took the girl for a date and brought her home to her apartment, she confessed to you about her affair with Osborn, and she said how the two of them were planning they should run away to New York right after the play closed. But she told you something else earlier that same night. She told you Lloyd Cunningham liked her so much dur-

ing the *Macbeth* rehearsals he asked her to play the leading part in the next production of the Mesa Grande
Players—*Oy, Wilderness!* She told him she certainly
would, and she was very excited at the idea because it's the
part of the mother and she never yet had a chance to act
like a character who's twice as old as she really is.

So explain this to me: How could she accept this part
and be excited about playing it if she was planning to run
away to New York right after *Macbeth* and wouldn't even
be in town for the next production? The answer is: By this
time, when she was offered this mother part, she knew—
she didn't just think, she *knew*—she wouldn't be going to
New York with Martin Osborn. By this time she already
overheard the long-distance phone conversation, and she
hated Martin Osborn in the guts, and she had no intention she should run away with him.

No, I'm not saying she's the real murderer of Martin
Osborn. I'm not saying she helped her father do it either.
She isn't that type girl, from what you told me about her.
She isn't the type that does things for herself. All her life,
when there were things she wanted should be done, other
people did them for her. Servants picked up her clothes and
cleaned up her room. Cooks brought her food to the table. Tutors made sure she got through school. And most
of all, her father, her darling daddy, made the way smooth
for her, popping up with his checkbook or his connec-
tions if only she expressed a desire for something she didn't
have.

It's a pattern, you follow me? People get into patterns
when they're little children, they don't get out of them so
easy later on. This little girl overhears the phone conversation, she realizes what Osborn is doing to her, she hates
him twice as much as she used to love him. Nobody does
a better job hating, in my experience, than spoiled little

children when somebody suddenly won't let them have their way. It would make her very happy somebody should do him a lot of damage, ruin his career, ruin his reputation, fix it he should get beaten up. Even if somebody should happen to kill him, she's ready to laugh all through the funeral. But getting revenge, hurting or killing somebody, is dirty work, and she isn't accustomed she should do her own dirty work.

Luckily, she knows all about what her father is like. He isn't so different from her, he also don't feel happy unless he's getting his own way. You give orders to other people all your life, and you get paid a fortune for doing it, pretty soon you start assuming this is the law of nature. She knows how much her father loves her, she knows he wouldn't sit by and let her be betrayed by this seducer. She also knows he'll never let himself be blackmailed, he'll never let somebody give him orders about his own pictures. In other words, she's as sure as anybody can be about anything in this world that sooner or later her father will try, in a big way, to get Osborn out of her life.

As long as he's got a reason to do it. But if she tells her father she overheard the phone call, if she tells him her love for Osborn has turned inside out into hate, if she tells him she'll never see Osborn again, her father wouldn't have no reason for doing anything bad to him. So what does she do? Nothing. She keeps her mouth shut. She don't say a word to her father or to Osborn about what she overheard on the phone. She pretends like she's still crazy about Osborn and wants to run away with him, and she lets him go on with his blackmail. Because this is the way to make sure Daddy will try to get rid of the man that treated her so bad.

Naturally she can't be positive her father will go as far as murder. Maybe murder isn't even in her mind. Or at least in the top of her mind. Who knows what's in the underneath part of her mind? Whatever happens, it wouldn't be *her* fault, would it? She isn't going to *do* a thing.

Incidentally, this is why she went into the wings on opening night and watched the scene of Banquo's murder. It wasn't on account of your legs, Roger, I'm sorry to break this to you. It was on account of she hated to let Osborn out of her sight. Any day, any minute even, she expected her father was going to make something happen to him, and she wanted, if possible, to see it with her own eyes.

Does this make her a guilty party in the murder? Not legally. Even if there was evidence that could stand up in court, she couldn't be put on trial. A crime is something a person *does*. People don't go to jail for what they *don't* do.

So whatever this little girl did or didn't do, to me it looks like she'll get away with it. Maybe the next time too. Maybe for the rest of her life. On the other hand, who knows, one day her trickiness and her coldness could come up and hit her in the face. This also happens in this world of ours, from time to time. Occasionally there's justice, otherwise how would we know what we're missing without it?

Meanwhile, there's one good thing that came out of all this. You found out what type person she is. You found out she's the type that sleeps like a baby no matter what she's got on her conscience. *Nothing* is on her conscience, in fact, because she never had one. Believe me, Roger, my darling boy, you'll feel better from knowing that what you lost wasn't worth having in the first place.

All right, I understand you're not feeling better right this minute. I understand this letter wouldn't do you much good, words were never any medicine for suffering. All I can say to you is, give it time. After a while, when you're feeling more like thinking it over, you'll thank me for telling you the truth.

Sincerely, with all my love, and I hope it won't embarrass you if I sign this letter

Mom

P.S.—How would you like it to come here for dinner next Tuesday night? I won't have Davie or his little legal secretary or any other old people. Only young people your age. I know a few of them, including some very nice young girls that are going to the college. You're under no obligation to like them. You don't even have to enjoy the dinner. Just humor an old lady and be here.

Love again,
Mom.

A DEB RALSTON MYSTERY
DEFICIT ENDING
LEE MARTIN

Ready or not, Ralston is back from maternity leave, haunted by the look of a young teller who is taken hostage and later killed— the first in a string of victims.

Deb Ralston is soon hot on the tail of the murderers and heading straight into deadly danger.

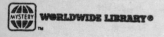

BARBARA PAUL

IN-Laws

and Outlaws

Gillian Clifford, once a Decker in-law, returns to the family fold to comfort Raymond's widow, Connie. Clearly, the family is worried. Who hates the Deckers enough to kill them?

And as the truth behind the murder becomes shockingly clear, Gillian realizes that once a Decker, always a Decker—a position she's discovering can be most precarious indeed.

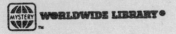